BLOOD
MOUNTAIN

by
Martha Novak

Quantity sales and special discounts are available for bulk purchases by corporations, associations and others. For details, please reach out to CSI Publishing, listed above.

Orders by U.S. trade bookstores and wholesalers, Email: ken@clientsi.com

The author can be reached through Ken Walls.

Manufactured and printed in the United States of America, distributed globally by CSI Publishing - www.csipublishing.com

CSI
Publishing

Dallas, Texas

Library of Congress Control Number: 2024920447

Paperback ISBN: 978-1-963986-07-5

Hardback ISBN: 978-1-963986-06-8

eBook ISBN: 978-1-963986-08-2

TABLE OF CONTENTS

CHAPTER 1

Her mother saw her struggling to swim in her lane at the community pool. It was hard for a serious swimmer. There were a lot of splashing children getting in their last hurrah before their mothers took them home. Beth Talmadge had just reached the wall at the deep end, clung on, and waved. Her mother waved back. She saw Beth rub her eyes as they stung from the chlorine and the garish night lights that shone directly on the water before she streamlined into her lane again.

Swimming was Beth's sport of choice, and she needed the workout. "She's Deloitte and Massey's youngest ad exec. Isn't that something? We're so proud of her," her mother told her young friend who was busy toweling off her seven-year-old.

What her mother didn't tell the friend was that she was there to protect her daughter from a killer. She would protect her with her life if it came to that. Beth resented all the hovering but put up with it. Her mother told her she was free to do as she pleased at work. Outside of that, she was going to keep a watchful eye.

The lane was almost empty now. She saw Beth's stroke lengthen, and she could tell that she was relaxing into her swim for the first time. She paid little attention to the shadow when it swam beneath her daughter. Only in retrospect did she scream, "Get out! Get out! Get away! He's here!" But of course, then it was too late.

She didn't think Beth felt the slash when it came. She'd just gotten to the shallow end and stood, a mystified look on her face as she regarded her mother and the water turning black around her. Her mother, incredulous but reacting to a silent alarm, stood and watched as Beth tried to speak.

Instead of words, there came a gurgling of blood, mucus, chlorine, and air. Her mother, fully clothed, plunged into the water then, but others were now in the water too and held her back. What was Beth trying to say? "Goodbye?" "Sorry for dying?" "I love you?"

Beth's last undelivered message tortured her mother's forlorn nights. Whatever her daughter had had to say, it sank beneath the dark water with the rest of her and was gone.

#

Seven-year-old Annie Hess sat in the parking lot of the mall in her mother's Mercedes. Slipping off her seat belt, she tried unsuccessfully to press out the wrinkles of her denim shirt with her hand. She wished she'd brought a sweater or that her mother had left the car keys in the ignition so she could have at least turned on the heat. Checking her phone, an hour and a half had passed, and she was upset.

"I'll be right back," her mother had said. She then went into Macy's to pick up the Christmas presents she'd had wrapped. Annie's mother was a very busy woman, an executive with AT&T. She didn't have time to wrap her gifts. Annie thought she barely had time for her.

Her mother had never left her this long. Annie hated to get her mother in trouble but didn't know what else to do. She dialed.

"Dad?"

"Honey Bunny!" He sounded glad to hear from her. "What's up?"

"Um…I'm in the car at the mall. Mom had some gifts to pick up and said she'd be right back, but it's been a while, and it's getting dark."

He erupted. "God damn it, Annie! Baby, this is why I want full custody. You remember this when the judge asks you who you want to live with. Okay? Okay?"

Annie heard him waiting for an answer. She didn't like it when he put her on the spot. "Yeah," she said.

CHAPTER 1

"Where'd she go? Do you know?"

"Gift wrap, I think. In Macy's," she said.

"Then get out of the car and go to gift wrap. Ask somebody where it is. And tell that mother of yours to call me immediately!" He hung up.

Annie got out and walked down the row of cars when she noticed she'd stepped in a red liquid oozing from under a car. It had gotten on her white sneakers.

Looking between the cars, she saw something familiar: her mother's camel coat. Packages lay all over the ground, everything absorbing the red liquid that oozed from her mother's throat.

\#

"The garbage has to go out tonight, sweetie," she said.

His wife, Sonia, had asked him multiple times, but it was tax season, and Jesse Turner had been concentrating. Sitting at the dining room table with his head in his hands, he stared at the computer screen and the multiple piles of receipts he'd created. Sonia's promotion to a directorship complicated things because she still maintained her freelance work. He needed a break. "Okay, I'll do it," he said, pushing himself back from the table and stretching.

"You don't have any shoes on," Sonia said.

"Yeah. I'll be right back," he said, ready to take the stairs to the bedroom two at a time.

"No, Jess, don't. I'll do it," she said, already pulling the bags out of the trash cans.

Jesse opened the door for her. Sonia, heaving the bags, scooted around him to the unlit side of the building where the dumpster sat. It was a clear night, and as he stood in the apartment doorway, Jess took a deep breath of air that smelled faintly of exhaust.

It'd been eight months since Sonia had found the killer's calling card: her underwear washed and folded on the bed. They had only been dating then, but Jesse knew he was in love and wouldn't let fear drive him away. He'd fiercely protected her ever since, and it sometimes worried him they might get laxer in their vigilance. Eight months was a long time to stay hyper-focused on every little anomaly around you.

He put his hands into the pockets of his khakis. He thought of their finances. They were trying to save money, but each month when the credit card bill came, he felt disappointed that they had made little progress in reducing their expenses. How were they going to afford to have a baby? Surely Sonia's promotion would help, but next year, he suspected he'd have to look for an IT job that paid more.

"Sonia?" he said, but she didn't answer. "Sonia?" he called, braving the cold pavement in his cotton socks.

He found her, limp and dying, on top of the bags she'd been carrying, as if she were a discarded plush toy whose stuffing had come out.

~ From the files of Kate Adair

#

I got to the bar a few minutes after ten P.M. Agent Bud Ramos and I met for drinks whenever he was in town, and we most often favored obscure bars on the east side. This one was as obscure as they went, off several labyrinthine alleyways that only locals knew.

"Kate!" Ramos called, his hand in the air from a back booth.

Bud Ramos and I had been friends for the entire nine years I'd worked for *The Express*. He'd started as a contact I'd nurtured at the FBI, always a good thing to have if you're an investigative reporter. We quickly became fast friends with a lot in common: a love of vintage scotch, a concern for our aging fathers—his was a cop, mine a lawyer—and dogs. He consorted with the enemy when he met up with me, but we were always discreet, and I'd proven myself to him in the past, printing only what he sanctioned and revealing nothing *verboten.*

"Sorry I'm late," I said, scooting onto the bench.

"The book?" he asked. "How's it going?"

"Don't ask," I said. I was ashamed to tell him I was playing with snippets, a story here, a story there, nothing yet coming together as a book. Some sort of writer's block. "I'm thinking of being a hairdresser."

He glanced at my hair all askew. "Stick to writing," he said.

I scowled. A couple of men punctuated our conversation by smacking billiard balls around in the back room. *Smack.* I stripped off my coat and balled it up beside me on the seat. It was October thirty-first, Halloween, and the weather had turned snappy cold. Pity the poor children who didn't get to wear their Halloween regalia without covering them up with a coat.

"What are you calling your book?" Ramos asked.

"Swan Songs," I replied, shifting in my seat and willing to talk about anything other than my book.

"Not bad for a book about dead women. You can't finish it until we catch this creep, but I'm glad you're keeping the story front and center in your column. I hear your newspaper articles on The Laundry Man might get you nominated for a Pulitzer. Congrats."

"It's just talk," I said. Secretly, I longed for that Pulitzer. I'd come up with the name "The Laundry Man" myself and had been writing about him for three long years.

"It'll give me great pleasure to say I knew you when. By the way, I've ordered you a scotch," he said.

"My hero," I said. I pulled a notebook and pen out of my bag. "What do you know about the recent Westchester murder?"

"Tom Cruise did it."

"His church won't be happy," I said.

The bartender brought my drink. We drank in silence.

"Seriously," I said, finally clicking my pen into action.

"Okay. She called us on March thirteenth. We interviewed her. He left his calling card by washing and folding her underwear, then leaving it on the bed for her to find. She didn't have a maid."

"So, it's been what?"

"Well, that was March, and it's now October. Seven and a half months?"

"The murders are so random. I mean…" I thumbed through my notebook. "…In December, he struck within two hours of doing the woman's wash. Last summer, he killed—"

"It can be hours, weeks, or months between the calling card and the murder."

"Do you see any pattern?"

"No. While we scramble around trying to find him, he wants us to know he's got all the time in the world." *Smack.* There was a great whoop from the back room. "It's only a game of billiards to him until he drops someone's life into the side pocket. Another one?" Ramos asked, pointing to my drink.

I nodded. One more wouldn't hurt. The bartender hurried over with two more.

"The Westchester woman was Christine Altermeier, by the way, and she owned—"

I wrote the name down, surprised. "I know who she is. Her clothing stores are famous. Very high end."

"Yeah, well, Christine is no more. She took her children to the playground, and they found her sitting in her BMW with her throat cut. Just waiting to pick the kiddies up."

"Poor kids." I shifted my weight to make the orange-sized knot in my stomach more tolerable. These women who'd received The Laundry Man's "calling card" were just going about their days, trying to keep some level of normalcy, and sooner or later, The Laundry Man got them.

"Lots of 'poor people' out there, and there'll be more if we don't find him." We got quiet and drank. The sixteen victims were from different states. They hadn't known each other. They didn't have a common link like a school, sorority, dating site, church, or club. Some of them were in relationships. A few of them were not. Some of them had children. Some of them didn't. Their commonality? They were all professional women who'd had their throats cut.

"Are you going trick-or-treating tonight?" asked Ramos.

"Yeah, I'm going as an investigative reporter."

"Not much imagination in that."

"None required at home."

We finished our drinks. "Can I give you some advice, kiddo?" he said. He got up and put on his coat and hat. "Watch your drinking. It makes you vulnerable, and there's a killer out there."

His words surprised me. There was no judgment in them, just concern. Looking back, I must have thought myself inviolate to the horror we were talking about, but there was an element of this conversation that brought the reality of it home.

Ramos must have read my demeanor, and smiled. "Now, don't feel sorry for yourself. I'm on the wagon too," he said. "Doctor's orders. Time to lose some lbs." He always referred to pounds as "lbs," spelling out the "l" and the "b", as if it made the excruciating thought of dieting less real.

Then he put on his fedora at a jaunty angle and shot the brim. "Want me to accompany you home, madame?"

"No. I'll be fine," I said, getting my things together. I knew a well-lit shortcut.

"Okay, then. Don't take any wooden legs…" and he sauntered out of the bar, waving like a royal.

I walked myself home then, losing no time, and jumping at every sound.

#

My rat hole of an apartment on East Forty-Second was five flights up over worn carpet. Arriving at my front door, I gasped for breath like an asthmatic. I should have moved a long time ago. I had the money but couldn't bring myself to go to the trouble. Inside, I poured a drink, wondering how long I could subsist on a diet of chocolate and scotch.

I inspected my feet after removing my athletic shoes and socks. I tried massaging them, but the pain was too intense. Some sort of indistinct anxiety had propelled me to visit my doctor the week before, and I was waiting for the results of the tests. Living with this agony for two years, it was the peculiar discoloration in my feet and ankles that made me finally seek help. Impatient for a prescription, I was ready to get back to normal.

I was hungry. In the refrigerator, there was a dried up half lemon and an unfinished bottle of water. I meant to bring home the Toblerone. Without it, I downed the first drink and poured myself another.

I was aware I drank too much. Somehow, it was justified in my mind because I spent my days looking at pictures of dead women. I wrote about their truncated lives and interviewed devastated family members as well as frustrated law enforcement who slept about as well as I did. It got to me.

CHAPTER 1

With my scotch in hand, I settled into my faded blue canvas sofa, the side that still had working springs. I thought of turning on the TV, but I was just too tired to search for the remote or follow a storyline. Instead, I reached for my bag.

Thumbing through my notebook, I asked myself what I knew about The Laundry Man. Other than law enforcement, I was supposed to be some sort of expert on him, but what I knew would only fill a paragraph: He was male. Organized and disorganized—that he was both was unusual, but he behaved in some cases as if he'd "lost it." Overkill and mutilation—but only sometimes. At a few crime scenes, a man's shoe print, size twelve. It would take a large guy to fill those shoes. The FBI's forensic psychologist speculated he was young, toxically narcissistic, and a substance abuser as sprinkles of marijuana and cocaine were left at a few crime scenes. The FBI had found DNA under the fingernails of a Virginia victim. Exposure to the elements had led to a partial degradation of the DNA, but there was enough of it to foster the hope it would, one day, lead us to someone. So far, however, there were no matches in the database. Other notes on the perp suggested he was "very intelligent," and that he could have been the victim of physical or sexual abuse, as there were no instances of victim rape or sexual mutilation. Oh yes, and the FBI profiler had included a PostScript: He was probably a compulsive masturbator. Geez. Just the guy you'd like to bring home to mama—if you didn't like her very much.

The notebook fell out of my hands. The alcohol was doing what it was supposed to do, and soon, my head lolled back, and I fell asleep.

Waking up at one thirty A.M., I stumbled to the bedroom in the dark, where I took off my clothes, leaving them in a pile on the floor. I anticipated how good the bed would feel and flopped on it, but it was lumpy and uncomfortable. I couldn't remember if I'd made it in the morning, and pissed off that I was going to have to wake up and do it now, I turned on the nightstand light. There was a pile of lingerie, neatly washed and folded on my bedspread.

CHAPTER 2

As soon as I could get control of myself, I dialed the police and Bud Ramos. I wasn't alone for long. Ramos, his team, and various other law enforcement were there within the hour, rushing in like a torrential downpour when I opened the door. Everyone had a job to do and set about doing it, while Ramos rubbed my back in an avuncular manner and led me to the sofa.

Someone brought me a cup of tea, and Ramos sat down next to me after glancing at the sprung side of the sofa. "So what happened?" Ramos asked. His voice was a comfort, deep and nonchalant, a practiced tone that in no way revealed who he was.

"Clean laundry stacked on the bed when I went to sleep," I said.

"And I assume you hadn't been on one of your rare cleaning frenzies," he said, looking around at my untidy apartment.

A young officer rushed into the room and interrupted us. "The back window to the fire escape has a broken latch," he said to Ramos.

"Okay, thanks. Listen up, everybody, this is a friend of mine, so do it right," he said, patting my ice cold hand.

People worked efficiently around me. I was a lump on the couch, which was about all I had in me. Ramos called a doctor friend who came over to check on me. He declared me shaken up but fine. All the while, I not only fretted about being hunted by a serial killer, but worried about my job.

I worked with great people and considered myself lucky to do so. Some men would rather pat a five-foot-three-inch tall, red-haired woman on the head and call her "cute" than acknowledge her as a person with opinions and talents of her own—even if the woman was a ripe thirty-three years old. Bruce, my professor in grad school, believed in me, so I jumped at the chance when he invited me to work with him as an investigative reporter. Shortly before becoming a widower, he received an appointment as the editor of a prestigious newspaper, *The Express*. After he lost Marjorie, he threw himself into work, as if it were all that mattered. The rest of us followed suit. He expected us to be smart and aggressive, and I was determined to be that and more. The third member of our team was Simon Chase, a brilliant photographer. He'd also been a classmate of mine and Bruce's student.

The three of us were wonderful friends. I waited to call Bruce and Simon until the authorities were thoroughly working the apartment. It gave me time to come down from the proverbial ledge. I knew they'd want to rush over even in the "wee hours," but I still felt "out of it" and didn't want them to see me so discombobulated. I thought I was being firm when I told Bruce not to come. But Bruce, simply because of his Bruce-ness, called back within the half hour.

"Look," said Bruce. "Simon and I talked, and he's picking me up in a few minutes. We're on our way."

"No, Bruce, there's too much confusion as it is," I said. "The police are here, and so is Ramos. They'll be here all night. I'm fine."

"You can't be."

"I am."

"No, you're not."

"Okay, I'm a little shaken up—"

"Simon just walked in—"

"Don't come!" I heard Simon sneeze in the background. He had the flu and had already missed two days of work.

"Give me the phone," Ramos said, and when I hesitated, he waggled his fingers with impatience.

"Who is this?" he asked me before putting the phone to his ear.

"My editor, Br—"

"Yeah," said Ramos. "Look, if you don't listen to Kate here, I'm going to arrest you for contaminating the crime scene and put you in the slammer. You understand me?"

Ramos handed the phone back. "Lovely man," he said, strolling back to work.

#

Bruce and Simon looked horrified when Ramos escorted me to Bruce's office at eleven o'clock the next morning. I was going on no sleep and plenty of adrenaline but in no way wanted to stay home worrying about myself and watching CSI come and go.

It was a typical noisy morning in the newsroom. Reporters sat at their computers typing their notes, phones chimed, chairs rolled, and people chatted and called to each other across their desks. Grant Maitland, my aggressive, arrogant, insufferable competition, wadded up a piece of paper, lobbed it through the air, and hit the new mail boy in the head. Poor kid. He didn't know how to react, so he pretended it didn't bother him and smiled. When Bruce banged shut his office door, it brought me out of my reverie about Grant Maitland being a jackass, and when Bruce turned, his face was red and blotchy, and I suddenly dreaded what was coming.

"You're off the story," he began. He stormed back to his desk as I lowered myself into a merciless wooden armchair across from him. Stone-cold sober, I needed a drink. My hands were shaking from fright, a lack of alcohol, maybe both. I crossed my arms and put my hands in the folds of my cardigan. It was time to appear to be the consummate professional—which lasted a good second or two.

"No, Bruce. I've worked hard for this, and you can't take it away from me!"

"You're going to be dead, Kate! This guy doesn't mess around." He paced and sputtered behind his desk, absolutely apoplectic. He turned to Simon, who'd been sitting, ever-so-still, on the brown leather couch listening to us shout at each other. "Talk some sense into this idiot!"

Simon, dark circles under his eyes and still pale from the flu, slid to the edge of his seat, anticipating a hard sell. "Kate, we care about you—"

"Look, I know you do. *I know* you do—" I said, trying to appease.

"Then—" said Simon.

"Then stop it!" I snapped. I dropped my head then, embarrassed that I'd hurt him.

"O-kay," he said. He sounded unsure or maybe just hoarse. Anyway, I wrote it off to his flu-y condition. He scooted himself back to his original position and leaned too heavily on the armrest.

I'd slept with Simon once, a drunken midnight clutch two years ago. The reason I did was that I was…sad. No…*despondent* about the murders and the horrors that humankind inflicted upon itself, and he was *there*. End of story. It was a mistake, and he'd been protective, kind, and solicitous ever since. I simply couldn't stand it. I didn't know what to do about it. His feelings were too strong, and I wasn't ready for them. I didn't know how to keep him as a friend and not have him as a lover, so I avoided the whole thing. And in moments like this, I wasn't nice. I wasn't proud of that, and I relied on his forgiveness each time I did something that, to me, was unforgivable.

"Look, Agent Ramos and I talked this morning before you got here—"

My spine stiffened. What was this? An intervention? "—and we've planned for you to leave town. You're going to hide out at my cabin in western North Carolina, where you'll be out of harm's way."

I'd never been to Bruce's cabin, but I knew that part of North Carolina. The thought of going back there made my stomach churn. I didn't want to see it ever again.

"I'm not going." My voice sounded thick and trapped halfway down my throat. I had no clue how to thwart their plan and an all-too-familiar bygone shame forced my silence. Thinking about going back to those hills, I was again five years old, barefoot, hungry, and pathetic, and there in Bruce's office, I suddenly caught myself chewing at a dry cuticle on my thumbnail. *Very* professional. I forced my hand down into my lap and held it there.

"It'll be in your best interest to go, Kate. You'll be safe there," said Ramos, standing against the wall. I'd almost forgotten he was in the room.

"How can you say that? I'll be out in the middle of nowhere!"

"Well, that's the point, isn't it? The killer won't be expecting you to disappear. Every one of his other victims stayed home with their families and their jobs. That's what he's expecting you to do. He won't know where to look for you."

"And what if he finds me?"

"I'm mobilizing some local officers now and setting up a discreet local watch force. We can't risk calling attention to you, but they'll be responsive if you need them. We've got a fine line to walk here."

Bruce, fidgeting with the papers on his desk, stopped. "Give me your phone," he demanded.

"No," I said. "Why?"

"Kate. Give it to me."

Rolling my eyes, I rummaged through my bag and handed it to him. To my horror, he dropped it in a desk drawer, closed it with a bang, and locked it. "We'll get you a burner. The only people who'll have the number are the ones in this room, the police, and the FBI."

"I need my phone, and I'm not going anywhere," I said again.

"You're not getting your phone back, and yes, you are," said Bruce, his jaw flexing.

"I have a job—" I said.

Bruce shot up from his chair and slammed his hand on his desk with such force, I jumped. "No, you don't! You're not getting it! You don't work for *The Express* anymore! I'm firing you! And if you ever want your job back when they catch this bastard and it's safe for you to come home, you'll do as I say!"

"Is this a good time to come in?" Grant Maitland asked as he let himself in the room. He didn't wait for permission. I was sure my jerk competition had been lurking outside the door for a while, and he marched in pretentiously and immensely pleased with himself.

This was too much. "Go to hell, Grant!" I yelled.

"Don't listen to her. Come in," Bruce said to the intruder. I could hear my teeth grind. "Grant is taking over for you."

I jumped out of my chair. "He damn well is not!"

Grant, taking the chair next to mine, crossed his legs and laced his fingers in his lap. "What were you…raised by wolves?" he asked, smoothing his silk tie just so.

Bruce ignored him and turned to me. "Kate, I'm not trying to be punitive. I'm frightened for you, and I couldn't live with myself if anything happened to you. I gave you this job, and if you die doing it, the onus is on me. If you care about me and this newspaper, you might try to see my point here. Please. I'd rather lose you as a reporter than lose you," Bruce said. He dropped into his chair, threw off his glasses, and pinched the bridge of his nose with his fingers. "Simon, can you drop in on her from time to time? I know you've got assignments coming up in Florida and South Carolina."

"Sure," said Simon.

I rose to my sore feet and tried to hold myself steady. I glared at each of the men in the room except for Grant. Screw Grant. "You're making a mistake," I said.

"Duly noted," said Bruce, who didn't meet my eyes.

I pulled myself up to my full, unimpressive height. "How long are you giving me?"

"How long will it take you to pack?" said Bruce.

Simon leaned over as I went by. "If you'd like, I can go with you to help get you settled."

"Leave me alone," I said. Raising my chin high, I strode to clear out my desk.

#

One of Ramos's men took me home and waited while I packed. *The Express* had made my plane reservation under the name Sarah Johnson. I was flying to Asheville, North Carolina, where I'd find a rental car, a Ford SUV. The agent took me to the bank, where I withdrew enough cash to keep me going since they didn't want me to use plastic, even under an alias. If I needed more, I would call Bruce, and Simon would bring it to me.

The agent was taking me to the airport, but I insisted first on stopping to see my father. I rang the bell of the assisted living community, and the receptionist buzzed me in along with Ramos's man, who wouldn't leave my side. I exchanged the usual cordial greetings with staff and took the elevator to the memory care unit where my father was sitting all alone in a corner of the common room, almost swallowed up by a hideous gold and brown upholstered chair.

He wore a faded navy-blue Aran sweater. He was always chilly, even in summer months, and he sat in his favorite chair positioned by the hearth where, today, a dwindling fire crackled. Witches, Frankensteins, and vampires hung from the ceiling, and black cats, their backs arched and mouths open in a hiss, cast ill-natured stares from the mantle. On this fall day, Da studied a honeycomb, fold-out ghost. Someone had hung a Harry Potter sorting hat from the ceiling above his head, and I couldn't tell from his expression whether he liked the decorations or was just confused.

"Da?" I said. He was, in truth, my stepfather, but he was always "Da" to me, and he liked it when I called him that. He had no family now except for me. My stepmom had slipped away quietly in 2014, lying beside him in their powder blue bedroom that hadn't seen a renovation since 1970. My stepparents possessed a rare thing called "true love," because despite having Alzheimer's, Da never forgot that mother had died. But I was his joy now, and this day, as it always did, Da's face lit up like a sparkler when he saw me.

"Well, hi, sweetie!" he said. "What brings you out here?"

"You, Da. I wanted to see you."

"How nice!" he said. "It's been a while."

I'd seen him two days before, but he didn't remember, and I was careful never to correct him. He'd been a proud man in his life, so at these times when he got something wrong, I'd lie—a snowy-white deceit I was glad to offer.

"Yeah," I said. "Sorry."

"Uh-huh." He found the honeycomb decoration fascinating.

I pulled over a side chair and put my hand on his arm. "Da," I said, "I'm going to have to leave town, but I'll be calling from the road. You understand?"

"Oh, sure. You work, don't you? Or are you in school?"

"Da, I work for *The Express*." I couldn't bring myself to tell him the truth: that I no longer worked there, that they'd fired me, that my life was in danger, and that my career had just gone down like the Titanic.

Ramos's man caught my eye and tapped his watch.

"I've got a plane to catch, Da, so I have to go. But I want you to take care of yourself," I said, getting up. I leaned over, kissed his forehead, and gave him a big hug. He wasn't looking at me as I pulled away, but at the decoration in his lap.

"Don't you know there's no such thing as ghosts?" he said. His tone was gentle, as if he were talking to a child.

I welled up at that. Getting control of myself, I smiled at him, hugged and kissed him again, and said, "I love you, Da." All the time, I was thinking, "Yeah, well, I hope to God you're right."

#

The next thing I knew, I was flying through the clouds on a puddle jumper with Ramos's man. His name was Henry. Nice man, but all business. Bruce had couriered an envelope to me while I was still in the city, and I opened it on the plane. Inside was a key and directions from Asheville to his cabin. There also was a note describing the nearest township, Bowden, twenty minutes away from the cabin by car. There was a map to the grocery store, a right turn onto the highway, and a left turn took me to the country "emporium."

I don't know what I was expecting, but the Asheville airport was a tiny place with only four gates. I felt relieved that I didn't have far to walk. A few tourists came in from the parking lot complaining of the cold, and someone sat waiting for an arrival with a yapping senior dog in his lap. I handled the car transaction as Sarah Johnson and was on my way to the boonies. I thought I'd feel agitated, but all I felt was tired, with a dull ache behind my eyes and an unnerving pulse in my temple.

On the way to the cabin, I drove around a bit, acclimating myself. Henry didn't seem to mind, and I could see him relaxing as we drove. While some of the scenery was familiar in some murky way, much had changed. I recognized very little, but that wasn't unusual since I'd left as a five-year-old.

And suddenly, I arrived at a place I knew too well. I didn't need the GPS to get there. While I told myself to avoid the place, strangely, I'd driven right there. If anyone wants to know why moths are drawn to the flame that kills them, come talk to me. I pulled into a small gravel lot opposite the gorge and parked behind a white Honda sedan.

"What's up?" asked Henry.

"I want to see the view. Coming?" I said.

He shook his head and got out of the car to stretch his legs and keep watch. I walked across the road to face the mountain, although I couldn't articulate why. Perhaps it was to prove to myself that the thing that had so haunted me all these years was just a mountain after all. Nothing to write home about. Nothing to drink myself to sleep over. During my teenage years, the mere mention of this place was enough to make me cringe. As an adult, the memories it generated influenced some terrible decisions in my life.

"It's beautiful, isn't it?"

I wasn't planning to have a conversation with the owner of the Honda, but there she was, being friendly. Meanwhile, a grouchy older man back in the car—no doubt her husband—shook and smacked his cell phone at his inability to get a signal. I smiled at the woman, hoping that would be all she wanted from me, and turned to face the view.

The enormous mountain looming in front of us was a true anomaly. A forest of black cherry, red oak, Flowery Dogwood, red maple, ironweed, and sourwood covered the rocky peak, which was almost entirely red. The trees seemed to shift colors before my eyes, broadcasting the entire spectrum of autumnal glory: scarlet, ruby, cherry, wine, flame, coral, vermillion, and more. These trees adorned most of the mountain, but right at the top, in the middle of all the splendor, a frightening granite overhang loomed. It ran out to a point where only the brave dared to go. I'd been there before and shuddered at the memory. But from here, I could hardly see it, and most tourists at the pull-off wouldn't have even noticed it. This last week of October was the peak of the season and leaf lovers from every state visited this spot to perch their children—already nauseated and green from the winding mountain roads—on the low, metal guard rail in front of me to take a picture. Never mind the danger as long as they got an excellent shot for Facebook.

"What's the name of it, I wonder?" my neighbor mused.

I hesitated. The tourist board had named it something cloyingly sweet to appeal to the grandmas in white shoes like the one standing next to me. The old name the locals had for it was unsettling to some people. And while there was a mountain in Georgia with the same name that was sacred to the Cherokee, local North Carolinians had appropriated it without apology because of the color of the mountain in the fall. I used the old name. I couldn't remember the new one.

"It's called Blood Mountain," I said.

"Holy Moly. Who named it that? Stephen King?" I could have sworn she paled before hurrying away.

I was glad to be left alone. The wind whipped a strand of hair into my eyes. I pushed it out of my face, feeling that my cheek was wet, and not from the sting of the hair. This mountain had earned the old name as far as I was concerned. There was a backstory that went with this place that no one knew but me.

About twenty years ago, the park service passed an ordinance to protect the flora on Blood Mountain, forbidding people from building there. However, they allowed the houses that were already there an exemption. As dusk fell, a few lights went on. Not many. Perhaps there were more houses that the thick trees and undergrowth obscured.

People who got lost here were often never found. The woodlands were menacing and famous for their tangled and overgrown vegetation. Granted, I'd forgotten a lot about Blood Mountain, but this I remembered: There was danger here, even without the threat of a serial killer.

A few raindrops fell in unenthusiastic splats around me. Bruce had once complained to me that rain was the norm in this area, as it was one of two official rainforests in the United States. Wetness was always in the air, and it amplified not only the sweet smell of flowers and pine, but also the cloying smell of decay. I reacted to the heady mixture, and a wave of nausea washed over me. I actually swooned but recovered my stance. Embarrassed, I looked back at my bodyguard to see if he'd noticed, but he'd glanced away.

I wished Bruce and Ramos had sent me anywhere other than these scenic hills. Bruce's cabin was not on Blood Mountain, thank God, but I guessed it was within five miles. Close enough to engender nightmares if I left myself unguarded without the fortification of alcohol. Perhaps staying in New York and facing down a killer would have been easier than facing my memories of Blood Mountain. I let everyone think I was a Floridian, but I wasn't.

I'd come home.

CHAPTER 3

I'd been right. Bruce's cabin wasn't on Blood Mountain. It was 4.9 miles away. I was relieved that I couldn't see it when I looked out the windows.

Bruce's "cabin" had surprised me. Even though his house was made of logs, it was quite large. A bear-themed welcome bell hung beside the door on the porch, and I rang it joylessly to welcome myself to my new digs. A jarring clang rang out, and I reached in to still the clapper.

To the left of the path to the house, there was a stone wall, and towering behind it was a colossal mountain. Despite the mountain's intimidating size, the cabin inside was cozy. It gave off a sense of warmth with its colorful hues of red, turquoise, and purple upholstery in tribal patterns. There was an overstuffed couch in the living room, a red cashmere blanket neatly folded over the back of it, and the overall feeling of the room felt nest-like. My feet and ankles considered it good news that the primary bedroom was on the main floor, which was really the second floor, and sliding glass doors opened onto a wooden porch, lakeside, running the length of the house.

The cabin comprised three stories, the bottom floor having a home theater setup. I followed Henry around. He was thorough, looking under the beds, opening every closet and pantry, and making sure there wasn't anything more lethal than the carcass of a dried wasp that had succumbed to old age near the window panes.

I was just about to ask him how long he intended to stay.

"You gonna be alright here?" he asked.

"Sure," I said. "You're not staying?"

"I'm supposed to get you here, check everything out, and report back."

"I'll have to drive you back to Asheville then," I said, confused by the inefficiency of going back the way we came.

"We had a tail. It's my ride back to the airport." He parted the red gingham curtains and sure enough, there was a black car waiting for him in the driveway. "You didn't notice?"

"I had no idea."

"Well, I'm sure they enjoyed the tour. But if you don't mind my saying, you're going to have to be more aware of your surroundings. Can you do that?"

"Yeah," I said, feeling as if the dog ate my homework.

"Good. Nice meeting you, Ms. Johnson. Take care now," he said and left.

Alone, I wandered around the cabin for a second look. I'd never known Marjorie, Bruce's late wife, but I could tell she and Bruce had excellent taste. There was stunning wildlife art all over the walls. Upstairs, a long trestle table filled the largest room. I claimed it as my office before remembering that I didn't have a job, so why would I need an office? Despairing, I closed the door.

As I was going down the stairs to take another look at the ground floor, I stubbed my left foot on a nail sticking up from a loose board, which sent paroxysms of pain shooting up my leg. A bit sickened, I gripped the handrail hard as I sank to sit on the stair and catch my breath. At JFK, this foot had hurt much more than the right one, and the pain I'd experienced before in both feet was nothing compared to what I was feeling now in the left one. Recovering from the impact, I took off my right shoe and banged the nail in place with no small amount of rage.

On the ground level, below the main floor, was another sliding glass door that gave access to the lake. Nice, but I wasn't going down there with my sore foot. I went back up the stairs and that damn nail was sticking up out of the step again. Someone must have built the stairs incorrectly. I put my weight on the stair three times, and each time, the nail rose a little higher. I hammered the nail down with my shoe again, wondering why I was making such an effort when I knew it wouldn't hold.

In the main bedroom, the desk displayed photos of Bruce and Marjorie on their wedding day and the celebration when Bruce took on his job as editor. The bed faced the lake. Marjorie's vanity was to the left, her sundries left untouched. A tall mahogany dresser stood angled in the opposite corner. And over the rustic bed hung a well-rendered print of Klimt's The Kiss.

I went back into the living room and got out the burner phone. On the plane, I'd studied how to set it up, and while there was a learning curve, I'd gotten it functional. I wasn't up to talking to anyone, so I took a picture of the living room and texted it to Bruce to prove I was here. "Lovely!" I wrote underneath the picture with an exclamation point I didn't feel. I threw the phone on the couch, unzipped my suitcase in the middle of the living room floor, and broke out the bottle of scotch I'd brought with me. Opening a few kitchen cabinets, I found a glass.

I walked out onto the wooden porch then, bottle and glass in hand. First, the sound struck me: birdsong. I'd seen a feeder in the kitchen, washed and ready to go, and made a mental note to find some seed and put it out the next day. Then there was the more subtle sound of waves shushing against the rocky sea wall. The sky reminded me of the finest cut crystal, and when the trees stirred in the easy breeze, light refracted everywhere and looked—if light could make a sound—like the air should ring or tinkle. The blue of the lake was an uncanny sapphire, darker than the sky, and it felt mysterious as it danced with light. Despite all this, I reminded myself that the peace that was settling over me was an illusion, and I pulled myself back from it to heed Henry's admonition to be more aware. I looked around again. Yes, this was a moment most city people would have relished, and I did—except that I'd lost my job, and a serial killer was after me. I must admit, it didn't seem real that I was being targeted by The Laundry Man, and I wouldn't accept that it was. I couldn't. The anxiety would have been overwhelming. I needed something to occupy my mind, but all I wanted to do was embrace self-pity. I can't say it was an unfamiliar state. Throughout my life, there had always been something troubling me. Perhaps I didn't feel good enough, or lovable enough, or smart enough. I always worked very hard to overcompensate, and I'd cultivated a professional image to hide behind and an arrogant faith in my intelligence. Now I didn't have those things.

A companionable breeze ruffled my hair. The odor of wood fires permeated the air and made me think of the roasted chestnuts sold from the hot dog carts in New York City. It was still fall, but I thought of winter in New York and how I'd purchase cones of warm nuts from my favorite vendor. My mouth watered. Instead of chestnuts, however, I drank my scotch, desperate to quell my homesickness and fear.

While sitting on a red-cushioned porch chair, a gray squirrel visited me, appearing as if he wanted something. What he got, however, was a front-row seat to witness the pitiful end of a promising career and a woman feeling bound and intimated by freedom: I no longer had a job, a schedule, people to report to, meetings to attend, deadlines to make, or friends to enjoy and work with. I even had to abandon my delicious chestnuts. Seated on that porch, I simply didn't know what to do with myself.

#

I digest alcohol poorly, though I still gave it the good ol' college try. I'd feel like hell the next morning, but it was better to deal with a blazing headache than be afraid, so I substituted one sensation for the other. It interfered with my sleep, of course, and I tossed and turned all during my first night at Bruce's and woke up in my usual ungodly, hungover state. I tried to go back to sleep, but as soon as I did so, I dreamed: Glass shattered and a hellish image of a man with a knife came bursting through a window. I woke up enough to tell myself it was a nightmare, but shutting my eyes again, the terrors returned with a vengeance. Now copious amounts of blood covered the furniture and walls. In the dream, I panicked and ran into the woods, disoriented, lost, with nowhere to go.

I awoke in a cold sweat with my heart racing. I stumbled to the kitchen to make a pot of coffee. Bruce had left a small supply of essential non-perishables. Thank God he considered coffee as essential as I did. It had just finished brewing when the burner phone rang on the couch. Anticipating a conversation with Simon or Bruce, my doctor was calling. Yes, yes, I had broken Bruce's rule. Knowing that Agent Henry would disapprove, I'd called from the airport ladies' room to give the doctor's office my new number. I needed whatever pill he was going to give me to get me out of pain, and I couldn't see any harm in that.

"Kate? Dr. Marsh," he said.

"Yes! Thanks for calling." I willed the brain fog to go away as I got the largest mug I could find out of the cabinet. My head pounded and ached and I could think of little else.

"I have the results from the tests, so we have a diagnosis. Is this a good time to talk?"

While I poured the coffee, I looked at the cramped galley kitchen, a perfect metaphor for what my life had become. "Never better," I said.

"Well, I'm sorry to have to tell you this, but it seems you've got a rare form of vasculitis. It's called Polyarteritis Nodosa. Ever heard of it?"

"Nope," I said. I thought of my blotched, grape-colored ankles, and, however irrationally, found myself panicky. I pushed the feeling aside and leaned on the countertop. "Okay, let's cut to the chase, doctor," I said. "What are you going to give me to make it all go away?"

"Uh, Kate…This is a little more serious than you seem to be taking it…"

When he paused, I pushed myself away from the counter and paced.

"I think you need to come in so we can begin treatment. This is a progressive disease, but if we treat it, we can keep it under control and possibly even cure it."

I loved the term "we." There was no "we" about it.

"I'm going to send you a rather high dose of corticosteroid, and if you can tolerate it—"

"And if I can't?"

"Well, there are other things to try, and down the road, we may even want to look into chemo…"

Now *I* was silent. "Okay, great. Only I'm not in town, so you can't send me anything, but I'll let you know when I'm back. When I'm ready."

He'd scared me half to death: *chemo.* I didn't tell him about my stalker. His damn sympathy and his corticosteroids were the last things I wanted. I could handle this on my own.

"Kate, this is serious—"

"Yeah. I got that." Geez. A serial killer isn't serious enough?

"I'm your friend and your doctor, Kate," he said, "so please don't take this as criticism, but it may be time to confront your overuse of alcohol. It's going to complicate this condition and—"

My rage skyrocketed. He'd crossed a line. "Sorry, doc. Gotta go," I said, and hung up like the phone was on fire.

Damn it all to hell.

#

I wouldn't use Bruce's office at the cabin. It became a metaphor linked to the acceptance of my condition, and I wouldn't do that. After a few days, though, I set up my laptop on the breakfast room table and Googled Polyarteritis Nodosa, a grandiloquent name for something that, according to several online sources, kills you twenty percent of the time. With that piece of information, I shut down the computer, poured myself a drink, and lay down on the couch to feel sorry for myself.

I remained incommunicado for two days until Simon called.

"How are you doing, Katie?"

Simon was the only one allowed to call me that. "I've died and someone has buried me in obscurity. No one noticed."

"You can't fool me. I hear you breathing," he said.

"How'd I end up in this godforsaken place anyway?"

"I'm sorry you hate it so much. I've always loved that area. A lot of New Yorkers travel down there to get out of the summer heat. I went to camp near there for years, and we'd build campfires in July to keep warm. Lost my virginity to a cute camp counselor, too."

"Too much information…How long do you think I'm going to be exiled?"

"They haven't caught the son-of-a-bitch, so does 'indefinitely' seem too long?"

I looked at the vaulted ceiling. "Twenty minutes seems too long."

"What are you doing with yourself?"

"Drinking," I said, surprised that I'd said it out loud.

"Always a poor choice," he said, but I could sense the smile on his face. "Why don't you write?"

"Great idea. What?"

"Well, do you feel like working on your book?"

The mere mention of it made my stomach ache. I'd put the book aside to gain perspective, I'd told myself, but it was an excuse. "No. Look, I know Bruce wants me to write it…"

"It'll be great publicity for the newspaper," said Simon.

"I have to get away from it for a while," I said. "Under the circumstances, it's freaking me out."

"Then why don't you write about what's happening to you?"

"What's happening to me? A gray squirrel visited me a few days ago."

"Well, there you go. A muse."

"At this moment, I don't know whom I hate more, you or me," I said, and hung up before he could say another word.

I combed my hair and went to the store after that. The roads wound through dense forests and thickets, and I got behind a slow Florida driver. They're called "flatlanders" here, and they're viewed with disdain, particularly when your car ends up behind theirs. I crept along, grouching "Come on, come on, *come on…*" through gritted teeth. When I finally got to Bowden, there was simply a crossroads at the town center and signs that said, "Keep our Crossroads! Block the roundabout!" which seemed to be a bigger issue here than the possibility of nuclear war. Cute little stores stood on each corner, extending about four blocks in every direction of the compass, and that was it. Bowden was no metropolis. I turned left to go to the grocery store. I bought cold cuts, mayo and bread, several bags of cookies, pickles, chips, and chocolate. At the liquor store across the street, I purchased a case of scotch from a wizened old woman who had unruly white hair styled in a youthful pixie cut. She stared at me a little too long. Her face scored with wrinkles, her deep brown eyes penetrated mine.

I felt prompted to ask, "Do we know each other?"

"No," she said, as her wiry arms thumped the last bottle of scotch into the box and closed it up.

Something niggled at me the whole time I was in town, however. I assumed, at first, it was what the doctor had told me, but I wasn't thinking about my physical problem anymore. It wasn't until I'd arrived back at the cabin that I realized it was what Simon had said about writing. I denied having anything to write about, but it wasn't true.

I had given up too easily. What's worse, I'd given up without a fight. That wasn't like me. My biggest desire in life was to help catch The Laundry Man, and when I couldn't achieve it, I'd simply imploded because I had a clear vision—a clear fantasy I realized now—of wanting it the way I wanted it. I wanted the FBI to catch this guy with my help. I wanted to be credited for this. And my intention was to write my book and have Bruce pleased as punch.

I suddenly realized that nothing was stopping this but me. It would not happen the way I thought it would. So what? It was happening in a different way, and there was nothing to do but drink myself to death or cooperate with it. After the conversation with Simon, I realized, with some hope, that this wasn't the end. I could continue to work on finding The Laundry Man, even from a distance. After all, I had a secret weapon, Bud Ramos, who'd feed me information. And if I stayed on top of all this, I might put clues together in a way no one else had. I suddenly felt a surge of energy, and before going to bed that night, I read through all my notes.

But I didn't sleep, not even as well as I usually didn't, and this puzzled me. My renewed sense of purpose didn't bring about the grudging peace I'd expected. I got up and paced, puzzled by my restlessness, and close to three A.M., I finally figured out what was bothering me.

There was a second story to tell…if I had enough courage to tell it. These mountains and I had secrets. But there in Bruce's cabin in the dark of night, I felt more courageous—or perhaps more foolhardy—than I had in recent times. It wouldn't hurt to research this second story. I didn't have to commit to writing anything if I didn't want to, and I wouldn't have to reveal myself unless it served me. Researching it would simply give me something to focus on, something to distract me from being hunted by a killer. I didn't know what the second story would even be when I knew all the facts, or even if it was going to be a good story, but there were mysteries to be solved, answers to find, resolutions to be had, and a writer to rescue from the Slough of Despond. I felt ready.

The Laundry Man would be my focus. But perhaps it was good for me to have a second project in the works. It could distract me from what was happening in the present time. Being adopted, I knew next to nothing about my birth family. What little I remembered, I'd spent my life trying to avoid, deny, and forget. Perhaps it was time to open that door and confront the memories and mysteries that had so plagued my life and that still loomed, dark and deep, in the dreary shadows of these mountains.

CHAPTER 4

The next morning, I was excited about work and moved my laptop to the office upstairs. Bruce's note had warned that internet access was unreliable, and that turned out to be an understatement. I waited several minutes, put my hair in a ponytail, and fixed a fresh pot of coffee in the kitchen. When I got back upstairs, I still didn't have a connection. Once I went to put on a warmer sweater, finally, there it was.

I first checked *The Express* online. I could barely stand to look at Grant Maitland's smug face next to his byline, but I persevered to scan his article. Same ol' stuff; nothing new. I was a bit let down, so I dialed Ramos.

"I'm withering on the vine here," I said when he answered.

"Whither thou goest…"

"Hilarious. Anything new on The Laundry Man?"

"He's gone quiet," he said.

"Why do you think?"

"Am I a prophet?"

"But you'll call me if there is anything?"

"Yeah. I don't have anything better to do with my time," he said.

We said goodbye and rung off, and I turned to research my second story.

This may come as a surprise to most people, but I didn't remember my birth father's first name. Since the Adairs adopted me, I put anything

I'd known before in a mind box somewhere and never got it out again. I didn't want the Adairs to think me ungrateful for the roof over my head and the lovely life they were giving me, and I went out of my way never to hurt their feelings.

I started my investigation with what precious little I remembered. My mother's name was Callie Moon. I found a birth certificate for her online, but no obit and nothing on Find-A-Grave. I searched for men named Moon and found twelve obits for Moon men all around the Carolinas over a fifteen-year period, but by the time I got to the tenth one, I scanned the pictures and didn't bother to read any more. No one looked familiar. The whole effort was proving fruitless.

I sat back and conjured any memories I could of my father. I remembered a boyish, even roguish smile, and a crease down one cheek which, in retrospect, had probably been a dimple. He was thin, strong, and energetic. I seem to remember him fixing things. I recalled he gave me a daisy when I was young and how important I felt. And that was it. The end of memory lane. I remember one time overhearing my step parents talking about him. Mother was telling Da that someone had murdered him, but when I walked into the room, they changed the subject and hustled me to soccer practice. Not wanting to appear ungrateful, I never asked about my life prior. I wish I had now.

Right then, the internet went down, and I couldn't bring it back. Restless, I got up to pour another cup of coffee when the thought occurred to me I might find a town hall or library where county records were kept. What county was I in anyway? I didn't know.

So I went into Bowden, sat at a table on the porch of The Coffee Freak Café, and ordered an espresso. The internet worked better there, and I searched my phone for a town hall or a library.

The town of Bowden had neither, but Bryson, down the mountain and a half hour away, was the county seat, and there was a town hall there. I resolved to visit soon, but before I could think more about it, a flurry of activity distracted me across the street. It looked like a fair, and people were hurrying into the park. Out of curiosity, I went to see what was going on. Two women greeters sat at a table tied on each end with balloons. They invited children to take candies, and I purloined a peppermint before anyone could disapprove.

There was a banner, "Welcome to the Leaf Lovers Festival!" There were tents and booths filled with crafts, paintings, sculptures, wood carvings, jewelry, food, and more, but I couldn't wish myself into the mood to shop. There was a small bandstand where a guitarist with an eyepatch sat playing. He was good, his fingers flying all over the frets. Two old women danced, unbridled, in front of him. They were hilarious to watch—turning, twisting, jumping, clapping. One tall and thin. One short and stocky. I looked at them with admiration. In my wildest dreams, I'd never been so uninhibited and free. But suddenly, my foot screamed with pain like I was walking on hot coals, and I sat on a bench nearby to give myself some relief. I quickly bored myself and looked in my purse for my phone.

It wasn't there. Panicked, I hightailed it, limping back to the café.

I recognized the barista. "Did I leave my—"

"You left your—" and she handed me the phone. Yes, Dorothy, you're not in New York anymore.

I went back to the table on the porch and turned the phone on, only to see the face of a strange man staring back at me as my screensaver. He had a head of unruly, thick chestnut-colored hair and brown piercing eyes that advertised that they didn't miss a thing. He wore a cocky smile and had very white teeth that matched his very white shirt. I didn't have a clue who he was, and I hadn't taken the picture. Puzzled, I glanced up to see him live and in person, leaning against the railing. He was looking at me, amused, and gave a small wave.

This unsettled me to no end, and I rolled my shoulders back to appear provoked. I was hiding from a serial killer, and perhaps he'd found me. But he didn't *look* like a serial killer, standing there, leaning on the porch rail with a glowing smile on his face. I found myself wanting to believe him harmless, but was angry that he'd scared me. The damn presumption, using my phone for a cheap bar trick. He strolled over to me. "Buy you a cup of tea?" he asked.

I continued to regard him. Warmth and a certain mischief radiated from him, and I've always been a sucker for that combination. Self-assured, he presented as a man who lived for the moment. He didn't radiate malice, and he intrigued me, so I said, "I'm hardcore. Espresso. A three shot." His eyebrows raised in surprise, and with a slight shake of his head, he went inside.

When he came out with my coffee and a cup of tea for himself, I was already worried that I'd made a mistake. Who was this guy anyway, and what did he want?

Taking a seat across from me, he commented, "You're new around here."

"You have that right."

"Are you a New Yorker?"

Suddenly wary, I said, "Why would you ask that?"

"Because you dress that way. In black. Comfortable shoes." He smiled as he glanced at my dirty Nikes and sipped his tea.

I tucked my feet under my chair. "Who are you?"

"If you promise not to laugh, I'll tell you my name."

"No promises."

"Damn. Okay. Well, you can call me Sal."

"And what's your real name?"

He cleared his throat. "Salem."

"As in the witch trials? As in people being hanged and crushed with stones?"

"Yeah, I thought you'd go there. But the answer is no. My mother named me after a spider in south India. She was an arachnologist before she retired. Early onset dementia. She lives with me now." I thought of Da. Sal took another sip of tea and glanced away, possibly embarrassed to have revealed something so personal to a stranger. He looked at me again and took another sip of tea.

"Are you from here?" I asked.

"Born and reared. And you?"

I sure as hell wasn't going to tell him anything. "I don't know you well enough to be having this chat," I said, swallowing my espresso and putting my phone away.

"How does anyone get to know you?" he asked.

"They don't," I said, standing up and slinging my bag over my shoulder.

"You haven't heard the rest of my story. About my name?"

"There's more?" I said, implying I'd heard enough.

He smiled. "Oh, much more…"

I'm a New Yorker, but when I'm in the provinces, I try to break the stereotype and I resisted the urge to roll my eyes. Instead, I sat down.

"Well, anyway, my mother named me after the Poecilotheria Formosa because of her love for spiders, but that's a mouthful when you're calling your kid for dinner. So I became 'Sal' because it's also called the Salem Ornamental Spider. It's supposed to be quite beautiful." He smiled his dazzling smile again and sipped his tea.

I returned the smile. I couldn't help myself. How fitting, I thought. Forget the spider. The *man* was beautiful: chiseled body, amazing jawline, and dense, dark eyelashes that fashionistas spend big bucks to paste on.

He smiled again. "And you are?"

For a moment, I couldn't remember my alias. That and me not knowing that this guy wasn't a deranged killer caused me to hesitate. I shook my head at my silliness. What was I going to do? Suspect everyone? Next: old ladies? Bag boys at the grocery store? Girl Scouts? I reminded myself of what Ramos said: "You'll be safe."

"Um…Sarah," I said. "Sarah Johnson."

He sat back in his chair. "Funny. You don't look like a Sarah," he said.

"And you don't look like a damn spider," I said. He laughed and so did I.

We talked all afternoon. Small talk. Pleasant talk, mostly. Here and there, I lied.

"Where are you staying?"

"I'm renting a place."

"What do you do for a living?"

I hesitated again. "I'm between jobs," I said, trying my best not to squirm, blush the color of a sliced beet, or look like a child caught with her father's dirty magazines. Sal stared at me, wanting more. "But when I have a job, I'm a writer."

"Wow," he said, "What do you write?"

"Doesn't everyone think they have a book in them?" I caught myself fidgeting with a paper napkin. "And you?"

"I'm a therapist."

I stopped with the napkin. "A shrink?" I felt horrified that I might have already disclosed too much about myself.

"Don't get excited. I'm a humble psychologist, with just a few remaining corporate clients. I'm thirty-five, but thanks to some family money and excellent investments, I'm already semi-retired. You don't look like you approve of therapists."

"I'd rather you were a bank robber," I said.

"A viable career move. I'll consider it." His broad, toothy grin was marvelous, and I smiled back.

We chatted for the rest of the afternoon, moved on to an osteria for dinner, and afterwards, he followed me back to the cabin in his car. I was being reckless and stupid. I felt guilty, too, that I was disrespecting Bruce and the generosity of his lovely home. Perhaps I was even putting myself in danger, but to be honest, that was half the excitement.

"Would you like a brandy?" I asked, thinking of Bruce's well-stocked liquor cabinet.

"That would be nice." He looked around at the cabin. "Nice place for a rental," he said. He sat on the couch. I handed him his drink and sat beside him.

"I suppose so," I said. He looked at me quizzically. "I mean, the house is lovely, but I'm not a fan of the mountains."

"You prefer the beach?" he asked.

"Let's just say that I prefer the action of a city."

He may have misconstrued my comment, thinking that I was asking for "a little action." Anyway, he leaned over and kissed me. A gentle kiss. An exploratory one. I responded a little more vigorously than I should have, but this was my pattern after all: sex without commitment, pleasure without thinking. My intention was just to invite him for a nightcap. I had no intention of sleeping with him, but alcohol once again became my boon companion, blurring the edges of good sense. Besides, he was altogether beautiful, and I hadn't experienced a kiss like that in a long time.

He pulled away. "Is this all right? Are you all right?"

I didn't answer. This wasn't the typical pattern of one-night stands, and it threw me.

"Look, you're lovely, but I don't want to move too fast. You shouldn't be uncomfortable," he said.

Talking was the last thing on my mind. I kissed him again. The kiss was needy and deep. He responded in kind, but he approached me with a tenderness I wasn't used to. Under his attention, whatever fears and concerns I harbored melted away. He held me with a genuine feeling of wanting to be with me, as if nothing in the world could call him away.

Sensitive yet demanding, he was a master at lovemaking. His body was hard and well-sculpted, and he knew what to do with his tongue, his hands, and other body parts. At least for the moment, all my frustration, fears, lost opportunities, and dashed dreams of fame and fortune vanished. He was smart, and I was certain we both knew that the sex was for one night. There would be no messy attachments or awkward silences at the end. Just a simple, "Enjoyed it. Goodbye," and something in me would be free, or at least freer, for a little while.

Encumbrances are not my thing, and I don't like intimacy. I don't trust people to be there for me. Once betrayed, only a fool will trust again, and I was no fool. I kept myself apart from all but a few. I was a modern woman, emotionally uninvolved, finding temporary pleasure with strangers who warmed the bed and released me from a repetitive mind prone to toggling between worry and anxiety. My narrative was that I was not like other women. I dedicated myself to my craft and the noble pursuit of worthy causes.

What an arrogant and shameless liar I was. My biggest skill was being a master at self-deception. The expectation of another betrayal, one that could be just as severe and malicious as the first one, I knew would do me in. I'd chosen a life with a ferocious guard at the gate, even if it meant that I'd be alone for the rest of my life.

Despite our marathon session, Sal surprisingly didn't leave as I'd expected. He fell asleep instead. I tried to rest beside him, dozed off for a few minutes, had one hell of a nightmare from which he woke me, and when he went back to sleep, I got up, slipped on my robe, and went to my laptop in the loft.

It was four A.M. when he awoke again. He followed the light to the office, and no doubt, the click-clack of my keyboard. I was trying to find my mother and if she were still alive, and if not, how and when she'd died, and where her grave was. Sal, logy from sleep, framed himself on the banister, watching me.

"What's going on?" he asked. "Why are you up? What are you doing?"

I shut the computer. "Please…Don't ask so many questions."

"Okay," he said. "I'm sorry." He came over to me, naked and hard again, without a shred of modesty. He squatted at my knee, undoing the sash of my robe, and embraced my pelvis. His touch thrilled me again. "Sarah, tell me what's going on."

"I don't know you. Why should I?"

He never answered. He went back to bed alone, and the next morning, as I predicted, he was gone. I was a bit relieved, but somehow I also missed him. However crazy the feeling, he was *there*—and this counted for something, at least to me.

The next evening, he surprised me by calling at five o'clock. We'd exchanged numbers when I'd felt in a particularly chummy mood, but honestly, I never expected to hear from him again. When I heard his deeply resonant voice, at first, I was sorry to have given him the number. Was I conflicted? You could say that.

"What are you doing for dinner?" he asked.

"I'm not eating," I said.

"Is that for tonight or ever?"

"What do you want?" I asked.

"A turkey Reuben with homemade kettle chips on the side. And you?"

I started to say, "to be left alone," but a turkey Reuben suddenly sounded wonderful. "O-kay," I said, dragging out the vowel. "Pick me up at six."

#

The turkey Reuben didn't disappoint. I'd spent all day at the Bryson Town Hall finding nothing I hadn't known before, and I'd forgotten to eat lunch.

He observed me devouring dinner with a wry smile on his face. "What?" I asked.

"You can tell how passionate a woman is by how she eats. Ever heard that?" he asked.

"Is that what you teach your corporate clients?" I said.

"Nope. It's an entirely personal observation."

A rivulet of thousand island dressing dribbled down my chin, and I wiped it off. "Why don't you go psychoanalyze a bowl of banana pudding for me while you're at it?"

"Two coming up," he said as he waved at the server.

Over coffee, I challenged him. "Look, Sal, you seem like a nice guy. But I don't know what you want with me. I just got here, and I'm leaving again as soon as I can."

"Plans change."

"Not mine."

"Okay," he said. "Fair enough. But can't we just enjoy each other for now?"

I didn't have an answer to that. The banana pudding came, and we ate in silence.

Scraping the last of the dessert out of his bowl, he said, "You don't impress me as someone who's used to being cared about."

I couldn't put my spoon down hard enough. "Wow. Let me tell you, that's not the talk that'll get me into bed again."

"I didn't mean to offend—"

"You're not my shrink."

"No. Sorry," he said. The silence that fell between us had a life of its own, but it was clear we hadn't reached the end of the conversation. "I think, sometimes, people don't see therapists as human. I'm being a little too human tonight, I suppose." Again, more silence. "It's just that...well, I care about you." "Oh, give me a blooming br—"

"I do. Look, I'm not asking for a lifetime commitment here. I'm just saying you intrigue me, and I care about you."

"Why?" I asked.

"You want a list?"

"Is there one?"

"Of course. First, you're a challenge."

"Not really. You got me into bed on the first date."

"Yes, the physical bodies merged, but the emotional body…you keep that locked away. Second, you're beautiful. All that cascading copper hair drives me wild. And those brilliant blue eyes. They're quite unusual."

I rolled my brilliant blues, but he continued. "Look, you asked for it. Third, you're smart. I don't know how I know that. Is it your lightning-fast comebacks or scintillating repartee? Maybe. Shall I go on?"

I looked into his eyes, which gave me the impression that they could see through me and read the small print engraved at the bottom of my stone-cold heart. He was so embracing, so sincere, so concerned. No one had ever looked at me like that, or maybe I hadn't let them until now.

This last thought brought me to an epiphany: I didn't want to be so alone, not anymore. I was emotionally exhausted, and while I didn't know this man, I resolved to tell him a little. Enough to satisfy him and unburden myself. And then we'd say goodbye—again.

"I'm from here," I said. "A long time ago. I left when I was a child. Someone murdered my father. I want to find out who did it."

His eyebrows shot up in surprise, but he didn't ask me to tell him more. We got in his car silently and drove to Bruce's cabin. When we got to the house, neither of us made a move to get out of the vehicle.

"Are you coming in?" I asked.

"Do you want me to?"

I'd already thought about it. "Yes," I said, and as soon as we got inside, he led me to the bed and put his lips on me. And after lovemaking, for the first time since I can remember, I fell into an undisturbed, dreamless sleep.

CHAPTER 4

In the morning, he asked the names of my mother and father. Puzzled, I told him my mother's name, and that I knew virtually nothing about my father. Then, in my old plaid, red flannel robe, I walked him to the front door to say goodbye. There, he turned to me and said, "I'm going to help you find your father's killer."

I felt a flare of anger. "I need you to go," I said. Suddenly, I felt he knew too much. Too fast, he'd intruded on the inner sanctum, and I blamed myself for opening that door. He didn't act hurt or surprised by my reaction. He simply got in his car and drove away without another word.

Something caught my eye as I turned to go into the house. Standing on the ridge above the cabin was a tan and white dog, wild, of unknown lineage. He had a white streak up his nose that ended on his forehead—and of all things—it looked like the end of a large Milk-Bone dog biscuit. I got the feeling that these were his hills and that he considered the rest of us merely visitors. I've always loved animals, but this dog considered me with such intensity, I found it unsettling.

He was still standing on the ridge, staring at me, when I closed the door.

CHAPTER 5

I'm not a complete fool. I'd heard what Dr. Marsh said. After Salem left, I rested and considered my situation. By the early afternoon, I'd decided to eat more healthily—that instead of abstinence. It was a start.

Determined to keep a low profile, I headed to the emporium to buy organic fruits and vegetables. But as I was climbing the stairs to the store, a man came barreling out, unbalancing me as he knocked into my shoulder. Instead of apologizing, he looked me in the eye, grunted, and kept going. My left foot had caught me from toppling over and this had exacerbated the pain, so I grasped the rail to steady myself and wait for the agony to subside.

I hadn't noticed the two women coming up behind me, one tall and angular, the other short and padded, the same two women I'd seen dancing in the park. The tall one looked serious and wore, what I guessed, was a perpetual scowl. The short one, wide-eyed and spacey-looking with wildly curling hair, was more animated and cheerful.

"Don't mind him, missy," said the tall one. "That's Alister Banks, the writer—"

"—or used to be," said the other, casting a knowing look at the tall one.

"—which is probably the source of his problem—" the tall one said.

"—but still no excuse," said the round one.

Their chatter sounded musical, one phrase segueing into another. I nodded, managing a small smile, and the three of us went inside.

The store was old, with a stamped metal ceiling, wood floors that creaked as I walked on them, and a wood-burning stove in the corner. There were two aisles, a cash register opposite the front door, and bins of fresh produce built into the wall to my left. The number of people in the store surprised me. Several of them stopped what they were doing and stared at me.

"Oh, don't mind them," said the tall woman coming up beside me with a basket. "Some folks in these parts ain't used to seeing strangers." No one here looked like they'd read *The Express* where my picture had accompanied my articles. Whatever their problem, a small group hurried out of the store as if I were Typhoid Mary.

I was admiring the fresh apples when the bell above the door jingled, and I turned to see the white-haired cashier from the liquor store come in. This time, I studied her. She'd probably been quite stunning in her youth, but her face was now a warren of wrinkles, as if she'd baked in the sun her entire life. She stopped when she saw me, an awkward moment, and then nodded. I nodded back and returned to picking out apples.

When I emerged with my bag of groceries about twenty minutes later, a tall, gaunt old man in black accosted me in the parking lot. He led a small group of people, several of whom were the people who'd stared at me in the store. They all wore black and had stern expressions on their sour faces.

"You!" said the leader, pointing a bony, crooked finger in my face as the others mumbled support.

"Do I know you?" I gave him a flinty stare, hoping he'd back off. He didn't, but to his credit, he withdrew the finger.

"Did you think you could sneak back here without us recognizing you?"

I froze. Did he know me?

A trickle of brown tobacco juice ran from the right corner of his mouth. "You look just like your mother, the *witch*!" He spat on the ground before wiping his mouth on his sleeve.

Wait. What?

"Tell her, Reverend!" yelled a stout woman who appeared to have six reddish hairs on her head.

"We don't tolerate witches—or their kin—living in our community," said the Reverend.

Gripping the bag of groceries more tightly in front of me, I said, "I assure you, I don't know what you're talking about." I tried to get around him, but he again stepped in front of me.

"Don't you deny it! You're the daughter of Callie Moon! The *witch*!" He spat on the ground again. A great big wad of something brown and gummy stayed perched on the gravel of the parking lot.

I couldn't tell if he meant the word "witch" literally or figuratively, but he'd gotten my mother's name right. I didn't know how he knew her, but I had a more immediate problem: The crowd, a hot-headed welcoming committee, was moving closer to me, noisy and excitable. My heart rate ramped up.

Suddenly, the Reverend grabbed me by the arms, his dirty fingernails digging into my flesh. "You ain't welcome here!" he shouted in my face. His breath stank of stale tobacco juice and undigested tomato soup. As I was reeling from it, my grocery bag split, and I watched my beautiful apples roll under somebody's car.

The crowd, meanwhile, closed around us. What the hell was happening here? Then a voice boomed, "Let her go!" As my accusers moved back a few paces, I could see that my defender was the tall woman who'd spoken to me as I was going to the store. The short one stood by her side, legs planted like a bulldog's.

"You know who she is!" boomed the Reverend.

"We do," said the tall one, as cool as an ice queen.

"We don't want her kind here," he said.

"Then you'll have to deal with it," said the tall one, "because here she be."

"Oh, is that so? Grab her and take her, boys," the Reverend ordered as several men grabbed me and started hauling me to a truck. I pushed, shoved, and kicked, but they were winning. Someone opened the door, and the crowd was getting ready to hoist me inside.

"Hey!" the tall woman bellowed.

The group stopped and turned back to the two women who, when they were sure they had everyone's attention, pulled up their shirts and flashed their naked breasts. My attackers and I were dumbfounded. A few mouths dropped open. I'm sure one of them was mine. The men who'd been holding onto me dropped me like a hot biscuit and ran to their vehicles. Their trucks peeled out on the loose gravel.

The women watched the dusty exodus and laughed. "You all right, missy?" the tall one asked me.

"I think so."

"You jes' met Reverend Thatcher. His cornbread ain't all the way done in the middle," said the round one.

I shook my head. "Well, you seemed to know how to handle him."

"We ain't in shape for anything else," said the tall one.

"Excuse me. I'm in shape. Round is a shape," the small one said.

"And, as long as we saved you from being rode out on a rail, I suppose introductions are in order. I'm Buttercup Swinehart; you can call me Cup. And this here's my sister, Bluet."

"You can call me Blue," said the round one, shaking my hand.

"Nice to meet you. I'm…" Again, I hesitated over my alias. Aw, hell, I thought, who am I fooling anyway? Certainly no one around here since they'd used my birth mother's name. "I'm Kate Adair. What was all that about? Why did he say my mother was a witch? Do you know her?" I asked as I went about gathering my groceries.

The sisters gave one another a knowing look. "Why don't you jes' finish gittin' your stuff together and throw it in your car there? Then follow us. There's nothing we can't discuss over a good cup of tea," Blue said.

I did as she said and followed them, walking a short distance down the highway and up a mountain road. They assured me they didn't live far, and we soon came to a sweet, blue clapboard house, situated up another winding gravel road in the middle of a wood.

"You okay, missy?" Cup asked, noticing my limp.

I waved dismissively. "Just a sprain."

The house inside was odd—one large room filled with shadows. The structure appeared to be a large kitchen. On several tables, liquids bubbled in pots of all sizes over hot plates, and herbs hung from beams in the ceiling.

Cup pointed to a wooden bench, and I sat at the long trestle table in the middle of the room. Blue then appeared with a cup of tea I hadn't seen her pour.

"Now you drink this, dearie," she said. "It'll settle your nerves."

The tea, a mixture of herbs, tasted milky and smooth, and there was honey in it. Whatever the elixir was, I felt better after finishing a cup and stopped shaking.

"Thank you. What was that crazy scene about? Who were those people?" I asked Blue as she poured me another cup.

"That's our cult," said Cup.

Blue shook her head. "The world don't have enough Kool Aid."

"They fancy themselves fundamentalists, but the real fundamentalists wouldn't have 'em, so they came here to start their own thing. They think that the flesh is of the devil. Nothing to worry about."

"Yeah? Well, tell that to the bruises on my arms." The spots where the Reverend's fingers had gouged me were turning as purple as my ankles. His nails had even broken the skin.

"Rub this in," said Blue, handing me a tube of ointment.

I did as she asked. "So what did they mean when they said my mother was a witch? They had her name right. Callie Moon—"

"Lawd, she weren't no witch," said Blue, laughing. Cup shot her a look. "Oops," Blue said.

I leaned into them, my elbows on the table. "You both know my mother?"

"Did. She ain't with us no more," said Cup.

"Okay," I said, sitting back. I told myself whether she was alive or dead didn't matter to me. The last time I saw the loathsome woman, I was five years old. "Why'd they call her a witch?"

"Jes' a rumor. That's all," said Cup. "She was half-Melungeon. Lots of prejudice and mystical nonsense comes with that. 'Witch' was one of the nicer things they called them people."

I sat, stunned. "I'm Melungeon?" I asked. I'd read about Melungeons, but I'd never thought of them as my lineage, although my mother was darker skinned than me. Melungeons were solitary Appalachian back hill people who kept to themselves. A mixture of European, African, and Native American ancestry. Not black, not white, and before interbreeding and recent acceptance by a "woke" society, they didn't fit in anywhere. Finding out that I was part Melungeon was, by far, the most exotic thing that ever happened to my white-bread existence, and I wanted to know more.

"Who was Melungeon? My mother's mother or father?"

"Your granddaddy. Your grandma was white as they come. You never wondered where your bright blue eyes come from? Or why you, as a little red-headed girl, tan?" Blue said.

"I guess I never thought about it. Mother had blue eyes and red hair."

"Well, those light blue eyes are straight from the Melungeons," said Cup.

"That's amazing. I never knew much about my family. You probably know more than I do. Back at the store, it even sounded like you knew me," I said.

"Well, no doubt you're Callie Moon's kid. You look jes' like her," said Cup.

"More tea?" asked Blue, appearing with a pot. She refilled my cup, and I drank it down. She then sat across the table from me.

I felt myself relaxing with these two eccentric women. Living in New York had prepared me for quirky. Now the conversation lagged, and they were waiting for me to say something. I wasn't about to tell them I was hiding from a serial killer. Instead, I offered something else. My thinking was that if I gave, I'd get, and I was looking for information. "I don't remember my mother very well. But I'm in these mountains to find out who killed my father," I said.

I think I might have gotten more of a reaction by saying, "This is damn good tea." There was no response from either of them. Cup kept leaning against the sink, still scowling but looking off in the distance, and

Blue, her head in her hand and her elbow on the table, was smiling at the live crow on a perch in the corner. I hadn't noticed it before. "*Wrack*," it said.

The minutes ticked by, a huge old train-station clock on the wall recording the seconds. No one spoke. No one moved. It was strange. Never one to be patient, however, enough was enough. I stood, and my movement seemed to wake everyone up.

"Well, thank you so much for the tea and the ointment, and for saving me, of course. I'm feeling better now. I'll just walk back to my car and head home." It was awkward excusing myself in such silence, but they didn't try to get me to stay, or even ask where "home" might be.

Blue walked me to the door. Then, when I'd stepped across the threshold, she whispered, "You're looking for Alister Banks."

Had I heard right? I swung around to ask her as the door slammed in my face. I knocked twice, but no one answered. "Hey, why do you think I'm looking for Alister Banks?" I called, and then, "Where do I even find him?" but I received no response, only silence. Clearly, the sisters were done with me. Reluctantly, I turned to go down the road and was surprised that it was already dusk. I'd forgotten how fast night fell here, the mountains and immense trees casting deep shadows before the sun had properly set. There was still enough light for me to pick my way back to the main road, but the gravel path seemed much longer than when I came up. It was rough going, and my ankles and feet hurt like they'd been torched. I pushed thoughts of my diagnosis away.

In the far distance, a tractor lurched over something, gave a great screech, and died. The silence that came after rattled me even more than the screech had. I walked on and then noticed a sudden, clamorous cacophony of tree frogs and cicadas. I also stepped around great piles of horse dung and deep ruts in the road that I could have sworn hadn't been there before. The gathering shadows were ominous and oppressive, the air too still, and there was a rhythmic pulse of something screaming from overhanging branches. I was spooked and wondered if I'd taken a wrong turn. I considered going back and asking Cup and Blue for help, but kept to the gravel road, worried about being caught by the night. Where was the damn highway? I felt my isolation keenly. Anything could happen to me here and no one would know. The scent of decomposition in the soil was too thick and intense and caused me to gasp for cleaner air. Slick, moldy leaves made me slide and nothing looked remotely familiar. Despite all this, I kept going, my left foot all but dragging.

Up ahead, I was equally relieved and frightened to see something move. Calming myself down, I was sure it was a dog, and I'm a dog lover. It was black and the size of a cocker spaniel or a young Labrador Retriever. I thought that finding a dog companion would make me feel better in this terrifying place. I hurried toward it, hoping not to scare it away. It was standing in the shadows and when I reached out my hand to pet it, whispering words of reassurance, I saw just how wrong I was. It wasn't a dog at all, but a young black bear. Before I could withdraw my hand, its mother came charging out of the brush. She roared at me, and I stepped back a few feet—not fast enough—because she advanced on me. It's a fallacy that bears hibernate all winter. Given a warm spell, you'll find bears using your hot tub and enjoying the birdseed on your porch as an *hors d'oeuvre*.

"Easy, mama. I'm harmless, I promise. I…I love animals…"

She stopped, observing me. I was shaking furiously and my unsteady legs felt about to give way. She snarled again, and I heard a snuffle behind me. Turning slowly so as not to spook her more, I saw a second young bear, about the size of the first, standing on his hind legs about ten feet away.

Oh, righteous hell, I thought. You never want to get between a mother bear and her cubs, and yet there I was. There was no place to run. I couldn't go forward and I couldn't go back.

I'd read the public service announcement posted on the wall at Bruce's cabin. *"When surprised by a black bear, back away slowly. If this isn't an option, yell, scream, and make yourself seem larger."* So all five foot three of me screamed for all I was worth, but the bear, who was supposed to run away, stood her ground and simply seemed confused. I opened my mouth to scream again when something came crashing out of the thicket.

Too surprised to scream, I only saw it was a dog. He leaped on the bear, and there were great, bloodcurdling roars of sound and fury from both animals. I couldn't tell who was coming out ahead until the bear swatted the dog with her huge paw, propelling him a good eight feet into the air. The dog slammed down on the side of the road with a hideous thud and lay still. The bear had had enough then. She roared at me once more, gathered her two cubs, and took her leave.

I ran to the dog. It took a minute for me to recognize that it was the dog I'd seen at the cabin. I can't say that I visually recognized him. I was too terrified to pay attention to details, and we were mostly in shadow. Yet miles away from Bruce's cabin, don't ask me how I knew it was the same dog, but I did. The poor little thing was bloody and unconscious, and I was crying as I took him in my arms. There was no time to think about the pain in my body. I did what I had to, limping and running with my would-be savior down the road to the highway as fast as I could go.

CHAPTER 6

The dog weighed at least forty pounds and my arms, as well as my ankles, felt as if they were giving out by the time we reached the highway. It had turned cold, and I was grateful for the small amount of body heat that my little companion radiated. There were no lights along the country road, so when a car pulled up behind me, I panicked. As I turned, the headlights blinded me, and I must have looked like a proper imbecile stepping this way and that, disoriented, when the vehicle pulled beside me. A fresh wave of terror hit when the car window whirred down.

"Sarah?" It was Salem's voice. He sounded as incredulous as I was.

I can't describe the relief in hearing his voice. I wasn't aware of holding my breath, but suddenly, I exhaled in a burst and gasped for air. "This dog just saved me from a bear! He's hurt!"

"Get in the car," he ordered. "I'll take you to a vet," and I climbed in the front seat with the dog in my arms.

"Are you okay?" he asked as I buckled up.

"I'm fine. It's the dog," I said.

"While I have a signal..." he said and dialed a contact number he had in his phone.

A woman's voice came through the radio. "Hey, you," she said.

"Hey. I've got a dog here that a bear has attacked."

"Come on," she said.

"You'll wait?"

"Come on," she repeated.

Sal drove like a madman, plunging down the mountain road, taking switchbacks at dangerous speeds, and riding the center line when he could to help straighten out the curves. It was a nauseating experience. Sal screeched to a halt in front of the veterinary facility down the mountain. I flew out of the car clutching the dog, before the car had even rolled to a stop, as a woman hurried out of the facility.

"A bear attacked this dog!" I shouted as she hastened us inside.

The examination room was neat and clean and smelled of antiseptic. Framed pictures of patients and grateful notes from their families lined the walls.

"I'm Dr. Hill," said the vet. "What happened?"

As I told her, she cradled the dog's head and raised his closed eyelids. "He's in shock," she said as she continued to examine him. "Looks like some deep puncture wounds and a possible concussion...What's his name?" she asked.

"I don't know. He's not my dog," I said.

"He's not? But you said he saved you? That's unusual behavior for a dog that isn't yours...What a beautiful animal," she added as she examined him further. "This is a breed called a 'Carolina dog.' Indigenous to these mountains. They make great pets when you can catch one. That's quite a distinguishing mark on his forehead. Did you notice?"

Now, in the bright light of the exam room, I could see how beautiful the tan and white dog was and along the top of his nose, there was the white streak that ended with the perfect image of the end of a Milk-Bone dog biscuit on his forehead.

"Look at that," I said, more to myself than anyone. This distinctive mark was probably why I recognized this dog from the ridge. I then glanced at Sal, wanting to share the moment, but he was leaning against the wall, hands deep in his pockets, staring at the floor.

"Hmm…Let's see if he's been microchipped," said Dr. Hill, as she took out a scanner and ran it around his neck, over his shoulders, and down his back. "Nope…No chip," she said, putting the device aside. "Okay. I'll clean up those wounds and want to keep him here tonight to watch how seriously he's concussed. He'll be in good hands with me. I live in the house you passed in front of the clinic, so I can come up and check on him throughout the night. Can you call me tomorrow? By then, we should have a better idea of how he's doing."

I took her business card. "I'm good for all the medical costs," I said. Despite her reluctance to calculate, I had cash in my purse and insisted on giving her more than the estimate.

After that, Salem drove me back to my car.

"Thank you," I said.

"No problem."

He was quiet, unusually so, and I was worried that he was angry at me, or worse, considered me a blooming idiot.

"I've got something for you," he said, handing me a folder from the back seat as we pulled into the emporium lot and stopped. "I know you're looking for information about your father, and I'm sorry to say that I've found nothing on him yet. It would help if you could remember his name. I found some stuff about your mom, though, at county records down in Bryson."

"Did you find where her grave is?" I asked, hoping that the grave was what he'd found and not something I didn't want disclosed.

"No. Sorry. There's something in there you should know about though."

"Yeah, what?" I thumbed through the file, but it was too dark to read anything.

"It seems your mother was in a mental institution."

Something shut down inside me. "Okay." I closed the file and stuffed it into my bag. That my mother was in a mental institution didn't surprise me. From what little I knew, her life could have gone in a number of terrible directions. Perhaps she suffered from the delusion that she was a witch and that's why she ended up in a mental hospital. Who knew?

"Thanks," I said and got out of the car.

"One more thing. Your mom didn't have a daughter named Sarah. Her daughter's name was Kate." A stultifying silence hung in the air. "Care to tell me about why you call yourself Sarah?"

I felt sucker-punched and vulnerable. "No," I said.

Another silence. "I hope one day you'll trust me enough to tell me. I won't ask again, but maybe the day will come."

Suddenly, I was furious. I didn't ask for therapy. I didn't ask for this *intrusion*. This was none of his business. I got out of the car, slammed the door, and leaned into the open window. I wanted to call him on something, change the subject, put *him* on the spot for a while.

"Let me ask you something: If you were down in Bryson today, why were you just coming up the road from South Carolina? It's in the opposite direction." I made no apology for the question sounding accusatory.

Sal looked taken aback. "If you must know, I went down to Bryson this morning to see my CPA and went by county records *for you*. And I lost a crown today at lunch and my dentist is in Greenville, so I canceled my afternoon appointments and went down there. I can give you the dentist's name and number if you want to check it out."

"That's a lot of driving to do in one day."

"Yeah. And I'm tired." He scowled as he gripped and twisted his hands on the steering wheel. "So tell me, is it me you don't trust or everybody?"

"Thanks for the help," I said, tapping the windowsill. "And...just so you know...it's you *and* everybody."

#

When I got to Bruce's, I made myself a drink. I felt disgusted with myself. Sal was trying to help, and I'd behaved like an ungrateful virago. I assured myself that he was getting too close, and it was alright to chase him away. Being protective, I guarded the truth about my family. I didn't want anyone to discover its secrets before I did because I didn't know what the truth would reveal about me. He'd found a piece of information I hadn't found and didn't know, and I felt raw and vulnerable.

I climbed into Bruce's king-size bed and read the file Sal had given me. Callie Talley, later Moon, was born in 1965, the only daughter of Alden Talley, Melungeon, and Alma Rogers, Caucasian, whose death records showed they had both died on the same day when my mother was three. That surprised me. What happened, and who reared her? The file contained additional information stating that she voluntarily admitted herself to a mental institution in 1986 when she was twenty-one years old. There was no mention of why. I calculated. I would have been a year old, too young to know what was happening then. But I had lived on Blood Mountain until I was five and still had very few memories. I wondered why. Who took care of me?

"What are your parents like?" my friends would ask me when they complained about theirs. I always felt guilty whining about the Adairs who'd given me a wonderful home. Still, I was an adolescent who wanted to fit in, so I complained with the best of them, all the while harboring a secret that stung like a wasp: I wasn't really an Adair. I didn't belong to anybody. Somehow it felt like my fault that I was not enough to be an Adair, that I wasn't enough to be anyone from the very start of my life.

There, propped up in Bruce's bed, I was overwhelmed with the feeling that I might not want to know my story. I got up anyway and went to the computer and searched for information about myself: Kate Moon, Kate Adair. Part of me was relieved when all I found were the articles I'd written and the papers Da had filed—maybe even forged—to make me his daughter.

But the thing about a mystery is you can't stop investigating it, certainly not when it's a mystery about you. I looked up Melungeon, and discovered that at one time, people used the name as an insult, possibly coining the name from a Turkish word for "cursed soul." I shuddered at that and pushed the thought away. I looked at pictures of them online. They were beautiful people, hard-working, with glowing skin and shining blue eyes. I found myself proud of my heritage, something I hadn't given much thought to before then. But now, at thirty-three years old, jobless and with time on my hands, I wanted to know more about who I was, and the stock I came from, and although afraid, I was willing to face the truth. Because substantial information on my life was so scarce, I sensed that there *might* be a good story here. I'd never asked Da—or my stepmother when she was alive—about my birth parents. I suspected that my mother was an appalling person, and after Sal's discovery, I asked myself, "Just how crazy was she?" It crossed my mind to wonder if I'd inherited something. *God forbid*, I thought. All these thoughts were going through my mind, but with sympathy for my Melungeon past, I knew now for the first time in my life, that I was going to press forward and go all the way.

The file said that Mother was housed in the asylum for a year. What had become of me during that time? Mother must have sent me off somewhere, but no matter how hard I tried, I couldn't remember anything. All my life, what I remembered, I'd tried to forget. Perhaps it was wrong to be so avoidant. It had only served me up to a point. Now I found myself considering ways to use the past instead of it using me.

CHAPTER 6

I researched the name of the mental institution where my mother had gone: the Bryce Home for the Insane. An awful name. The internet showed a huge, old wooden structure and said that it had burned down in 1988, a kerosene heater fire. Eighteen people died. Feeling conflicted and weak in the knees, I forged ahead and started a journal.

CHAPTER 7

I woke early, feeling better than usual. The scotch I'd poured the night before stood untouched on the nightstand. That was why. I made my way to the kitchen for coffee, and while it was brewing, I called Dr. Hill about the dog as I'd worried about him until I fell asleep. No one answered the phone. It was probably too early for them to be in the office, so I left a message.

I checked *The Express* website for additional details about The Laundry Man, but there weren't any. He was still lying low. I put that story aside because I had two more missions for the day and had to get on with them—and I wasn't looking forward to either. First, I dressed for hiking around Blood Mountain. I pulled on my jeans, a white t-shirt, and a tan corduroy barn jacket. In the closet, I found some boots, most likely belonging to Margaret, well-worn and slightly too large, just right for my painful foot.

Driving onto Blood Mountain, I passed a sign that said, "Private Road. Trespassers will be prosecuted," and stopped at the gate that kept out the curious. There was an entry code for the few people who lived there, but I didn't know what it was. I parked in a gravel turnabout and stepped out of the car. I remembered this old road. It didn't go all the way to the top of the mountain. This main road only served the few houses along the way. But the mountain itself consisted of a warren of old Cherokee hunting trails. I was going to follow them. I felt sure they'd take me past what most people saw and into the realms of the beyond, whatever that was going to be.

Starting the climb, I prowled around the mountain, hoping to find something recognizable: a house, a field, a stream, a rock, anything that might trigger a memory and launch me in a direction. The vegetation was thick. It was a tough climb; the trails disappeared and then reappeared more deeply in the woods. They always required more laborious climbing. And while I recognized nothing, the mountain *was* eerily familiar. I don't know how to describe it—but the uneasiness was overwhelming: Not only was this mountain familiar to me, but I was familiar to it, as if two disparate energies, when they came near one another, magnetically accommodated each other, and snapped insistently into place.

I looked around for my mother's grave. After all, we'd lived here and her ultimate resting place could have been on this mountain. Of course, it could have been anywhere, and finding it was more important to me than it probably should have been. I'd made it some sort of ill-defined metaphor, blurry at its core.

I hiked up, down, and sideways, but nothing looked familiar and there was no grave to be found. There was a small shack in a deep ravine about a quarter of the way up the hill. There were two more houses, one large, impressive house, neglected by the looks of the overgrown yard, and one more that was higher still. It had a scratched front door as if a big insistent dog had tried to get inside. The entire house was in serious disrepair, the white paint peeling off and black mold growing up its south side. Dull black shutters hung catawampus to the windows that once they'd abutted, and metal poles that had supported a clothesline stood at an angle, rusted and impossible to use. Despite the house's horrible condition, it looked occupied as there was an old dilapidated truck parked at the side. I kept walking, this time around the mountain, where another more modest home stood. Someone had taken meticulous care to groom this house and yard.

Heading back down, on a weedy, barely visible gravel road, I came to a burned-down shack. A couple of scorched beams where the house once stood stuck up from the undergrowth. Two ravens sat on a collapsed split-rail fence nearby, watching me.

CHAPTER 7

"Hi, boys," I said. The birds, affronted, flew away.

Nothing looked familiar, not the road, the landscape, the mountains, the trees, nor the long grass growing in the field across the road, but it *felt* so. Some gut feeling close to terror told me I'd found *something*, so I stood there trying to experience what I could before approaching the shack. I could sense an uncanny feeling in the air, as if something were lurking, ready to suck the soul out of my body and into oblivion if I wasn't on guard. I shuddered but pressed forward, watching my step. The house lay in rubble under my feet, nature having claimed the space as her own. Tall, wet weeds pressed upwards through the wood rot, and I smelled char, which still emanated from the decay, even though the fire that had brought this place down appeared to have done so years before. Nature hadn't completely erased the sickly sweet odor of someone's life in ruins, and I couldn't help but wonder if it was mine.

#

After leaving that rubble, I sought the car and drove back toward the cabin. I stopped in Bowden, however, and bought a copy of *The Express* from the grocery store. I sat at the coffee shop reading Grant Maitland's article on The Laundry Man and had to admit that, with some consternation, his article was good. There was still nothing newsworthy, however. The Laundry Man's unusual silence unnerved me, as there had been no recent attacks.

Pulling out my notepad, I read through the notes I'd made on my family. I then re-read The Laundry Man notes. I slapped the notebook shut, feeling frustrated that I wasn't making headway on either story.

In the car outside The Coffee Freak, I called Ramos.

He answered, "Ramos Esquire."

"Well, you obviously know it's me."

"Yep. How's doings?" he asked.

"That's why I'm calling you."

"All's quiet on the eastern front. We can't figure out why," he said.

"You'll let me know?"

"You're a pushy broad, you know it?"

He rang off, and I took advantage of the good cell signal to call Da.

"Hey, Da! It's Kate. Guess where I am?"

"I don't know, sweetie, but I'm going to town." This was his version of remembering that I was *out of town*.

"I'm in North Carolina. Near where you used to live."

"Uh-huh."

I choked up. "I miss you very much."

"Uh-huh."

"I love you, Da."

"Well, I love you too, sweetie. You're the apple of my eye."

He often substituted words, but he always got that line right. I was always "the apple of his eye." When I got off the phone, I felt guilty for so relentlessly researching my past. *Da* had been there all along. *He* had been my father, more than the real one ever had. The boundaries for love, loyalty, curiosity, and what I owed myself to find out confused me. I was simply a mass of irreconcilable differences.

I called the vet again too, and this time, the receptionist answered. "Hello! I'm calling about the dog I brought in last evening. A bear had attacked him. I want to see how he's doing," I said.

"I'm so sorry, but I'm new here and just filling in. May I ask the doctor about your dog and get back to you?"

Frustrated, I gave her my number, even though the office already had it. I drove back to the cabin to change out of my hiking gear. Getting ready for my second mission required me to clean up, and as the afternoon arrived, the temperature dropped drastically. I learned that people in this region often experienced four seasons in a day. The weather forecast even predicted a light snowfall.

I'd just pulled on my heavy Aran sweater when I heard the clang of the bear welcome bell on the porch. When I opened the door, there stood Sal.

Adrenaline hit my bloodstream and I could feel my heart pounding. "I didn't think you'd be speaking to me," I said.

He chuckled. "I didn't expect *you* to speak to *me*. But I brought you a peace offering." He held up a can of aerosol spray with a little waggle of his hand.

"What's that?"

"Bear spray. If you're going to pull stunts like last night, you'll need a case of it."

"Thanks," I said, taking it from his hand as he entered the cabin.

"And I bought you a holster, too, for it to go in," and he handed me a paper bag he pulled from his pocket as he slid out of his coat. Inside, there was a holster that could hang from my belt, but instead of a six shooter, it fit a can of bear spray.

"It shoots up to thirty-five feet, so you don't have to get close, and they recommend you practice with it first. They don't want you to shoot your eye out. Directions are in the bag."

"Thanks," I said again. I wasn't about to tell him about my solo excursion this morning. I didn't want him to be upset with me for hiking all over Blood Mountain without bear spray. Grabbing my coat from the rack, I said, "But you'll have to excuse me. I'm on my way out."

He watched as I got into my coat, hat, and scarf. I was self-conscious about my foot, which these days hurt most of the time, and I tried not to limp as I bundled up.

"Have I done something?" he asked. "I don't know what I've done."

Because I'd been so unkind to him the night before, I felt myself flush. I angled my body away from his so he wouldn't see how embarrassed I was.

"No," I said, "You haven't done anything. I apologize for my temper last night. It's difficult to find out your mother's been in an asylum, and I overreacted. Thank you for extending friendship, but I haven't been quite honest with you. I didn't come here to get close to anybody. I don't want your help finding out who killed my father. Once I figure things out for myself, I'm going back to New York."

"Ah-hah! You *are* a New Yorker," he said.

To my horror, I snorted with laughter. "You're a pain in the ass," I said, turning to him and shaking my head.

"So are you," he said, his eyes crinkling at the corners. "So…where're we going?"

"I just informed you I don't want you in my life!" We stood staring at each other for a moment, and then we burst out laughing again, so I reconsidered. I was on my way to do something that I was unsure about, and perhaps I'd be more comfortable if I had a witness to the proceedings. I wanted to find Alister Banks, and I was unsure about where to find him and how he'd receive me. A witness had unexpectedly shown up at my door with bear spray, of all things. "Okay, I'm sorry. Put your coat back on. You can do me a favor."

He was already sliding back into his coat. "Goodie. A road trip! Where're we going?"

"Well, if you must know, I met some old women the other day who seem to know more about me than I know about myself. They're sisters, Cup and Blue Swinehart. Ever heard of them?"

He struggled into a pair of gloves he took from his pocket. "Nope."

"I told them I was looking for information about my mother and father and one of them said to see Alister Banks." Gloves seemed like a good idea, and I dug a pair out of a tote bag by the door and started putting them on.

"The writer?" Sal asked.

Surprised, I stopped wrestling with the gloves. "Yes. Do you know him?"

"Only through local gossip. He's a bit of a recluse and has a reputation for being surly. I know where he lives on Blood Mountain, though."

"You do?"

"No need to be impressed. Everybody knows where he lives. He has one of the biggest houses on the mountain, family money, and the return of the famous literary bad boy was big news in these parts. I'll drive you there."

"Thanks," I said.

At the door, he stopped me. "So it's good to have me around."

I smiled. "We'll see," I said, plunging into the cold.

#

That's how we ended up in Alister Banks's front yard, but from the time we turned onto Blood Mountain, I was again uneasy on home soil. Here I was with a therapist who could probably size me up in a New York minute. I chatted amiably, acutely aware of how I was coming across: a little too chatty, but even keeled and in the range of "normal."

We parked at the gate and hiked the rest of the way. Alister lived in a small mansion, although in its present condition, it looked neglected. I was getting my bearings: Alister's home was further down the hill from the run-down house with the scratched front door, and it stood around the mountain from the well-tended, but more modest house I'd observed.

Up close and standing in the yard, the old house looked pitiful. The yard was a mess, filled with long grass, fallen branches, and rusting farm equipment. There was even an old Underwood typewriter in the unmowed grass. The wind picked up, and the chimney whistled. The trim was so rotten that the windows rattled in their frames.

I stepped in front of Sal and knocked on the door. I could hear someone moving around inside. The drooping lace curtains at a window flicked open and closed.

"Mr. Banks?" I called out. "Callie Moon was my mother. I understand your need for privacy, but I have a few questions about my mother and hope you can help me."

Nothing.

"Mr. Banks? I'd appreciate you talking to me…"

Nothing.

Just then, the front door creaked open. I barely registered the shotgun barrel before it went off with a blast. I grabbed Sal, and we ducked, a little late, but better than nothing. Another blast followed. Buckshot hit the trunk of the large red oak tree behind us, sending splinters flying.

"Holy crapola," I whispered. After the initial shock, I stood, my ire up, ready to tell him off. "What the hell do you think you're doing? Mr. Banks—"

But Sal had had enough. He grabbed my hand and ran me down the mountain, not letting me go until he threw me in the passenger seat and ran to get behind the wheel. He spun the car around and drove like he couldn't get off Blood Mountain fast enough.

"You all right?" I asked.

"Doing you a favor can get a guy killed."

"Yeah," I said. "What a peculiar reception...Can I ask you for one more favor?"

"Wow. No..."

"It'll be safe, I promise. I want to ask Cup and Blue why they sent me over there. What did they think he'd tell me?" I gave Sal directions to their house. He drove with a tight jaw, his hands white-knuckled and glued to the steering wheel, no doubt in silent protest about granting me another favor.

But try as I might, I couldn't find the path from the main gravel road that led to the Swinehart property. As a matter of fact, there weren't any routes off that main road at all—no gravel path and no blue house, only something that looked like a defunct granite quarry at the top of the hill, which was nothing more than a large pit dug out of the side of the mountain. Sal stopped the car. There was no place else to go.

There was an icy drizzle now, which did nothing to improve Sal's mood. He thwacked on the windshield wipers.

"Enough?" he asked me, his nails thrumming on the steering wheel.

"Just a minute. I'll be right back." I jumped out of the car before Sal could object. He was in a non-negotiating mood, and it was a relief to get out of his car, even if I got soaking wet. Besides, I wanted to look around, puzzled about how I'd gotten so lost.

To my left, there was an abandoned, rusty trailer that, I guessed, served as a makeshift office for the quarry. Mangled venetian blinds hung in every window, as if a bear had found its way inside and redecorated. All around the yard, unidentifiable parts of old machinery lay wet and rusting, and the only sound was the chitter chat of an annoyed squirrel in a tree somewhere.

"Enjoying yourself?" asked Sal. He'd walked up behind me holding up an umbrella. He sighed, displeased to have his time wasted and to be out in the rain.

My head had started to hurt, and I rubbed my forehead. "I'm sorry. I just don't know how I could have gotten the directions so wrong."

"Yeah, well, I don't think you're going to find what you're looking for here. Can we go?"

A breeze ruffled his gorgeous hair. Touching his arm, I looked into his eyes. "I'm sorry, Sal. I genuinely am. You've been nothing but kind to me, and I keep dragging you into my problems."

"And getting me shot at. Let's not forget that," he said.

"Yeah. That."

He smiled, a bit begrudgingly. "But I kind of invited myself to this party, so I guess I have little right to complain."

"Look," I said, "Why don't we go back to the cabin? I'll pour you an enormous glass of wine courtesy of my host's wine rack and cook you some sort of fantastic dinner. Okay?" I asked.

"If you insist," and after he shrugged, a small mischief returned to his eyes.

#

We went back to Bruce's cabin, where I assembled a rump roast and some vegetables I'd bought at the market. My stepmother had been an excellent cook and had taught me a culinary thing or two, and while I didn't cook hearty meals for myself, I knew how to "put on the dog" for someone else. I also poured both of us a fine cabernet.

After we ate, I excused myself for a few moments and moved to the bedroom. I still hadn't heard from the vet and checked to make sure I hadn't missed a message. Nothing—so I called again. Certain the office was already closed, I wanted them to know I was worried about the little dog and was getting impatient for information.

"Can you tell me about the dog that saved me from the bear? I've yet to hear from you and am quite concerned…" I also dashed off a text message to them.

"Still haven't heard about the dog?" Sal asked from the doorway.

"No."

"You know, they could have had a day full of emergencies, and he could be a low priority right now because he's doing fine."

"Yeah," I said and tried to smile. The other scenario was that the dog was dead, but that idea broke my heart, so I went back to the kitchen and got busy clearing the table and putting the dishes in the dishwasher.

"I've got to go to Boulder on business tomorrow," he said as he restocked the pantry with items I'd left on the counter. "How about a ride to the airport in Asheville? I'd say you owe me a favor," he said, grinning.

And since it was a pretty good bet that no one would shoot at us, I told him I would.

After that, we were quiet. I washed Bruce's fine crystal goblets by hand and turned them upside down on a kitchen towel. I'd been standing on my feet too long and my left foot was excruciating with what felt like sharp needles penetrating the skin and burning their way down to the bone. As I stood, I held my foot up like a flamingo, then put it down, but no position helped. The pain was constant.

Sal was watching me as he dried a big pot that we couldn't fit into the dishwasher.

"What's with the foot?" he asked.

I was dismissive. "Sprain," I said.

My condition wasn't any of his business, but in truth, it made me feel "less than" to have something wrong with me in front of this handsome physical specimen. To his credit, he didn't press further. Later, when I went into the bathroom and took off my shoes and socks, I felt alarmed to see that my left foot and toes were curling under like a claw.

Sal stayed that night. I hid the foot.

CHAPTER 8

Sal asked me to walk him into the airport, so I put the car in hourly parking and plodded to the terminal, trying to minimize the limp. At the security check-in point, he swept me into his arms and kissed me ardently before striding away. I watched him for a moment and asked myself how we'd gotten this far. I should have kept him at arm's length, but there was something so immensely attractive about him, and it wasn't just physical. He had accused me of holding back emotionally, but he did too. I could feel it, and it made him more interesting.

I turned to leave when I all but crashed into Simon, standing a few feet behind me in a heavy green anorak, suitcase in hand. He was scowling. I could tell he'd seen it all.

"Simon! What are you doing here?"

"Who's that?" he asked, nodding toward Sal, who'd disappeared.

I flushed. "Just a friend. Why didn't you call?"

"I thought my popping by would be a delightful surprise. I'm supposed to be checking on you, remember?" he said, putting down his suitcase with a loud plop. He studied me for a few seconds and made an effort to be less irritating. "I'm on my way to Florida to take photos for a story. Iguanas, apparently stunned by the cold weather, are falling out of trees."

I laughed despite myself. "That's a serious story?"

"Well, the iguanas think so," said Simon, breaking into a smile. "Slow news week."

"Can you stay overnight?"

"I thought you'd never ask."

Simon and I walked out to my car. You might ask why I'd asked Simon to stay, having just said goodbye to Sal. But we always shared rooms. It would have been strange not to offer Bruce's place. We'd collaborated on many stories, slept in the same room, separate beds, and shared the bathroom like people married—not to each other—but to the job. It was always easy to be with him, and often wacky and fun. But this time, another reason crowded my mind: I was getting too close to Sal. I didn't want that, even though I'd let it happen. Simon's company was a pleasant distraction, and I counted on him always pulling me back to center.

"Do you mind if I take a quick detour?" I asked as we got to the car. "I'm on the prowl for someone's house."

"You're the captain," said Simon.

When we got back to Bowden, I went up the road I'd driven up with Sal the day before, and still found nothing. No gravel driveway, no blue house. I stopped the car at the top.

"Since when are you fascinated with old quarries?" asked Simon.

"Since never. I must have taken the wrong road."

I turned the car around and headed back to the grocery store. It had started to snow, large, luscious flakes that were sticking to the ground. While Simon dashed in for food and wine to replenish Bruce's supply, I sat in the car and dug out the vet's phone number. No one picked up, and this time the clinic's voice mail announced that they were closed due to inclement weather. Frustrated, I jammed the phone in my bag when I saw Simon coming.

At the cabin, I made a hearty beef, vegetable, and barley soup while Simon opened a bottle of red wine and lit a fire. We talked easily, exchanging trivialities, and laughed about inconsequential, funny things. It was our way. Simon was my best friend. An excellent photojournalist, he saw things that other people didn't, capturing the unseen moments between the moments people pay attention to. He was blond, a man of perpetual youth, curiosity, and generosity when it came to me. He brought me ridiculous gifts like an entire fish skeleton covered in sequins, presented formally in a beautifully wrapped tie box; a highly polished board with random holes bored into it he'd worked on for hours—the finished product absolutely useless—and a resin pig. There was no reason for any of this. As for the pig, he just thought I needed one. The only problem was that Simon loved me, and I knew it. I loved him too, but was terrified of such a good man. I wasn't sensitive enough for him, kind enough for him, joyful enough for him. He deserved the best, and it wasn't me.

I smiled across the table at him.

"The soup is fabulous," he said. "You certainly know how to feed a starving artist."

"How long are you staying?" I was concerned that Sal would come back before Simon's departure and wanted to spare myself any craziness.

"Gotta push on tomorrow. Iguanas, you know. They don't wait."

"Well, I'm sure you'll do justice to their little bodies floating from the trees like falling leaves," I said.

Simon guffawed. "Believe me, they're heavy as lead. If you don't hear from me, a flying reptile has taken me out. Not the epitaph one hopes for. Shall we go sit in front of the fire?"

I joined him on the sofa. He refilled my glass, and I drank with too much enthusiasm. I was leading up to something.

"I saw Grant's latest article. It pains me to say he's doing a good job."

"All's quiet right now, but that means nothing," Simon said. "We're all on edge. Grant's doing a great job finding new things to write about even when there's absolutely nothing to write about."

"Screw Grant," I said, downing my cabernet and helping myself to another.

Simon's eyes widened, and I resolved to be more prudent about drinking in front of him. I started to top off his wine, but he placed his hand over the top of his glass. "What's your beef with Grant, anyway?"

"He's good," I said.

"You're good, too."

"Yeah, but until The Laundry Man came along, he got all the stories. I don't think Bruce exactly trusted me until I proved myself."

"Well, you certainly have now," said Simon.

"Yeah, well, my Pulitzer's in the closet with my Nobel Prize," I said, toasting myself.

After a moment, Simon scooted closer and took my hand. "I'm sorry for the way this has turned out."

I pulled my hand away and shrugged. I tried not to chug the wine. When he pushed a lock of my hair behind my ear, his intentions were clear. I got up, but he caught my arm.

"Don't do that," he said.

"Do what?"

"Leave. Push me away."

I got up anyway, taking my wine with me. I crossed the room and turned to face him. We stared at each other before he reached for his glass and took a sip of wine.

"Is that a serious relationship?" he asked, not doubting I would know whom he meant.

"No. Absolutely not. But neither is this," I said.

"Okay." He mustered a dejected smile. "At least I know where I stand."

I stepped forward defensively. "I haven't led you on."

"No, you certainly have not. Hope is a wonderful mistress, though. She's kept me warm at night."

"Shoot her. You'll thank me later," I said, downing my wine.

He sighed, rubbing his finger around the rim of his wine glass. "Well, I'd better turn in." He rose. "Guest room?"

I pointed him in the right direction, and off he went with his suitcase. Once he'd left the room, I finished up the wine and was going for the scotch when an odd rustle at the door stopped me. A footfall on crusted ice. A swishing sound as an envelope came sailing through the small crack under the door. I gasped, my hand covering my mouth. Scared witless, I took a moment to react and when I did, I jumped to the door and flung it open. It crashed against the wall behind, and outside, no one was there. Not so much as a footprint. I closed the door and picked up the envelope. Just then, Simon reappeared, clad in a towel, drying his wet hair.

"What the hell sound was that? Did you go outside?" he asked.

I tore open the envelope and pulled out a single sheet of paper covered with letters in all sizes and shapes cut from various magazines and newspapers. It said:

Get out or you will die.

I must have paled. Simon came over and took the letter from me. The police and sheriff were called, and the FBI, and there was a call from

Bruce, and another sleepless night ensued during which I had my hand held and barely felt it. So much for lying low.

#

By morning, the high drama had, if anything, intensified. We were getting ready for a Zoom call. Ramos had gotten to the house about an hour before, having grabbed the first flight he could out of Washington. He'd brought another agent with him who was hovering by the door. Simon and I sat on the end of the couch as Ramos positioned the computer camera so it picked up me, Simon, and him, and he flopped in a nearby chair, positioning it further. Bruce joined in from his New York apartment, as he'd already received a briefing on the situation. He and Simon had spoken, *ad nauseum*, off and on all night.

"I want to start off by saying that it looks like The Laundry Man is here," said Ramos.

"Oh no," I moaned.

"The preacher's wife over on Blood Mountain got a visitation. They own the house in the ravine," said Ramos.

"Oh, my God. Reverend Thatcher's wife? Is she all right?" I asked.

"Oh, yeah. Nicely washed underwear, but otherwise *nada*. We don't understand it though. She doesn't fit the profile. A young professional she is not. She must be at least...what?" he asked the other agent.

"A hundred and fifty?" the man said, snickering.

"The murderer must be here on Blood Mountain. It's too close," I said. "He's discovered me." I felt myself trying to hyperventilate and made myself slow down.

Bruce raised his voice to get everyone's attention. "Now listen. We've got two situations here. The preacher's wife—who doesn't fit the profile—"

"And the poison pen note. That doesn't fit The Laundry Man's M.O. either," said Simon. "This looks like somebody else."

"It's the real thing, a copycat, or two incidents that are unrelated," said Ramos. "We're investigating all possibilities."

"He's right, Kate," said Simon. "There're a lot of unanswered questions here, but for sure, The Laundry Man doesn't leave poison pen notes."

"Does anybody here have anything against you, Kate?" Ramos asked.

"Anybody you've pissed off? She's good at pissing people off," said Bruce to Ramos. "No offense," he said to me.

But I *was* offended. "For God's sake, Bruce, I've only been here eight days! I don't work that fast." I turned my attention to Ramos. "Nobody comes to mind..."

But the Reverend and his flock did. Then I thought of the sisters. And there was Alister Banks and his warning shot—but were any of those incidents serious enough to bring to the attention of the FBI? I didn't think so. Provoking these individuals wasn't a good idea. I needed their cooperation. Besides which, I didn't want law enforcement hanging around, looking over my shoulder, forbidding me to leave the house and interfering with my own investigations. I'll admit this wasn't the reaction of a sane person. But I'd begun doing what I always did when anything scared me senseless, and that was to wrap fear up in a box, tie it neatly, and put it away.

Even with all this going on in my head, I attempted to appear rational. "Look, I'll keep my eyes and ears open, I promise, but I'm agreeing with all of you. If this were The Laundry Man, he wouldn't have left me a warning note; he would've killed me. This is somebody trying to scare me."

"But why? Simon, I wonder if we should bring her home," said Bruce.

"That's not your call. It's mine. And I don't think so. Not yet," said Ramos, "She has multiple locks on the doors. She's as safe here as anywhere if she'll stay put. There is no evidence suggesting her cover is compromised, and look, if you all think she'd been less of a target on the streets of New York than here, you should have your heads examined." His eyes bored into me as if I was nothing more than a two-by-four at the mercy of a carpenter's drill. "This operation is still uncompromised, isn't it? You haven't done anything stupid you should tell me about?"

I bold-faced lied. "No."

He watched me for another moment. "For your sake, I hope you're shooting straight." And then he turned his attention to the others. "Okay, moving on. The FBI now has a presence in Bowden, and I'm staying here too, so we're close by." He turned back to me. "I'm sure you know that some mountain folk don't take kindly to strangers, so it could be nothing more than that."

"And the Reverend's wife?" I asked.

"Well, after struggling to take their wacky statements, I can think of a lot of reasons people wouldn't like the Thatchers," said Ramos. "But…"

"But?" I asked.

"Aside from the age factor, it *is* The Laundry Man's M.O."

Simon, with deep purple shadows under his eyes, looked at me. I read his message; he wanted me to ask him to stay. I pretended I hadn't gotten the memo and looked away. Finally, Ramos signed off Zoom and everyone left, Simon having to follow a story in South Carolina. I was alone, exhausted, and slept all afternoon. When I woke up, it was dusk and about four inches of icy snow slicked the ground. I had plenty of food, but eating was the furthest thing from my mind. The only thing I absolutely knew I wanted was the Carolina dog and I tried once again to call the vet. The inclement weather message still played on the recording.

CHAPTER 8

That night, it snowed another four inches. I woke around midnight, got up, and looked through the front window at the mountain facing me. The night was finally clear, and the sky was bursting with stars. The moon was full and bright and the mountain, covered in snow, glistened. I put a few more logs on the fire and sat on the couch, but I was restless. The pristine snow was calling me, and I suddenly felt I was drowning and would die right there if I didn't breathe some wintery, crisp air into my lungs that hadn't worked to capacity since the note had sailed under the door.

I told myself I'd only be a minute. Without bothering to put on a coat, I turned on the porch light and hobbled into the night. Bruce's front yard was nothing more than a path leading to the parking area where I'd left my car. The stone wall ran to the right of the path and held back the formidable mountain that now lay covered with billowy drifts that made it seem softer and friendlier. I took a few deep breaths. The silence was so profound, it was almost loud, and I pulled my sweater tighter around me and stepped off the porch to get a better view of the moon through the trees.

Had you asked me before this happened, I would have told you that my intuition was plenty good. But before I could react, there was a man's arm around my shoulders, and I was being pulled backward against his body. A seven-inch knife blade coming for my throat caught the moonlight. I reacted without thinking, grabbed his arm, and bit the hand that held the knife as hard as I could. The man screamed and threw me to the ground. My right temple hit something hard under the snow.

After the immediate shock, I saw my assailant scrambling away from me. He must have dropped his knife. I got up and started running the opposite way, my left foot dragging. He grabbed my ankle and pain shot up my leg. I fell, and he pulled me toward him, his body climbing mine. As the knife once again came for my throat, I turned over and kicked, twisted, and grunted under him. I grabbed the arm that held the knife with both my hands to keep it from landing.

In my struggle, time slowed. I was aware I was about to die. I'd read about this phenomenon, this pausing at the threshold, a threshold where human beings who are close to death take stock. It flashed through my mind that I was sorry for the life I'd lived and wanted to make it a better one. It was revelatory, this feeling that I didn't want to die, and it was absolutely clear to me.

There was an echoing crack, a sound that only a bullet can make in frigid air. At first, I was simply aware of the man's sudden dead weight and the certainty of my impending death. I couldn't tell you which was heavier. But after a moment, I realized I wasn't dead. Surprised and relieved, I pushed and shoved his thick bulk off me, grateful that he didn't put up a fight. Struggling through the snow, I forced myself forward and crawled to the stone wall. I willed myself to breathe and get my wits about me. I leaned my back against the wall. Not much of a hiding place, but all I had.

I seemed to be alone; the night was eerily silent, and a dead man was lying in front of me. Blood and brain matter saturated the snow; I felt it all over me as well, and as I came to my senses, the reality of my situation hit full force.

"Help! Help!" I screamed, aware that I was heavily perspiring and desperately cold at the same time. I wiped the stinging sweat from my eyes. When no one answered me, I pounded my thighs in frustration. I remember thinking for the first time in my life that I was beyond helping myself.

"Help! I'm begging you…" I cried again, but no one answered.

Tears, burning cold, poured down my face. Whoever had killed this man was still out there and could kill me, too. If he meant me no harm, neither was he coming to my aid. What the hell was happening here? Before I could figure it out, I had to get myself up. Literally, I was a sitting duck. With shaky legs, I pushed myself up, only to fall back down on the icy ground. I pushed myself up again and, plunging my hands deep in the snow, grabbed the top of the wall for leverage. I steadied myself, took a handful of ice, and rubbed it on my face. Whatever was happening, I would have to be more alert than I was if I were going to live.

Still nothing. Still no one. I lurched through the snow and into the house where I locked the door, called Ramos, and then, in all honesty, freaked the living hell out.

CHAPTER 9

And then we did it all over again on steroids: the police, the sheriff, and the FBI. There were photographers and crime-scene analysts, and I sat on the couch drinking tea, telling my tale, and answering Bruce's and Simon's phone calls. The FBI presented me with my attacker's face, which remained intact, despite the back of his head being blown off. They wanted me to identify him, but I'd never seen him before in my life.

The coroner came and took the dead man away. Everyone agreed it was The Laundry Man, but no one knew who he was or who'd shot him. The police assured me that his DNA would soon provide the answer to at least the first question, and they hoped that I'd produce a gun. But I didn't have a gun. *Someone* had one, but it wasn't me. Then they tried to get me to go to the hospital, but I refused to go anywhere. I could take care of the head wound myself, and I didn't want anyone finding out about my foot.

They sent me to a hotel in Bowden with a guard at my door while police, Ramos, the FBI, and crime unit analyzers stayed on the case, processing the scene for the next four days. I kept calling about the dog. No answer.

Ballistics determined that whoever had shot the 308 Winchester, a gun used for hunting deer and elk, had been standing a little higher up the mountain than I was and that I was lucky he came by—or he'd been watching me, an unsettling thought, but not as unsettling as the thought I had once the police let me return to the cabin. Was the dead man the actual target or was I?

Bruce had insisted I come back to New York, but Ramos had other ideas. A dead person dictates certain protocols, and for that reason, I had to stay put.

"Then I'm sending Simon to protect you," said Bruce.

I couldn't believe my ears. "Thank you for your concern, Bruce, but if you send in the cavalry, you're going to blow what little cover I have left. It's just not smart. There's been enough activity here already. Everything just needs to settle down now." That might have been true, but I was still fearful that Simon and Sal would turn up at the same time. The very thought made my head hurt.

Bruce grumbled, but that was that, or so I thought. By late afternoon the next day, I opened the door to find Simon, with a suitcase in hand, and Salem, who was back from Boulder. Wherever each man had come from, they'd arrived on my porch at exactly the same time. I hadn't slept the night before and was ill-equipped to handle the inevitable drama. Unable to hide my displeasure, I said an unenthusiastic "Oh, great," and walked back inside, leaving the door open. They were coming in anyway. Might as well get it over with.

"I heard what happened," Salem said. "I heard that the man who attacked you was a serial killer." He looked horrified. So was I.

"Who told you that?" I asked.

"I did," said Simon. "I want him to go away and leave this to the FBI." Without an invitation, Simon went to the bar and poured a short drink. He wasn't facing me, but I could see his jaw clenching and unclenching.

"That doesn't fly with me," said Sal, offering an apologetic smile. "I need to hear what's going on from you."

"Okay, so here're the facts. The police say it could be a serial killer called The Laundry Man. We're just going to wait and see. There was a threat against Mrs. Thatcher, the preacher's wife, as well."

"Well, I'm just glad you're alive," said Salem, dropping his full weight into a chair.

"She's okay. I'm here now," said Simon, turning. "You can leave."

Sal looked at me. "Is there something going on between you two that I should know about?" he asked.

I glared at Simon. "No."

"Then I want to state that I can't leave," Sal said to Simon. "I live here."

Simon's eyebrows shot up.

I said, "He didn't mean that literally. He has a house somewhere." I don't know why, but at that moment, I wanted to laugh. All this chest-beating was ridiculous. I suddenly wondered if a woman had ever suffocated from too much testosterone in the room.

In the next moment, I felt done with the histrionics and wanted both of them to leave. I took a deep breath. "Okay, listen up, you two," I said. "The police will have the answer in a few days regarding the identity of the man who attacked me. I'm not hurt except for this cut on my forehead. Despite being scared, I'm fine, and I am damn good at looking after myself. Plus, if either of you were any kind of friend to me, you'd realize I don't need this imbecilic drama right now, and you'd know that I want you both out of my house! …Bruce's house…" I said, correcting myself. "Simon, go back to New York. Salem, go wherever it is you go, but both of you, get the hell out of here, and leave me alone!"

My declaration hung in the air. My arm hung in the air, too, with a finger pointing toward the door. I was getting damn tired of holding it there until one of them spoke.

"You're right," Salem said. "I'm sorry. Call me if you need anything," he said as he got up and went through the door.

Simon and I just stared at each other. Eventually, he shook his head, picked up his suitcase, and left.

CHAPTER 10

I looked ragged and unkempt the next morning, having slept on the couch fully dressed, with a carving knife in my hand and an ice pack on my foot. When I opened the door to Sal, who arrived at Bruce's door at a decent hour, he seemed contrite and kind, and had brought me fresh bagels and cream cheese, which was a sure-fire way to make me let him into the house.

We ate at the kitchen table. He tried not to look as hyper-focused on me as he was. "How are you, Ms. whoever you are?"

Damn. I'd never had the "Kate Adair" conversation with him. I resolved to tell him today, but I wanted to finish my bagel first. "Fine. No need to worry about me," I said, shifting in my chair.

"Did you get any sleep last night?"

"About as much as I usually get. What's with the third degree?" I asked, but he acted as if he hadn't heard me, opening a small tub of cream cheese and slathering his bagel with a plastic knife.

"Any word on anything?" Sal asked.

"From the police? From the FBI? How fast do you think they work?" I said, eating a bite of bagel.

"I brought you something," said Sal. He got up and walked to the coat rack by the door and retrieved a folded newspaper from his pocket. It turned out to be the current issue of *The Express.*

I stood up, grabbed it, and walked away from the table. The headline screamed that The Laundry Man had claimed another victim in West Virginia, and Grant's picture had somehow grown much larger than mine had ever been. Not only that, but Grant had practically plagiarized a paragraph of mine and didn't credit me for it. I was over-the-top indignant.

"Damn it all to hell! Damn it! Damn! Damn! Damn!" I screamed. I threw my empty coffee cup across the room, where it shattered against the stone hearth.

"What the hell, woman?" Salem yelled, jumping up from the table.

"My name is Kate. Kate Adair…" Sensing his apprehension about being in the house with a crazy woman, it was time to explain. I took a deep breath. "Okay, Sal, I was going to tell you everything. I just hadn't gotten around to it." The rage came up in me again. "But that goddamn Grant Maitland! He's going to win my goddamn Pulitzer!"

"Okay…Kate," he said, emphasizing my name with the hard consonant at the end. At first, I thought he was mocking me. But he came over, took the paper out of my hand, and looked at the article. "Is that all this is to you?" he asked. He was in his therapist mode now, chastising me, although there was a slight smile playing across his lips. I wanted to smack him.

He moved out of range, continuing to peruse the front page. "Hmm. A woman has died. 'Marlene Ferguson.' She was the CEO of a manufacturing company, a wife, a mother, and pregnant with her third child. That must have been a bonus," he said.

"A bonus?" I asked, fuming.

"A two-for-one murder." He shook his head and put the newspaper down on the table.

"Who are you, Kate, or whatever your name is? What's all this about? Don't you think I deserve an explanation?"

"No!" I said. "No! Leave me alone!" My heart was beating out of my chest, and I was ready to be vicious. I wanted him to get the hell out.

But Salem surprised me. Instead of fleeing, he sat back down, crossed his long legs, and his arms in his lap, and waited. We stared at one another. He wasn't going anywhere.

Maybe he was right. Maybe it was time to come clean. "I…Oh, *hell!*" I said, screaming at the top of my voice. That did it: I felt like such a fool, I calmed myself down. "Listen, Sal, if you ever tell a soul what I'm about to tell you, my life could be in danger."

His head jerked back. "What? Really?"

"I'm serious. If you say anything to anyone, I could die."

He nodded. An understanding.

"I'm a reporter for *The Express*," I said. "Or was. My name is Kate Adair. I worked on The Laundry Man story for three years until he came after me. That's why I'm here in these godforsaken mountains. I'm hiding out. He threatened me."

"And the story about your dad?" he asked.

"It's all true. They shipped me off and never saw him again."

"Shipped you off?"

"Stop asking questions!" I hit my hand on the table so hard, I hurt myself. "I'm trying to tell you everything, but I've got to do it my way!" Spent, I collapsed into the chair opposite him. He just stared at me with that practiced, therapeutic gaze. And after a few moments, to my horror, I burst into tears.

"Kate," he said. He got up, came to me, and kneeled in front of me. "What's wrong? Tell me…"

"I…" I tried to say it, but I couldn't. Throughout my life, I hadn't uttered those words. I always felt that if I said them, I would be inviting in the pain, the loss of me, the sense of self blown to bits atop Blood Mountain.

"My mother sold me when I was five years old." There it was, and there was no taking it back. Sal sat back on his heels, dumbstruck. His eyebrows knitted, and he stood up. He dragged his hand through his hair and looked—what?—disbelieving, horrified, unnerved? I couldn't read him. He put his hands in his pockets and looked at me for further explanation.

"She sold me. She sold me to a family that reared me in Florida. The Adairs. My mother sold me. She didn't want me. I didn't matter. So for all the hoopla, my picture in the paper, my illustrious career, and my putting myself in harm's way, I'm nobody and have lost it all. I'm a big fake, and it's all been for nothing."

I sobbed, and to my surprise, he came over to me and held me. He built a fire and sat with me, holding me all afternoon. Using the ingredients I had in the house, he made us a light dinner. He helped me to bed and held me throughout the night and into the next morning. There was more to tell, and I felt entirely raw and had given up the fight. We lay in bed, face to face, his eyes like deep brown tunnels through which I was ready to go.

"We lived on Blood Mountain. I've been looking for the house. I didn't really find anything. But I remember my last day there as a child. I was five.

"It was very windy. I didn't know where my mother and I were going, but I didn't want to go with her. She was in one of her frantic moods. When she was like that, it never turned out well. She told me to dress in layers and hurry, and I did—although I didn't move fast enough. I remember she jerked my arm and pulled me out of the house and up the mountain. At the top, she told me to wait behind an enormous pile of rocks, and I did. But when she didn't return, I climbed to the top of them to see what was going on.

"On the other side, she was with the Adairs. She'd gotten close to them since we'd been on Blood Mountain. They were long-time summer residents. I always thought they felt sorry for us, for our poverty, and they brought us things—old clothes, things for the house, and toys. They'd send us a turkey or ham for Thanksgiving and Christmas. We took their handouts, and when they came up for the season, mother cleaned their house to pay them back.

"Mother was hysterical that day. Sally Adair, my stepmother, had an arm around her, and Ben, my stepdad, looked worried, as if something bad were about to happen. Mother was crying so hard that I could barely understand her. When she saw me, she tried to pull herself together. 'Come down,' she said. 'I need you to come here.'

"I climbed down, in a hurry, of course. Mother was upset. Can't do anything to upset mother because I didn't want to get into any more trouble than I was already in. I cut my hands and knees to shreds, crawling over the rocks as fast as I did, and I remember blood running down my legs in streaks. She didn't see it or she didn't care which was more like it.

"'You're going to go live with the Adairs,' she said.

"'No…' I said. 'I want to go home! I've got to go home! Don't I wash and clean for you? You said you'd show me how to cook! Dad and Asa need me! You need me!"

"Asa?" Sal asked.

"Asa was my brother…I don't know what happened to him. 'Listen to me, Kate,' my mother said. 'These people are going to take care of you now—'

"'No…' I said. I pulled away from her. She grabbed me back and tried to put me in their hands, pushing me into one or the other of them as I tried to run away. 'No!' I screamed.

"'Stop acting like that! I need you to go with them now!' she said, and she slapped my face so hard that sometimes I think I can still feel it. When she did that, I hit the ground hard. I couldn't believe it. She'd never hit me before. I glared at her, and she glared back at me. Then she changed into the mother I guess she'd always been, but I'd never seen. 'Don't you see? I don't love you anymore! Don't you see that you're nothing but trouble? I'm exhausted from taking care of you! Do you think I like you? I want you to leave! I can't stand the sight of you anymore! Get her away from me!'…Or words to that effect.

"She kept screaming at me. I tried to scream louder than she did so I wouldn't hear the hateful things she was saying. As if I could forget. I grabbed at her clothes.

"'Get off me! Get away from me! Take her! Take her!' she screamed as if I were some sort of disgusting thing, not worthy of being picked up off the ground. Ben grabbed me then and carried me down the mountain. I shrieked the whole way.

"But I stopped for just a moment and looked back. 'Take this!' Sally said as she thrust money at Mother. At first, Mother didn't react. I assume she'd exhausted herself. She'd certainly exhausted me. They mumbled to each other. Then Sally said, 'Please! You must! You know you must—' and my mother grabbed the money and ran.

"And before you say anything, Sal, offering words of comfort, before you say, 'Perhaps you don't know the whole story, Kate,' or 'I'm sure she was doing what she thought was best,' or 'I'm sure she didn't mean the hateful things she said,' or 'Maybe she had second thoughts about selling you and didn't want to take the money,' or any other bull I've told myself through the years, let me tell you this: This is the mother I believe she was, and this is the woman I'll never forget."

Salem said nothing. The silence was profound, as if the conversation were taking place inside a vacuum. "And what about your father?" he said. "Where was he when all this was going on?"

"I don't know," I said. "There's so much I don't remember. I never saw him again, and, sometime later, I overheard Sally saying that someone had killed him. I created a fantasy about him though, that he was a good guy."

Salem smiled.

#

By noon, I was exhausted, and Sal had confused me. He'd said and done all the right things, the expected things, but I found myself surprised that, after a night and a morning of revelations, I didn't feel closer to him. Perhaps from his point of view, he was keeping a therapeutic distance, but I attributed his behavior to my delivery of the information: I never wanted to let on that I needed anyone or anything—a ploy that most people bought. I wondered if he did.

After lunch, I asked him to leave. Craving solitude, I wanted to resume my research. I also tried to take it easy. Trying to be kind to myself, to comfort myself, to bring myself down from the trauma of the last few days, I snacked too much, went down to the lake, got bored with sitting there in the autumnal sunshine, and dragged myself and my pitiful foot back up the hill. I listlessly read a book before I gave up resting altogether. Resting was causing me more stress than being active ever did. I also knew where I wanted to go.

I drove to Blood Mountain, parked in the usual spot, and hiked to Alister Banks's house. With my pulse pounding and muscles quivering, I knocked on his door. The shotgun be damned.

"Mr. Banks? It's me again. Only my name is not Sarah Johnson. I'm Kate Adair, Callie Moon's daughter. This is the truth. And I'm here alone."

There was silence from inside the house, but I could feel him listening.

"Cup and Blue Swinehart told me to talk to you; they said you had information I might need about my mother. Please…" I sounded like a supplicant, so I stopped, cleared my throat, and lowered my voice. "I'm trying to find out who murdered my father—"

There was a belligerent huff from inside, and then a flurry of activity. It sounded like he was throwing things around, tearing boxes open, and cursing.

It surprised me when the front door flew open and crashed against the back wall. I was getting ready to duck, but instead of a shotgun blast, Alister threw what looked like a box of printer paper out on the porch. It made a terrible bang when it hit the wood and there was a second bang as the door slammed shut.

"There!" came a gruff voice from inside. "That's what you came for. Now get off my porch. And don't you ever come back here. Next time, I'll call the police on you."

His tone left me too shocked to move. I'd been expecting him to be enraged, but he didn't sound that way. He sounded broken, even as if he were crying.

After a few seconds, I scooped up the box and lumbered back down to the car before he could change his mind and shoot at me again.

CHAPTER 11

I kept looking at the box on the car seat beside me, and curiosity got the better of me. I pulled off the road in Bowden and looked inside. It was a typed manuscript. I didn't know what I'd been expecting, but not that. I went straight back to the cabin, fixed myself a drink in case I needed it, and started reading.

That day, as I were standin' in my kitchen, I coulda swore that ol' yellow wall phone lifted itself out of its cradle, floated across the room, and right into my hand.

Who was speaking here? I couldn't tell.

I'd seen her at the country store. In a small town, you see everybody. Whether you know 'em or not don't matter. She were a pretty girl, my boy Jimmy's new kindergarten teacher.

So when she called that day, I knew who she were. "Come quick," she said. "Somethin' bad's happened to Jimmy."

I threw the phone down and run.

A scrape on the knee, I thought. At worst, a broke arm. "What could happen at a school?" and I raced the old red truck along Highway 107.

Parkin' in the lot, I run inside. Not knowin' where to go, I headed toward the sign that said "Office".

"Mrs. McCall phoned me about my boy, Jimmy Moon," I said to the young woman behind the desk.

Oh, my God. This was my mother! She'd used the name, "Moon." Putting the manuscript down, I covered my mouth with my hand. I trembled uncontrollably. I stood up and walked around shakily. Reaching for my drink, I took a sip, but the alcohol sickened me, so I poured it down the kitchen drain. I took several sips of water.

Be careful what you wish for. I'd wanted to know more, and boom, here it was. In my mother's voice. I went back to the manuscript despite feeling completely disoriented. The book didn't have a date. Had I been alive at the time of the writing? I didn't remember any of this, and I didn't remember a brother named Jimmy. Perhaps I'd been too young. I picked up the manuscript again.

"She's in class right now," the woman said.

"Then you gotta go get her 'cause she tol' me somethin's happened to my boy," I said, tryin' not to be hysterical.

"What's the trouble out here?" A severe-lookin' older woman come out o' the back office to the left side o' the picture window. I guessed she were the principal. She were all starchy and suited up in gray.

"I got me a call from Miss McCall sayin' somethin' was wrong with my boy, Jimmy. He's just started kindergarten here. You should know him," I said, beginnin' to lose my cool.

"Okay," said the principal. "Go get Miss McCall, Vilma, and she'll clear this up for us. She'll be here in a minute," the principal said to me. "Why don't you have a seat while you wait? May I get you some water?"

"No...No!" I said. It were harebrained to think of me drinkin' water while Jimmy were layin' in sickbay somewhere. Perched on a metal foldin' chair near the door, my foot were tappin' on the floor, my knee goin' up and down. I were so nervous, but I didn't wait for long. Miss McCall swooped in, lookin' all colorless and strained.

"Hello," she said. "I'm Loris McCall. Can I help you?"

"You called me!" I said. "I'm Jimmy Moon's mama and you called me and tol' me somethin' happened to Jimmy. Where is he? What happened?"

"I'm so sorry," she said to me. She turned to the principal. "I'm genuinely puzzled by this," she said. "I don't have a boy named Jimmy Moon in my class. What grade is he in? I teach first grade—"

"He's in kindergarten," I said. "Enrolled him myself. I dropped him off here this mornin'. You lost my boy?"

"There's some misunderstanding here," said Miss McCall.

"Have a seat, Ms... Moon, is it? Let me see if I can find out who called you. He's in kindergarten?" the principal asked.

I nodded.

"You go back to your class, Miss McCall. I'll handle this," said the principal.

Then she turned to me. "Now, if you'll pardon me, I'm going into my office to make some phone calls to see if we can straighten this out. You'll be all right here?"

I nodded again.

"Okay. Try to relax. I'm sure this is nothing serious," she said, "and we'll find him."

But I couldn't relax. They'd lost my boy! How could a school lose a boy? And he were such a little thing, small for his age, his hair as tow-headed white as the summer sun at noon. My precious little boy Jimmy...

Somethin' didn't feel right at all.

I waited, petrified, for close to a hour. The girl, Vilma, in a sleeveless, orange, flowery dress, throwed nervous glances at me while she typed on her little machine. Tap-tap-tap. Tappity-tap-tap. And I think there were a big clock on the wall that ticked off the seconds. I could hear that too. Everythin' seemed too loud. I felt like I were goin' to lose what little mind I had.

Then the principal's door opened and so did the door to the hall. Two policemen came in. I didn't know which way to look first.

"This is she," said the principal, noddin' at me.

"Ms. Moon? I'm Officer Slater and this is Officer Daltry. Would you come with us?"

"What?" I asked. "No!" I said, jumpin' up, and the officers tried to take me by the arms. "No!" I cried. "Get your hands off of me! My boy's missin'! These people have my boy!"

"They don't have your boy," said Officer Slater. "Now just lower your voice and come on quietly with us—"

"I ain't goin' nowhere! These people have my boy! They've lost my boy! What don't you understand?" I asked and somebody somewhere set to keenin'.

"Is there anybody who can look after you at home?" asked the first officer. "Somebody you'd like us to call?"

"You got a husband?" the second officer asked.

"What? No!" I screamed. "I mean, that ain't the point, is it? They lost my boy!"

Officer Slater looked at his partner and their grips on me loosened some. "Listen, Ms. Moon. I'm sorry to inform you that your boy is dead. He died several months ago, don't you remember? Ms. Moon? Your boy never went to this school. He never got old enough," he said.

But the colors of the books on the wall behind him run together like a child's finger paintin'. It smeared into the colors o' the window, oozed into trees outside, and then came back and blended into Vilma's orange dress and the principal's scared face, which was meltin' like a pat of butter in a hot pan...

"We're losing her!" somebody yelled.

I set the manuscript aside. My whole body was quaking and I was more confused than ever. My mother wasn't illiterate, but she was uneducated, and writing a book like this would have been beyond her. And who had typed these pages?

It was necessary to go back to Alister Banks. I didn't know any other way to get answers.

But first I had to hide the manuscript. I didn't want anyone to see it. Some things were too personal to share, and while I didn't exactly know what I had, I knew it was for my eyes only, and I wanted to keep it that way.

I remembered the loose board and the nail that just wouldn't stay in the step going down to the lower floor. I got a hammer off the wall of the garage where Bruce's tools hung and pulled the nail out. The box just fit the space, and I nailed it shut.

That afternoon, I went back to Alister's house.

CHAPTER 12

He must have seen me coming. Before I could knock on the door, from inside the house he said, "I told you not to come back."

"I'm sorry, Mr. Banks, but I have to be here. I don't know why my presence is upsetting you, and I would like to honor that. But please understand that I don't know what's going on, and I don't have anyone else to ask about any of this. If you could speak with me for a few minutes, it would mean a lot to me, and if I can just understand some things, I won't bother you again."

The door opened, and I walked into a dark room. When my eyes grew accustomed to the gloom, I'd never seen so many papers and books in my life.

"You look like her. She had that shock of thick red hair and light blue eyes too," he said.

I said, "Thank you." I flushed, embarrassed at the inappropriate reply. He hadn't exactly complimented me.

He sat down as if he carried a lot of weight—which he physically didn't—and gestured to the sofa opposite. I sat. "What do you want?" he asked, rubbing his head. His sparse salt and pepper hair now stood straight up. His arm dropped heavily to the armrest.

"Thank you for the manuscript," I said, "but I'm puzzled. Did my mother write it?"

"It was her story," he said.

"But you helped her, didn't you? My mother was uneducated."

He looked as if he wanted to scold me for that remark, but said nothing. "I collect a lot of stories and have filled these shelves with them. I used to be a writer," he said.

"Aren't you still?" I asked.

"No. Your mother's was the last story I collected."

"Were you going to write a book about her?"

"Maybe," he said. "I don't know. Look…" He stood up. "I've got things to do, and I think the manuscript explains it all."

I didn't feel insulted. He looked as if he were fading away right in front of my eyes. His was some kind of torment I didn't understand.

I also stood. "Thank you for your time," I said. "I'll try not to bother you again."

He nodded, and I left.

#

I went back to the cabin, pried up the board on the stairs, and read.

All I ever wanted were to be a mother.

The words stunned me. That was not the woman I knew.

Momma and Papa died young before I even knew 'em. My pa was a dark man, my mother white. That's about all I remember of them, that and the singin'. We'd been to a revival, and I was little, maybe three? When I look back on it now, comin' home in the blackest night, we sang them hymns to calm us down. It were pourin' rain, and our ol' truck with its bald tires were skiddin' all over the road. Momma held onto me too tight. She were spooked, and I were squallin' 'cause she hurt me. She didn't mean to, but that's the last memory I have of my momma, her squeezin' me too tight, and all of us tryin' to sing.

Folks tell me at some point we wasn't on the road no more but crashin' through trees and goin' straight down to the swole-up river. They tol' me I was throwed out, and onto a riverbank, jes' like the little baby Moses in the bullrushes. A king's daughter got to him, but we don't have no kings in these parts so I jes' lay there till the old ladies, Cup and Blue Swinehart, found me. They took me in and sent me to grammar school. To this day, I don't recollect more'n' I've said. I jes' didn't have no family no more, and that much were pretty clear, pretty fast.

Cup and Blue Swinehart reared my mother? Cup and Blue looked to be in their sixties when I met them. If Mother was three years old, this must've been around 1968. If Mother describes them as being old in 1968, they would have to be more than a hundred years old by now. But all young children think adults are old, I told myself. Perhaps this was the explanation.

In 1981, I was fifteen. I met Big Jim Moon, and he was all I'd ever hoped for. I was in a family way within a month, but my baby didn't live. Then, in 1984, I had little Jimmy, and I loved that boy with my whole heart. I called him my firstborn, even though he weren't officially, and he were beautiful. Kate, feisty and never satisfied with anythin', come along in 1985, and everybody said she looked like me. She were a lot more difficult than Jimmy, but that were like me too.

I remembered the obituary of James C. Moon that I hadn't bothered to read. I hurried to the computer in the loft and found the item again.

"Entered into rest on September9 [th] ,1986 ,was James C .Moon ,loving husband of Callie Moon .James is survived by his beloved wife ,Callie Moon ,and a daughter ,Katherine .His son ,Jimmy Moon ,preceded him to his heavenly reward by five days".

I was stunned. How could this man be my father? I didn't recognize this picture in the obit. Yes, I was just a toddler when he died, but to have absolutely zero memory of him? I kept remembering someone in my life, somebody I thought was my father, and had an indistinct picture of him in my mind's eye. He was tall, wiry, and tanned. The man in the picture was portly, with very white skin as if he'd never seen the sun. I kept going back to the laptop to stare at him again and again, but he was a perfect stranger and I couldn't see any family resemblance.

One day, when I was five or so, Sally, the mother I had now, received a phone call. I had only been at the Adair house for a few weeks, and I was still disoriented and didn't understand why my life had changed so abruptly. When she answered the phone in the kitchen, I saw the blood drain from her face. I heard her say, "I know nothing about it. We sold our house there. It was getting too tedious to go back and forth like we were doing…" When she hung up, I saw her shaking.

Later that night, I overheard her talking to Da. "It was murder," she said. "I'm sure that's why the police were calling. And who didn't want to kill him?" And they promised each other that they'd never speak of it again, so they didn't, and I didn't either. I guessed they were talking about my father. They might not have been, but it was part of the mythology I created about my life in lieu of facts. I wondered about it now, that phone call, the mystery surrounding it, and Sally's apparent anxiety.

I went back to researching. There was nothing in the obituary about a cause of death and no mention in the newspapers of any murder involving a James C. Moon around that time. Frustrated, I did and didn't want more information, and I dithered between these poles until I wore myself out. I kept glancing across the room at the book as if it were an enemy at the gates. I'd had a real prejudice about my birth mother and didn't know if I wanted to read excuses about her treatment of me. Perhaps she didn't think I was even important enough to talk much about. At odds with myself, I finally took the book and curled up on the sofa to read.

CHAPTER 12

In 1986, my world come crashin' down, and I went to the home for crazy people. There, it took months for me to come to my senses, but folks was nice to me. They taught me to draw and paint and make little things with my hands. I ate good, and there were a doctor who talked to me real nice most every day and who, over time, helped me recollect.

The first thing I remembered were that Kate, who'd just started walkin', followed me to the barn to feed the chickens. We found Big Jim hangin' from the barn rafter, a rope 'round his thick neck. Big Jim were a drinker and a good one. He were cuddly, funny, and generous when he were full o' liquor— which were most of the time. That's why his friends down the road at the juke joint never seen his drinkin' as much o' a problem.

But that were how Big Jim were to his pals at the bar; inside our house, things was different. Big Jim never worked a day in his life. Oh, he tol' stories about workin' and made people laugh aplenty, but he never brung home a brown penny. He were jes' happy for me to work like a mule. I were the one sent to clean people's houses, and it weren't beyond me to work in their yards pullin' weeds and movin' heavy things. I'd do anythin' somebody needed me to do to put food in front of my young'uns. Big Jim never noticed when I'd come home pained and so bent over I couldn't stand straight. He had everythin' he needed: money for drink, food on the table, a ol' mattress to flop on, so he jes' didn't care about anythin' as long as I kept it comin'.

So, in the barn, Kate got an eyeful of Big Jim hangin' there despite me hurryin' her away. She never spoke o' Big Jim after that, never in the years I had her, never asked where he were, or when her daddy were comin' home. It were as if he didn't exist, and to my shame, I were glad. I jes' don't know how I could explain Big Jim's hangin' hisself to a young'un.

And when they sent me to that hospital, Kate had to go somewhere, so she went to Cup and Blue. If anybody could have made her forget Big Jim in the barn, it would've been them that could do it.

In the hospital several weeks later, the doctor suggested that it were safe to remember why Big Jim hung hisself. After having me some false starts, the nightmares come, and one day, it all spilled out.

I got me a waitressin' job. On the day it happened, I were starting the job and were excited. I never had money o' my own. Big Jim drank up most every cent I brung in. I also didn't consider myself much use to nobody. But now I were goin' to do somethin' important, and as I recall, Big Jim supported my efforts to be somebody—after all, for him it meant booze money. We was so dirt poor that we had only three plates to eat off of, two forks, and four chipped cups, and we was one of the last families on our mountain to still have a outhouse. But that day, I had me a real job, and I made Big Jim promise to take care o' Jimmy and Kate. He tol' me he'd stay sober till I got back, and I had the early shift anyway, so I were gon' be home by three.

But Big Jim broke his promise, and when I come home, I found him asleep on the tore-up couch. Kate were okay, playin' in a corner by herself as she liked to do. I called and called, but little Jimmy were nowhere to be found, so I panicked. I jumped on Big Jim and pounded him with my fists to wake him up, screamin', "Where's Jimmy? You were supposed to watch Jimmy! Where is he?" I must've scared Kate half to death. She started howlin'.

Big Jim come to then and tol' me to calm down, that Jimmy were jes' in the outhouse takin' a dump. Thank God, I thought, feelin' relief. And then Big Jim said, "What you doin' home so early in the mornin'? They fire you?" and he seen the look on my face. It were almost four in the afternoon.

I run outside, scannin' the fields right and left, lookin' for my boy. The grasses was tall and I remember the wind were blowin' and the red leaves comin' down. I went runnin' everywhere. Thinkin' my boy might've fallen, I raked at the tall grass with my hands, and even run to the top of the ridge to look into the valley, but there were no sign of Jimmy at all. So I went to the outhouse.

Somethin' were wrong before I got there. Things went too still. The birds stopped singin' and it were like the insects, busy in the long grass, held their breath. And when I opened the door, my hands was shakin' bad, and there were Jimmy, slumped against the side of the outhouse lookin' like a pure angel, his blue eyes open wide, surprised-like, his skin as pale and see-through as spilt milk on a wet floor.

It were a spider bite, the doctor said. That's how he died. He were allergic.

And that's why Big Jim done hisself in five days later. He couldn't live with hisself. And I were mad at him, really mad, and may God strike me down for bein' the sinner I am, but when I seen him danglin' up there in the barn, part of me were glad. As he hung there in the rafter, I finally seen his pure uselessness. I worked hard for the comfort o' this man and he couldn't be bothered to watch a child. I were so filled with rage and grief over what life had brung me that for a while, even though Big Jim were dead and gone, I let him do his worst and break me.

#

Behind my back, the townsfolk said wolves raised me. I heard 'em whisperin'. Maybe I didn't keep myself as clean as I should have or comb my hair nice. All desire to live that way plum run out of me that day I found Big Jim in the barn. I were easy to pick on, a little half-Melungeon girl who nobody trusted to begin with. Daddy had been one and I'd heard more 'n one man call him "a dirty, rotten piece o' shit." I even saw a man spit right in his face. But Daddy said we had to hold our heads high 'cause we descended from some sort o' "lost tribe" like the children o' Israel, but unlike them, we was better off hidin' in the hills, away from folks who judged our kind. Over time, he said, our kind started looking more like everybody else, 'cept for our eyes. They always gave us away. They was a strange light blue, Melungeon blue, and different from other blue-eyed folk. My skin were dark like my father's, jes' not as much. But my wild curly red hair come down from my mother, and all my life, I were easy to pick on 'cause I didn't look like nobody else. I were glad my baby's skin were lighter. Kate took after Big Jim, who were a great big white somebody, so I hoped my baby might grow up more passable than me. Then things might be easier for her.

After a few months o' folks gossipin' behind my back about what a crazy woman I were when I come out of the hospital, and me stealin' from their gardens and chicken coops, I got Kate one warm spring day and we left the town of Bowden in our ol' truck. We didn't take nothin' with us 'cause we had nothin' to begin with, save for the truck and some nickels, dimes, and quarters I'd squirreled away from Big Jim drinkin' 'em up. Besides, I wanted us a new start, with nothin' to remind us o' past misery. I didn't know where we was headin' neither, but I kept us goin' into the woods, past the fields of buttercups and bluets, up into the highest mountains, away from folks who talked behind our backs. We passed occasional communities and stores that served local folk, and I stopped here and there to steal my babe a tittle o' food.

We come a distance when the ol' truck clanked and rattled itself out. I were goin' down a hill, so I pulled to the side of the road and opened the hood while little Kate slept in the front seat. I weren't expectin' to figure the problem. All I knowed to do was check the oil, and we had enough o' that. I crawled back into the driver's seat, looked at my darlin' child still sleepin', and wondered what I were gon' do.

Soon, though, a pickup pulled beside me. The driver rolled down the window. "You havin' trouble?" he said. He wore hisself a Carolina Panthers baseball cap put on backwards.

"Yes," I said. "My ol' truck won't start up." And without another word, he parked his vehicle in front o' us and got out to look. He were wiry and strong lookin'. He had grease under his fingernails and poked 'round under the hood for a while. From the look of him, he'd be somebody who knowed what he were doin'.

"Looks like somethin's wrong with the gearbox," he said. "If you want my advice, I'd get rid of this ol' clunker and buy somethin' newer," and then he closed the hood.

"Ain't nothin' can be done?" I asked.

"Naw, and it'll cost you more than the truck is worth if you try to fix it."

"Well, thank you kindly," I said, and I thought about the change in my pocket. I didn't want to give it up. "I don't have no money—"

"Ain't necessary," he said. "I didn't do nothin'. I work over to the Shell station in Claymore so if you want to get it towed…"

"No. But thank you kindly," I said again, and he went on his way.

I sat in the car with Kate for a while. Havin' no truck were a terrible thing. I wanted to cry myself a lake of tears. I couldn't afford me no tow truck and what good would it do anyway to pay for pullin' a plum dead car to a gas station? Finally, I figured somebody might haul off a no-good truck sometime, so I put Kate on my shoulder, and we jes' plain walked away.

When Kate woke, she'd missed most o' her nap so she were cranky from the get-go. She were hungry, too, and tapped out most all the time—despite me feedin' her a hunk of bread or apple from my pocket that I'd stole.

We made slow progress. Kate dragged her feet and had to speak to each little snail she found on the leaves of a bush. She rooted 'round in every muddy creek for garnet stones and played with all the dogs we passed along the way. It were sweet, watchin' her, and it were easier lettin' her enjoy herself than fightin' with her to hurry. Besides, I didn't know where I were takin' us. I weren't too worried at that point. Little communities was here and there, and I were sure we'd come on one before it got dark and find us a place to bed down.

But by nightfall, we was lost, and there were thunder and lightnin' rollin' in fast over the mountain in front of us and there wasn't no little towns. We needed to find shelter fast. We hurried past a church where, next to it, a tent revival were going strong with the preacher shoutin' and flailin' over God's word, lightning cracklin' behind him.

"You're a sinner! Admit it! You get a little toe outta hell if you admit it, don't you see? And if you're honest with the Lord, he may look at you with jes' a speck of mercy! But if you wear that black soul of yern and flaunt it, and take his fine name in vain, he'll smite you down and grind you into dust and never look back!"

I moved us on, sayin' to myself what a sinner I were and hopin' for jes' a speck of mercy like the preacher talked about. The first raindrop fell as we come on a deserted shack by the side of a ol' loggin' road, and Kate were delighted to collapse in the tall, soft grass of the yard. For once, she were so wore out I didn't have to worry about her stayin' put.

It weren't much of a shack. In fact, it were barely a shelter: two rooms, a dirt floor, a caved-in wall in what looked like a kitchen, a roof half-collapsed in room number two that, at one time, coulda been a bedroom. I took a big stick and pounded on everythin' to drive the vermin and critters out. I turned over multiple boxes of stuff where animals had made nests and beat on the heavy pans and cauldrons still lyin' about. When nothin' come flyin' or crawlin' out, I relaxed and called to Kate. I were jes' turnin' over the last box of sticks, when a big ol' rattler come slitherin' out, curlin' up to be deadly, and shakin' that terrible rattle at the end of its tail and there were my baby, runnin' to her mama.

"Stop!" I screamed, but she didn't. "Stop!" I screamed again, "Move out the way!" And I hoisted up that snake on the end of a stick, run it to the door, and slung it with all my might. In my fright, I threw the stick out too. Then I grabbed Kate and hugged her so hard I were afeared I'd break her.

When I calmed down, I laid a ol' canvas on the dirt floor. I took Kate's wet clothes off and made her a bed out of the clothes I were wearin', puttin' my sweater on her for a nightdress. It were freezin' in my underwear, but I curled up beside her and pulled the canvas over the two o' us. When the heavy rain come later that night, we moved to another corner o' the house where the roof didn't leak. Kate were sleepin' hard when I picked her up, and she didn't seem to take no heed at all as I put her on a dry pile of pine needles. I sobbed after that. Quiet, so as not to wake her. I didn't know what to do or where to *go. My life were over, and yet there in front of me were my baby girl. I could hardly see her through the half-light, but I could hear her breathe, a soft little purr sound that were innocent o' the awful things that could happen to a body. I tried not to think about little Jimmy and how he died, and it were all I could do not to wonder if, in my haste to get away from the mean talk, I hadn't headed Kate and me into the same fate.*

In the mornin', the weather'd turned clear, and I had a good look at the shack. It were ol' and tumbled down, but nothin' I couldn't fix, given time and a few tools I didn't have. It were gon' serve us to stay put, and I went to cleanin' out the place as best I could.

Several days later, Kate and me was out walkin' when we seen a stout woman with little hair on her head gardenin' in her yard.

She spoke to me first, "Yoo-hoo! You on the road! Whatcha doin' there?"

I were scared, but I poked out my chest and said, "We live here!"

"You live here on Blood Mountain? I ain't seen you before and I know everybody. I'm the preacher's wife."

"We keep to ourselfs," I said and kept walkin'.

So that's how we found out where we was—on somethin' called Blood Mountain. And Kate and me made our lives there, foragin' for whatever food we could find in the woods like I learned from Cup and Blue, and raidin' the preacher's garden for potatoes when the findings was slim. There were a creek with fresh clean water not too far away. Sassafras grew in the woods for tea. Fairy potatoes and burdock abounded, and there were so much kudzu and mushrooms around that my skirt was full of them things by the time we come home from our walks.

One day, Kate and me went almost to the top o' the mountain, and we wandered into a clearin' that was a sight to behold. There, we found a real lawn and a little white clapboard house with a red door, where a woman were singing and laundry in wonderful bright colors were hanging on a line. And right in the middle o' the breezin' sheets and such, were a beautiful blue ribbon, the color o' a robin's egg.

I put my finger to my lips. Kate were little, but she knew what that gesture meant, and we crept forward to get a better look at the pretty place.

We fell back and hid behind some wet sheets when the woman come out. She were beautiful, with raven-colored long hair and black-colored eyes with lots of makeup. She were tall and seemed like someone who had everything and could get more. Wearin' a flouncy skirt with red flowers on it, she also wore a red scarf 'round her neck, and she flipped her hair back like that famous singer, Cher, I seen on a TV once in a storefront window. She wore a clean, white blouse, too, that had little white flowers embodied into it as if sewed by the sweetest hand.

Stoppin' for a moment, she acted like she were sniffin' the air before removing some sheets from the line. Not our sheet, thank the good Lord. If she had, there weren't nothin' for me to do but die of mortification. She went back inside, and I don't know why I done it, but I snatched me that pretty blue ribbon off the line and stuffed it in the pocket o' my dress. Then I grabbed Kate's hand and run.

We went home, and I boiled us kudzu root for dinner in a rusty kettle on an outside campfire. After we ate, Kate played with some sticks on her make-shift bed, and I kept touchin' the ribbon in my pocket. I loved it; it were somethin' o' my very own.

#

It took me several days to wear it. I were scared to be found out as a thief. But eventually, it were so pretty that I wore it, and one day, it got the attention of some people hikin' down the road. Sally Adair and her husband, Ben, was long-time summer residents of Blood Mountain and they saw me when Kate and me was out in the yard boilin' clothes.

"What pretty red hair you have!" Sally called. "And that blue ribbon just sets it off in the nicest way."

I touched my hair and the ribbon, nervous-like. She might've guessed I stole it. But then, with a big smile, she come into the yard, and held out her hand.

"Hey" I said, shakin' it. "I'm Callie Moon."

CHAPTER 12

Her man stepped 'round her and come at me kinda fast. As he went by her, the lady put her hand on his arm and said, "Be nice, Ben."

He nodded. "You know that this is our house and land?" he asked me.

My heart jumped outta my chest. "No! No! I didn't know." I wanted to run, but Kate were too far away to grab. I were shamed. Being desperate, I done somethin' terrible wrong. "It were rainin' one night and me and my baby…I can clear us out right now," I said.

"I should call the sheriff on you," said the man.

I set to quiverin'. "Oh, please, mister. Oh, please…"

Then the lady come forward. "Oh, Ben, stop being such a mess. We'll do no such thing, honey, don't you worry. Where are you from?"

"Outside of Bowden," I said.

"And why are you here?" she asked.

"I run away—"

"From the law?" the man asked. He seemed keen on thinkin' the worst o' me.

"Naw. From meanness," I said. That shut 'em up, and we all stood 'round lookin' at each other.

"Well, I, for one, am glad to see the old place being used," said Sally.

"This is our place, and she's squatting!" the man said, raisin' his voice.

"Oh, for God's sake, Ben! You've done nothing with this place for forty years. When were you going to start? Today?" Then she looked at me. "My grandparents owned this land and built that old house. Ben and I bought a place of our own a couple of miles away around the mountain—so we don't live on this property. We were going to sell this place one day, but never got around to it. Sentiment, I suppose. My name is Sally Adair, and this is my husband, Ben."

"Howdy-do," I said, tryin' to be nice, but my heart was thumpin' faster 'n' a jackrabbit's. I didn't want 'em callin' no sheriff who might snatch Kate away.

"As I see it, you're doing us a favor being here and fixing the place up," she said.

"What?" Ben asked, lookin' at his wife like he'd never seen her before.

"And if you'll come over to our house, we can let you borrow some tools."

"My tools?" he said.

"What would you rather do, Ben? Have this house fixed up or let it rot where it stands? You've done that long enough," and then she turned to me. "If you fix this place up, you can live here rent-free. How does that sound?"

"I—"

"And I think we have some lumber you can use," Sally said. Ben started to pipe up, and Sally shushed him. Ben then threw up his hands and give up.

My head felt swimmy. Sally was talkin' too fast for me, givin' me too much to decide all at once. This mighta been some sort o' trick. If so, I could end up losin' Kate and see myself in jail. "No," I said. "Thank you, but I can't take handouts. It ain't right. I gotta work for what I get."

Sally stepped closer. "Does she have to suffer, sweetie?" and she nodded her head toward Kate sittin' in the grass. "This'll give her a good roof over her head and a better life. Besides, you will be working for it—fixing up the house. This is mutually beneficial for both of us, don't you agree?"

I seen the right thing to do. Kate deserved so much more than a life like me, and I wanted somethin' better for her. It were as if Sally could read my mind 'cause she smiled and stepped closer. "Sweetie. Let us help," and that were jes' what I did.

#

CHAPTER 12

From then on, I thought o' my ribbon as a good luck charm, so I wore it every day. The Adairs was wonderful to me and Kate. They was more than generous with food, toys, and clothes to keep us warm. When they seen we needed somethin', a teakettle, a stovepipe, a washboard, or anythin', it'd appear on the porch, leanin' up again the front of the rickety ol' house as if by magic.

One day, Sally and Ben brung me some black tea and sat down at the table and chairs I'd jes' made. I were so proud o' havin' furniture and Sally brung the special tea to celebrate. The drink were bitter until I added me some sourwood honey, and then, it tasted like love itself—that is, how love would be if somebody really, really loved somebody.

Sally held Kate on her lap and leaned over and kissed her soft hair. "I love this child," she said. "We never had children of our own, you know. The doctors said I was infertile. Ben and I tried everything—"

"Everything," Ben echoed. "I hate to tell you what I had to do."

"But it wasn't in the cards for us. I'll just have to love your baby, darling," she said to me and kissed Kate again. Kate smiled at her and offered her a doll that Sally had brung her.

"Are you sad about not havin' babies?" I asked.

"Oh, yes," she said, hesitatin' before she said, "Devastated." She took a big breath. "But one gets used to reality, eventually." Then she got up and plunked Kate down on Ben's lap. Ben hadn't exactly warmed up to me, so I was right surprised by this. I got myself up to snatch her back, but before I could, Kate surprised me by pushing herself up, takin' hold of his head, and givin' Ben a big, wet kiss on the cheek.

I never seen a man melt before, but Ben did. His face got all red and his eyes got teary. "Well, look at that," he said, "Look at that…" and he give Kate a squeeze.

Kate and me went to their house a lot after that, and they come to ours. They brung us many kinds o' food and noticed all the improvements I made to the house and land no matter how small and they seemed to like 'em. They spoiled Kate rotten, too, and babysat her so I could get some of the big work done, and when Kate were with 'em, she were always happy.

#

The first thing I done were to give us a wood floor. Then I started on the roof. I were up there, nailin' some shingles the Adairs had give us, when Billy Mars come by.

"Hey!" he said. He had the waviest brown hair and nice green eyes. 'I'm Billy Mars. Live up the road a piece. What you doin' up there with your flamin' red hair and blue ribbon?' He acted all full of himself, puffin' out his chest when he talked to me. Then he come into the yard with his cocky self, actin' like he knowed he were a cute piece o' work.

"Fixin' my roof, as if it was any business of yours," I said.

"Ain't you worried about fallin' down?" he asked.

"Ain't you worried about curiosity killin' your cat?" I said back.

"Don't have no cat. Always wanted one, though. I could do that fer you," he said. "I'm a fix-it man."

"Don't have no money for a fix-it man," I said, "but thanks anyhow."

He went off whistlin' with a twinkle in his eye, and I didn't think no more about it.

Despite the kindness of the Adairs, money were tight. Every night, I counted out the nickels, dimes, and quarters we still had left. I planted me a garden with vegetables and herbs, but nothin' much were comin' in yet, so I were goin' to have to get me a job. There weren't no town on Blood Mountain and there ain't no jobs without a town, so whatever work I were to find required a trek. One day, leavin' Kate with the Adairs, I set off back to Bowden.

CHAPTER 12

The fancy hardware store didn't want me. Then I went to the grocery store and applied. I tried one or two other places. They all said they'd let me know, but nobody seemed too interested, so I come back home. Walkin' down the road near the shack, I heard bangin'. When I got to the house, I seen where it come from. Billy Mars were on my roof, puttin' on shingles and doin' a dang fine job too. As good as my own hammerin' and nailin'.

I were plenty surprised and maybe a little mad. If he were expectin' me to pay...

Shieldin' my eyes from the sun, I said, "Hey! I tol' you there ain't no money for a fix-it man!"

And he said, "Well, that works out just fine 'cause I don't have me no dinner tonight less'n you cook it." He come down from the roof then wipin' off his hands on his dungarees. "I finished it fer you. If'n you have trouble with it, I'll fix it back."

"I got to fetch my child," I said 'cause Kate were at Sally's. "So there ain't no vittles for you until then."

"Well," said Billy. "I best go along with you to make sure you don't queer the deal."

"Listen you," I said. "Why're you helpin' me and bein' so nice?"

"Would you believe that's me?" he asked, his eyes sparkin'.

"No," I said.

And he laughed. He laughed so hard he doubled hisself over.

I come home with Kate and fixed us pork chops and turnip greens, which the Adairs give us. I made some cornbread to go with it, and we all agreed it were a mighty fine spread.

#

Billy turned up regular after that. He didn't disappear, and he didn't hide hisself inside a bottle. We worked on the house together when he weren't busy helpin' other folks and home come together fast. There were a nice steep roof, the kind that rich people have on their houses, and inside, the high ceiling made the main room look big. There were a sittin' room that had the kitchen in it and Billy made a long table for that. In the bedroom, he made me a double bed and another little bed up against the wall for Kate. Billy even built us a bathroom off to the side of the bedroom and I had inside plumbin' for the first time in my life.

I decorated the house with whatever I found outside: a bird's nest, pine cones, a pretty lichen-covered stick that I stood in a corner, a tree branch I nailed to the wall and hung things on. Billy took me to a thrift store and bought me some drinkin' glasses that matched and a fake pumpkin wove with reeds. He brung us food and firewood and left little bouquets of meadow flowers at the door. He had hisself a shotgun and shot us squirrels and rabbits for dinner.

Billy were fallin' for me. He tol' me once that he liked me 'cause I were kind. He said nobody'd been kind to him his whole life, no woman anyways, but for a sister. "She ain't no real sister, mind, but a sister-friend," he said. "I never knowed a proper family. As far back as I can recollect, I lived wherever I could find in the woods. I met up with my sister-friend stealin' fruit from a stand. She were better at it 'n' me." He laughed, but then somethin' come over him and he turned the color of wet ashes. I went to live with her and her ma." I asked more questions, but he were done with talkin'. It seemed somebody hurt him bad. With almost nobody lovin' him, I always tried to make him feel special. I cooked his favorite foods and my arms would go 'round him when he looked sad. I often reminded him o' the good times we was havin' and tried to make him laugh and not take hisself so serious. Then one day, I looked at him with softer eyes and realized all this had growed into love.

Billy never pushed me for sex, but he'd gape at me all-smitten, and I knew what he wanted. Losin' my family twice, though, had made me twice scared, and I didn't want to lose nothin' again. I didn't know if love lasted neither. Maybe it was just a thing in storybooks, designed to keep us desperate folk puttin' one foot in front o' the other. But Billy had built us a fireplace, and one chilly night in May, he made a roarin' fire in the rusty grate, and I put Kate down to sleep on a ol' blanket in the corner.

"You want to know how I knowed you was the one?" Billy said. He were lyin' on his side in front of the fire with his head propped up on his hand.

"The one what?" I asked. I knowed what he were goin' for, but I wanted to hear him say it.

"You know—the one. My girl," he said.

"Oh. I'm that now, am I?" I said, but inside, I felt my heart all swole.

"It were the ribbon," he said. "The blue ribbon. A month ago, Conjure Man over to Claymore said that one day I'd know my girl by the blue ribbon in her hair. Ain't that somethin'? And there you was," he said, wrappin' a lock of my hair 'round his finger.

I closed my eyes and smiled.

"He also said you was a witch."

CHAPTER 13

I laughed and laughed. Me...a witch!

"But I ain't smart. Cup and Blue taught me things, like how to cook and nail a plank, and which foods I could eat in the woods, but I ain't book smart, and witches have to read big words out of a book. How'm I gon' be a witch?"

"Cause yer my girl and the Conjure Man said so," and he leaned over and touched my breast. I felt alive inside, my heart jumped, and that was all the invite I needed. We tiptoed out o' the room where Kate were sleepin' and made love and a bond.

"I want you to be my girl ferever," Billy said, lyin' there in bed. "But it's only a lastin' bond if you promise somethin' too."

"Aw, Billy, I don't know what to say," I said.

"All right. I'll go first. 'I promise my heart to you, Callie Moon, and I promise to protect you against any meanness for the rest o' time.' Now...what you gonna say back?"

"Oh, I'm dizzy," I said. "Them pretty words..."

"Empty as a bucket full o' air if you don't promise me somethin' back."

"Okay," I said. "'I, Callie Moon, take you Billy Mars to be my love.'"

"'Ferever,'" he said. "Say 'ferever'."

And I said it.

#

One late afternoon after that, Billy wanted me to take a walk, so off we went with Kate. He were laughin' and cuttin' up. He picked her a flower and hoisted her up on his shoulders, and I wished I could have had a moment as happy as that child were, ridin' high with a fresh-picked flower.

I seen 'em first in the shine of the late afternoon: the sheets breezin' in the wind. It felt like my heart was gon' bust, but Billy turned us into the yard. I stopped dead still.

"Well, c'mon," he said, "I got somebody I want you to meet."

Scared, and without Billy seein', my hand went to my hair, where I snatched the blue ribbon and stuffed it down my shirt. Billy gave a whistle, loud and ear-rattlin', and that same raven-haired girl come out glad to see him. Lopin' after her was two wolf-dogs that scared me half to death. They was the biggest dogs I ever seen and they watched me with hard eyes. Billy give me Kate to hold, and the woman and him hugged real friendly-like. When he swung her 'round, her big yellow skirt went flyin'. Then a man, skinny as a rail, who looked like one bad thought could blow him over, come out of the house and watched 'em from a distance.

"This here's my sister, Helenne, with an extra '-ne' on the end, but it's pronounced Helen. She gets pissed off if you don't pronounce it right. And she ain't really my sister, but as close as we come, huh?" he asked her. And when she didn't answer fast enough, he pulled her tight and jostled her, forcin' her to smile. I half watched 'em 'cause I kept my eye on them wolf-dogs. I didn't trust 'em 'round Kate, and I didn't want her thinkin' they was ordinary dogs.

"And this here's Frank," Billy said as an afterthought, pointin' to the skinny man. "He's Helenne's husband."

Frank and I nodded to each other. I felt sorry for him. He looked as bothered by all the hoopla as me.

"Where you been, Billy? I was missing you!" Helenne said, play-swattin' at him. And then she turned to me. "And who's this?"

CHAPTER 13

Billy puffed out his chest and said, "This here's my girl, Callie Moon."

Her eyes opened wide. "Your girl?" she said. "Since when?"

"Since she said she'd have me," he said. "What kinda vittles you got? We come fer dinner!"

Billy were a rash man, and I were sorry he said that. I wanted to go home, but he'd already clapped poor ol' Frank on the back and gone inside. I stayed standin' in the yard. Helenne, pretty as she was, smiled too much. She sashayed over to me, grinnin' all the while.

"About time Billy got himself a girl," she said. And then she asked somethin' that chilled my bones. "Do I know you?"

"No," I said, "No, I don't know you at all."

There were somethin' kinda scary 'bout the way she stared at me, so I held onto Kate even tighter in case we'd have to run. A excellent judge of character, my babe started frettin', knowin' somethin' were wrong, but not knowin' what.

"And who's this?" Helenne asked, noddin' to Kate.

"This here's my daughter," I said.

"Does she have a name?"

I didn't want to give it to her. I cleared my throat to say it. "Kate."

Helenne kept smilin', and about the time I were hopin' to fall in a hole to China, she looped her arm through mine and said, "Well, we all know each other now, don't we, and we're gon' be good friends."

We walked through the red door, the dogs waitin' for her go-ahead before racin' inside. The house wasn't as neat as I expected. There were a pile of clothes junked in a corner. Someone had thrown more clothes over an old chair. There were a corner full of paper bags and ol' boxes. The wallpaper were peelin', too, the little blue vines in the design lookin' like they'd shriveled up and brung the paper with 'em. There were a long table in the room that looked jes' like the one Billy made me. We sat ourselves down there, and I put Kate in the middle o' me and Billy.

Helenne cooked good, I'll give her that. We ate hearty, all but Frank who pushed a potato 'round on his plate. The talk 'round the table were nice, and Helenne and Billy laughed and laughed. Frank didn't say nothin', just kept his head down, and forsakin' his potato, started pushin' peas 'round with a fork. I tried to relax, but I felt foreign. I smiled from time to time, 'specially when somebody asked me somethin', but inside I felt like Frank who jes' sat there lookin' gray.

Billy were happy though, and that made me happy. It were as if he had all he ever wanted in that room: me, Helenne, Frank, and Kate, who he seemed to love like a natural-born daughter. By the time we left at one o'clock in the mornin', Frank had dozed off in his chair at the table, Kate were sleepin' on Billy's shoulder like he were her pa, and Helenne made me promise we'd get together for dinner regular-like. We never did.

#

That June, a few days after the dinner, Billy's nightmares come. He'd be screamin' in his sleep, and when I tried to wake him up, he wouldn't come alive. I wiped him down with a wet rag and would even get him up out o' bed and walk him 'round the room to get him to wake up. He'd stumble, and his knees would buckle as he'd try to go back to the nightmare he'd left. Long after my back felt like it were breakin' from holdin' him up, he'd finally come around. His bad dreams coulda had somethin' to do with Helenne in our lives now, and I thought she coulda reminded him of some terrible time. She were always comin' by. Billy and me'd been livin' in a little bubble, and the outside world hadn't touched us for over a good year. But it were four o' us now, and I tol' myself that it were jes' the way it were gon' be, and I had to be good enough to change 'cause it pleased Billy.

Besides, I had dreams of my own that caused me to wake with a fright. Billy'd put his hands on me, and it were a comfort. For months, life went on like this. I didn't ask where his nightmares come from, and he didn't ask me about mine. Sometimes I wished he would, but I once tol' him about Big Jim hangin' hisself in the barn, and Billy turned pale, walked out o' the house, and didn't come back to us all day. For that reason, I never tol' him anythin' else. I didn't want to add to his misery.

And there were plenty o' misery in him. One summer night, while Kate played on the front porch and the crickets and tree frogs was as loud as a train comin' through, we was settin' the table inside so we could eat like a proper family. I looked 'cross the table at him, and I coulda sworn he were somebody else, all white and made of bleached bones.

"I didn't have no ma and pa, y'see," he said. He stared at the fork in his hands like it were gon' come after him. "Hel's momma took me in. She said the good Lord spoke in her, but she were mean and beat us and…she…she made us do things. Me and Hel, we ran away. That's why we're here," he said.

Then he put the fork on the table and called Kate in, and we ate corn pone and gravy, and never spoke o' his ol' life again.

CHAPTER 14

Lying there on Bruce's sofa, all I felt was heartsick. For the first time in my life, I questioned my perceptions of my mother. Had I so misjudged her? Or was she all the things I thought she was and only different in the early years? I didn't remember those years when she professed, at least in this document, to love me. And who was Billy Mars? Was he the "father" I remembered? I tried Googling him, his birth, his death, and came up with nothing. I tried all the search criteria available to me. Nothing. It was as if he'd never existed. And if I stayed with Cup and Blue Swinehart as a child, why didn't I remember them, and why didn't they tell me our association? I researched them too. Nothing.

I remembered a little brother, Asa. The Adairs hadn't adopted him when they did me. I wondered why. With no knowledge of what happened to him, I neglected to search for him through the years. Then I felt ashamed about not searching for him and didn't look for him for that reason. What was I going to say when I found him again? *Sorry, but I was awfully busy.* There was simply no excuse. I was protecting myself, knowing that it would break my heart to find him and have him reject me. Now I knew it would break my heart not to find him, whatever the consequences. At the computer, I searched for him. Nothing. I vaguely remembered a sister named Gilly, too, and that she'd died. I searched for her, her birth, her death, her grave. Nothing. And where were the other people mentioned in my mother's book? Helenne and her pitiful husband Frank. I looked for all of them, but my efforts to find answers had hit a wall.

And then I thought of the Adairs. These sweet, dear people, so seemingly transparent and innocuous, were suddenly mysterious. What had they kept from me? They'd been wonderful parents. I thought of them as "perfect": loving, kind, generous people who saw the bright side of everything. There were no formal papers of adoption that I knew of, and we didn't talk about my family of origin. If anyone asked how I'd turned up in their lives, they said I was the daughter of a long-lost cousin who'd passed away. Da was a lawyer, and this must have come in handy as he went about creating an official identity for me. I'd never had trouble gaining a passport, a driver's license, or a social security card, and back then, I never asked questions. I was more concerned with fitting in with all my friends. Now that I'm full of questions, my dear Da's memory was gone, and my mother took any secrets she had to the grave.

I was thinking more about my backstory than The Laundry Man. When I thought of the murderer, I hoped a fervent hope that the dead man was him. But I couldn't shake the feeling that this madman was still out there hunting me. It rattled around in my head, never far away, and it puzzled me. Perhaps I was just in the habit of being afraid, so I sought a distraction and reached for my mother's book again.

I was about to read it when I heard the car. Sal had stopped out front, and I jumped up too fast for my foot and turned it. Pain shot through me, and I limped as fast as I could to return the book to its hiding place. I barely made it. Sal came in—by this time we were beyond ringing the doorbell—and caught me with the hammer in my hand.

"Whoa!" he said, an arm not yet pulled out of his coat sleeve. "Is that for me?"

"If I say 'yes,' will you go away?" I teased.

He smiled and shrugged the rest of the way out of his coat. "No, I'll just look for a picture to hang. Besides, you dare not kill me. I brought us dinner." He held up a brown bag he had set on a small table by the door. "This is no ordinary bag, my dear. It is full of the most succulent fried chicken and french fries these mountains offer. The chef is famous."

I had to admit, it smelled divine. Sweet, greasy, and full of carbs, it made my mouth water.

CHAPTER 14

My cell phone rang. "This is Kate," I said.

"Ramos."

My blood pressure jacked up so high that I swear I could feel the blood rushing through my arteries. "Any news?" I asked.

"Yeah. I'm sorry, Kate, but the DNA didn't match," he said.

I was incredulous. "What? How could that be?"

"He's not our guy, that's all. His name was Boris Purdy. Plenty of priors, some violent, but nothing like the attack on you. And he was from Brooklyn. Any of this sound familiar?"

"Not one word. But you know, I'm not surprised by this. I haven't been able to feel like this was over."

"Great. Next, you'll be trying to get the FBI to hire you as a psychic."

"Well, I need a job…" I said. He chuckled to be polite. "Bud, I don't understand this at all: He came at me with a knife. He had The Laundry Man's M.O." I needed Purdy to be the murderer, even if he wasn't.

"What can I tell you, Kate? The guy's still out there."

"Have you told Bruce and Simon?"

"They know. We all want you to stay put. We're assigning an officer to monitor you, so if you see someone lurking around the cabin, that's our man. Mrs. Thatcher is getting a police officer, too."

That didn't make me feel better for either of us. No amount of security had stopped The Laundry Man before. "Okay…Thanks for calling."

"Keep your door locked," he said and rang off.

Sal was setting the table. "You look like you've seen a ghost," he said.

"The DNA didn't match. The man who attacked me wasn't The Laundry Man. They're assigning an officer to protect me."

He sat down and put a brown paper napkin in his lap. He was ready to eat. "Hmm. I suppose it's good they have the killer's DNA."

"Partial DNA. It's a good partial, but…partial," I said. I told myself to sit down and eat, but I'd lost my appetite.

#

After dinner, I asked Sal to leave. I was weary, and I wanted to call Da to hear the warmth of his voice. I wanted to hide, if just for a few moments, in the old safety of him.

One of his caregivers handed him the phone.

"Da? It's Kate."

"You're the apple of my eye," he said. I teared up.

"And you're my Da." He said nothing, so I jumped in there to fill the gap. "I'm still out of town, but one of these happy days I'll come back home, and we'll go for ice cream. What do you say?"

He fell silent again, and I could sense his distraction. No telling what was hanging from the ceiling in the common room today, if that was where he was.

"Da? Can I ask you a question? Who was my biological dad? Do you know?"

Silence. I could feel his confusion through the phone. "That's nice," he said.

"It would have been when you still had your summer place in North Carolina."

"Is it nice?" he asked.

I closed my eyes and sighed. I told him again that I loved him and let him go. Alone now, I paced and went to retrieve the manuscript. Then the phone rang.

"It's me," Simon said. "I guess you heard."

"Oh, you betcha," I said.

"I'm sorry."

"I guess I'm just someone people want to kill," I said.

Ignoring my self-pity, he asked, "Did you know this guy?"

"Boris Purdy? No."

"Any idea why he came after you?"

"Not a clue."

"I've been researching him. Can't find any connection to you at all. He drove a truck, was divorced twice, has an autistic child he never sees, and was a petty thief. Oh, and he got in a bar fight one time and the other guy almost killed him. I'll keep digging, but right now, it looks like the attack on you was a one-off."

"Wait! Did you say he was a truck driver? That was one of the FBI theories."

"Yeah, but DNA doesn't lie, and right now, there's nothing to tie Purdy or anyone else to these crimes." Silence passed and his tone changed. "Are you going to be alright, Katie?" he asked.

"Oh, hell, Simon, I don't know. How should I know?"

"Bruce wants me to tell you he's thinking of you and if you need anything–"

"Yeah," I said, feeling homesick. "Thanks for calling," and I rang off.

I poured myself a drink in the kitchen and stared at it. I didn't want it, but I left it there on the counter in case I changed my mind. Meanwhile, I settled into the overstuffed couch with the manuscript and pulled the cashmere blanket over me.

I'd finish the book, I told myself. Then I'd decide what to do.

CHAPTER 15

It were a perfect day in July when I left Kate with Billy and set off to the little store to get some supplies: a bright blue sky, a slight, friendly breeze to push me along, and buddin' trees the color o' hope. Billy and me was scrapin' by with the money he got from being a fix-it man, and things was a little easier, so I planned to buy us pork for dinner. We couldn't afford meat most of the time, and that I could afford it that day made me feel right sassy. I dressed up in my best dress and wore my blue ribbon.

I were almost to the front of the store when I heard growlin', like dogs that was in a fight or fixin' to be. Goin' 'round the bend to where the store were, Helenne's two wolf-dogs had a man in a wheelchair cornered, and he were tryin' to fend 'em off with his cane. He weren't screamin' like I woulda been. He were jes' quiet and swingin' that stick. I could see he were plenty scared though, and I don't know why I done it, but I run over and got between him and those dogs.

I were about to raise a ruckus like you do to scare off bears when Helenne appeared, gettin' between me and the wolf-dogs. She looked me square in the eye, pointed at me, and said, "Don't. Don't raise your voice." I stepped back, more 'n glad to let her handle it.

"Home," she commanded. She said it once and the wolf-dogs looked at her, and when she repeated herself, they run off for home.

Before I could breathe a relief, Helenne, who were usually okay-nice to me, gave me a look, puzzled at first, and then like I'd done somethin' bad wrong. She stalked off after her animals without another word. She didn't even look at the man in the wheelchair, much less apologize to him. I heard footsteps runnin' up behind me.

"Are you okay? That was very brave of you," a man said.

I turned myself around. He were a tall somebody and had kind eyes, but compliments, which I hardly ever heard, left my brain empty to reply.

"I'm Alister Banks." His hair were premature gray 'round the edges and his eyes was hazel, a greenish gray that reminded me o' misty summer twilights that would sometimes settle between the hills. He held out his hand, knowin' full well I'd take it. Now that the wolves was gone, I were beginnin' to shake. "You alright, Horace?" he said to the man in the wheelchair, all the while keepin' hold o' me.

"Thanks to this young lady, I am," said the cripple man, who waved me over and shook my hand. "I'm Horace Stein. Sorry about the left-handed shake. Right side doesn't work anymore." Poor ol' Mr. Stein. He were bent over fierce on the right side and had a humpback. His hands was full o' the rheumatism, too, and when he reached for me with his left hand, I could see the fingers on both hands had angled themselves like he were reachin' for somethin' to the side. When I looked in his eyes, I expected to see pain, but he were concerned for me.

"I'm Callie Moon," I said, still tremblin' hard. In hindsight, I seen that those dogs coulda tore me apart. Mr. Banks were watchin' me, maybe thinkin' I were gon' faint.

"How about we get out of the sun and go sit under that tree to get ourselves calmed down?" He didn't wait for no answer, jes' started pushin' the wheelchair to a shady spot 'cross the road from the store.

"You should have seen those dogs from my vantage point! Holy mackerel! Dire wolves are not extinct!" Our experiences was sinkin' in, and Mr. Stein looked mighty shook up. He were shakin' like he didn't have a solid bone in his body.

Mr. Banks wheeled him into the shade of a large oak. There was a big log there, and I sat myself down, watching Mr. Stein and fearin' for him. "Shouldn't we get Mr. Stein to a doctor?" I asked.

"As you might or might not know, miss, there aren't any doctors or hospitals up here," said Mr. Banks .

"Or police," said Mr. Stein. "We're pretty much on our own unless you factor in a one-or-two-hour car ride. They say we may get all those things one day, but don't hold your breath. Besides, I'm fine. No harm done."

"Tough ol' coot," said Mr. Banks, smilin'. He patted Mr. Stein's shoulder and put the brake on his wheelchair. "Horace was a judge down in Florida before he retired, Callie."

Me. Knowin' a judge!

The Judge waved his fame away. "Listen, Alister here is the celebrity. He's a well-known writer. Has books in stores around the world. Thrillers."

My eyebrows poked up and my mouth dropped open. Mr. Banks laughed. He looked like an important somebody, tall, tanned, and sure o' hisself.

"Where're you from, Callie? I haven't seen you around here before," he asked.

"I'm over to Blood Mountain."

"Well, that's something we have in common," said the Judge. "That's where we both live, too."

"No kiddin'?" I said.

"I assume we were all going to the store today. That was lucky," said Mr. Banks.

The Judge smiled at me. "Without you, I might have gotten all chewed up and not been my good-looking self anymore."

The men laughed. I tried to, but my chin quivered. The men, easy with each other, chatted on and tol' me where they lived on the mountain. Mr. Banks weren't too far from me, but higher up. Judge Stein were a good stretch of the legs 'round the slope. Then they asked about me and seemed impressed that I'd fixed up the ol' Adair place. I tol' 'em Billy Mars helped.

"Billy Mars?" asked Mr. Banks.

The Judge wrinkled his brow. "He's the wolf-girl's brother, isn't he?"

"Yeah. I guess so," I said. "I kinda stay away from her. Them wolf-dogs scare the bejesus outta me."

"I think that's the point," said Mr. Banks.

"Aside from the obvious reasons, you two know why those wolves are so dangerous?" asked the Judge. I shook my head for both Mr. Banks and me.

"Helenne has trained them to attack anything that screams. She trained 'em on rabbits she keeps for that purpose. A rabbit screams in its death throes, you know, and that makes the dogs go at it harder."

"What?" said Mr. Banks. "Why?"

"I think it's how she protects herself."

"From rabbits?" Mr. Banks asked.

But I knew what the Judge were sayin'.

"That's why you was so quiet," I said. "I'd a been screamin' bloody hell if those dogs come after me."

The Judge motioned to Mr. Banks to unlock his chair so he could be wheeled over to me. I'd clasped my chilly hands in my lap, and the Judge reached over and took them.

"Promise me you won't ever do that. If you're ever cornered, don't scream. They've never killed anybody that I know of, but they could. That's why Helenne trained them that way. Better than a bodyguard."

"That's pretty scary," I said.

"Yeah, but she saved your life, Callie, so you must be on her good side."

"Yeah, and I was jes' about to let loose, too."

"Never do that, honey. I need you to take this seriously, as far-out as it sounds. And those wolf-dogs get out from time to time and jump the pen out back where she keeps them, so I think it behooves all of us to be careful. Bears aren't the only predators we need to worry about."

"Wolves trained to attack anything that screams. Now I've heard everything," said Mr. Banks.

"Oh, stick around, Alister. As yet, you don't know half of the eccentricities in these hills," said the Judge. He swung his wheelchair around.

"Want me to run you home?" asked Mr. Banks.

"Hell, no. I'm going shopping. Old Perkins wheeled me down, and he'll wheel me back to the mountain. He's in the store now." Judge Stein looked at me. "Since just one side of me works, I'm only good at going in circles."

I smiled at him. "I'd be happy to help you whenever you need."

"Well, that's kind of you," said the Judge.

"Okay, then. Let me get you across the road to Perkins," said Mr. Banks.

"Perkins!" bellowed the Judge before Mr. Banks could get behind his chair.

The man named Perkins come runnin' outta the store. He were a pudgy fella. He sucked on a ice pop and throwed the stick in a nearby bin before bustlin' to take his place behind the Judge's wheelchair. Perkins pushed, but the Judge raised his hand. "Hold up, Perkins," the Judge said. When the chair stopped, the Judge turned to us. "There's a dearth of pretty girls to talk to in these hills. You ever notice that, Alister?"

Mr. Banks smiled.

"But here's the thing: I wouldn't mind a visit from one of them once in a while. Would you come visit an old man?" the Judge asked me. "Not to help, mind you. Just for a visit."

"Sure," I said.

He nodded once like we had a deal, and Perkins pushed his chair across the bumpy gravel. "Sayonara, suckers!" the Judge called, wavin' and laughin'.

"He's nice," I said as we watched the Judge cross the road.

"Finest man I know," said Mr. Banks.

"Well," I said, gettin' off the log. "Goodbye, Mr. Banks." I offered my hand like he'd done me.

He took it and looked me in the eye. "Will you call me Alister? 'Mr. Banks' was my father. He was a drunk, and I would rather not have any reminders of him. Besides, I'm not much older than you."

"Okay. Thanks, Alister." His name felt nice in my mouth. I turned 'round to walk away.

"Hey, wait!" he called as he leaned down and picked a big dandelion growin' by the log. Then he come over to me and put it behind my ear. "There. That suits you," he said. I laughed and went to the store.

#

When I got home, I'd forgotten about the flower, but not about the two men I'd met. I wanted to tell Billy all about them, but Billy noticed the flower behind my ear soon as I got in the door and pulled it out of my hair.

"What's this?" he asked.

"Jes' a flower," I said, sensin' somethin' weren't right. I never seen Billy like that before, mean and wily. I didn't understand it and until I did, I lied. "I forgot about it. Thought Kate might like it." And he gave me a stare down like he knew the words in my mouth weren't words at all, but the devil's own deceit.

"Girl!" he yelled and Kate come runnin'. He held the flower out to her, and she took it.

CHAPTER 15

I didn't move. I felt froze.

Billy took a big sniff of air and pulled hisself upright. He looked like a man turned to stone. "Git dinner on, witch," he said. I wanted to say, "I ain't no witch" like I always did whenever he called me that, but he were in no mood to hear from me so I went to scurryin', glad for somethin' to do.

All night I wanted to tell him about the day and the interestin' gentlemen I met. But I didn't dare, and that were probably a good thing.

CHAPTER 16

Far back as I can recollect, these mountains was magic to me. All my life, I seen trees growin' straight outta rocks and thought, if they can do it, so can I, and I'd have the courage to keep goin'. Tree roots risin' up above the soil looked like they could walk off by themselves. I would imagine them doin' jes' that when people weren't lookin', and if they could have a secret life o' their own, so could I. And I liked the Carolina jessamine's ropy vines that growed up trees and hung down again, and I imagined me like Tarzan—which were a book Cup and Blue read me—swingin' from them vines and callin' to all my animal friends.

But the place I most loved in these hills were the top of Blood Mountain. Up there, there's a big rocky overhang over a deep, green valley. Some folks might've feared the drop, but there was things in life a lot scarier. Sittin' up on that rock give me time to think. I'd find peace up there, and sometimes I took Kate, but I had to watch her every move. She seemed to have no respect for heights or the dangers all 'round. Once in a while, Billy were with me, too, although he didn't like it and stayed 'way back from the edge. I come to realize the top of Blood Mountain were my place—and sometimes, sittin' there, I imagined God talkin' jes' to me.

When Billy were livin' with me, there was times I didn't know what to do or what to say to him and Helenne. When she come 'round, I were left out. I started thinkin' more and more about Cup and Blue and missed 'em. The sisters was kind to me and never once made me feel like somebody they didn't want, even when I done somethin' they didn't like. They explained things to me, things I wouldn't know about. How to look past a dyin' animal's body to see its soul ascend. How the moments of life cooperated with each other to form one big whole. They taught me how to feel at home with nothin' more than a canopy of trees overhead.

I ruined a dolly they give me when I were six. It were my one doll, and I loved her, and I had tore off her head by accident 'cause a rubber band broke inside. I run downstairs—what house we was livin' in, I can't recollect. They was always changin' houses. This time, there was a curvy set of stairs that I had to come down—and I were cryin' for my dolly the whole way, scared o' telling them I broke her, scared they'd think I didn't care. I stood outside the parlor door, terrified to interrupt, and I heard Cup and Blue figuring out a spell. The 'Pure of Heart Spell,' they called it. It were a marvelous thing to hear about. I think they was readin' it out of a book of magic, and they sounded so sure it would work, and it made me feel like, if somebody could ever put that spell on me, I might be a bird and fly myself above all the sadness in the world.

Cup read with a low, steady voice. "Saving the dying is never a straightforward thing to do, and that's why the Pure of Heart Spell is so effective. But it demands something in return," the book said. "It demands that you sacrifice what matters most to you, and the spell is only effective when death is imminent..."

Don't know why, but them words has stuck with me all these years. But then I creaked a board, and the next thing I know, Cup come clatterin' out, closin' the door behind her, and takin' me by my elbow into another room so Blue wouldn't hear us.

"Kate, what goes on in that room ain't for little girl ears. How much of that did you hear?"

Sniveling, I said, "You was creatin' a spell for the pure of heart."

"I need you to forget what you heard. Children don't make sensible decisions, and you could hurt yourself, or somebody else, and die. Do you understand what I'm sayin' to you?"

"Yes'm," I said.

"I command you to forget what you heard."

CHAPTER 16

"Yes'm," I said.

"And your dolly's hurt. Let me have it, and I'll tend to her. You'll get her back after we've finished. Okay?"

"Okay," I said.

I never wanted to displease them, but that were a time I did, and Cup had protected me from the switch Blue threatened to use when somethin' weren't to her likin'. She rarely used it, mind you, but she'd run 'round wavin' it until Cup distracted her. They was good women that I never understood, but who I loved with all my heart. And sometimes in the night with Billy, my face turned away from him, I'd cry for missin' 'em and feel guilty for not even sayin' goodbye when I left Bowden. I prayed that they'd still love me despite my selfish ways, but I didn't know if I'd ever see 'em again.

And then one day in early fall, I left Kate at home with Billy while I went foragin' for food on Blood Mountain. Leaves swirled 'round me like there were no color in the world but red. I'd found me some big orange mushrooms growin' off a tree trunk and was fillin' my skirt with 'em when a familiar chatter twined through the scarlet woods.

"Get offa my robe," said a voice. "You're always steppin' on it."

"Why don't you wear clothes like normal people? Why do you have to be so... bohemian?"

"Bo...? Shh...Is that her?"

They called to me from the white balcony of a yellow house way up in the woods. "Yoo-hoo! Callie Moon! Look who's here!" said Blue, posin' like she and Cup were famous folk. They was happy to see me, and I ran to them, overjoyed. When I got growed up and on my own with Big Jim, I never knowed when they'd pop up, but pop up they did, even when I hadn't tol' 'em where I were.

That day, their house were one o' the bigger ones. Lots o' chandeliers hung from the ceiling and bounced light off all the mirrors linin' the walls. From

*floor to ceiling, mirrors hung in frames with the biggest one I ever seen leanin'
up against a wall. And runnin' down the middle of the large room were the
wooden trestle table I remembered as a child, scarred and elbow-worn, but so
sturdy I knowed it were bound to outlive me.*

*They poured me a cup o' tea, and we gabbed all afternoon. They wanted
to know all about Kate, and I promised to bring her by, knowin' full well
that it probably wouldn't happen 'cause they wouldn't live there no more. It
felt good being with them that day. I didn't feel alone anymore, and I were
lonesome with Billy. I were always the one set aside 'cause he had Helenne.*

"Your hair is longer," said Cup. "Very pretty."

*"And you got yourself a blue ribbon," said Blue. "Where'd you get that
'un?"*

*"I..." I were about to lie, but what good would it do? Cup and Blue
always knowed the truth. "I stole it."*

*The sisters looked at each other, serious-like. "She don't know," said Blue.
Her head swept back and forth as if somethin' bad were on its way.*

"Nope," said Cup, "but save your fussin'."

"Tell her," said Blue.

*Cup took a deep breath. It were like I were in a room full o' dread. The
air got heavy and hard to breathe. I thought they was gon' tell me I were gon'
burn in hellfire for sure, like the revival preacher preached.*

*"When you is full of greed, and steal something like that, you steal the
destiny of the person you stole from," said Cup.*

At first I thought they was kiddin'.

*"What're you sayin'? That I'm goin' to turn tall now and get all dark-
haired and beautiful and have a pretty house and a fine yard? That don't
sound so bad." The sisters looked grave, and my joke fell flat, squashed like a*

mighty hand had pressed down on it, and at the same time, had taken all the colors outta the world.

"You gon' live her life in some real important way," said Cup.

I felt a chill then. Being afeared of Helenne and her wolf-dogs, I knowed I'd screech up a lung if they ever come after me. I didn't want to get too close to her from the start, but because I did something stupid, it sounded like I were going to be tied to her forever.

"Suppose'n I don't want her life," I said.

"Look," said Cup. "You stole the ribbon. No one forced it into your hand. It was your doin', and there ain't no one to blame but you."

"Well, I'll give it back," I said.

Cup shook her head. "Don't work that way."

"There ain't nothing we can do, Cal," said Blue. "There ain't no spell on earth that can break this 'un."

"But I didn't know what I was doin'!" I said, sweat springin' out of me.

"Don't make no difference. You did it. You gon' live with it," said Cup.

"But—"

"Ain't no 'buts,'" she said, and I stared at her for a while before the tears come.

Blue filled my teacup, and I drank the potion down. I knowed it weren't tea in that cup, but I needed whatever it were. Soon, I were calmer.

"I guess I better be goin'," I said, puttin' the chipped china cup in the rosebud saucer and standin' up.

"Yeah, you better," said Cup.

At the door, I threw myself into their arms and held on tight, but they pushed me away and waved me off.

#

When I got home, it were nighttime, and I weren't happy to see Helenne's truck outside our door. Her husband, Frank, never come to visit with her, and I hadn't seen him for a long time. My suspicions tol' me he weren't there at their little white house no more, and that he'd run off somewhere. I'd o' run off too if I belonged to Helenne.

Relieved there was no wolf-dogs runnin' 'round, I heard raised voices coming from inside the house. I took me a deep breath and walked inside. Helenne and Billy was standin' there glarin' at each other from across the kitchen table, ignorin' Kate who was bawlin' in the corner on a blanket. I went and picked her up.

"Where you been, witch?" said Billy. He had a sly smile on his face.

"Don't you call me that, Billy. I ain't no witch," I said for the umpteenth time, all the while pattin' on Kate's little back. I'd gotten to hate when he called me that, but he always said it with pride—like what he most admired 'bout me was what I weren't and never would be.

"You are, too. Don't deny it," he said.

"Look at her," said Helenne. "She's flaunting it. Where'd you get that ribbon, Callie Moon?"

Suddenly, I knew why she were glarin' at me on the road with the Judge and Alister: I'd had the ribbon in my hair.

"I bought it in the town I used to live in," I said. I were shakin' now, and Kate screamed even louder. My mind were in chaos, and I had to give my baby and me some relief. "I gotta put her down," I said and ran to the bedroom with my little girl. I tried to quiet her but couldn't and had no choice but to go back to Billy and Helenne and let Kate cry herself out.

"You stole that ribbon from me," said Helenne when I walked back into the room.

"No, I…" but I knowed defendin' myself were useless. I were about to confess when Billy spoke up.

"Leave her be, Helenne. She ain't yours to torment."

I pulled the ribbon from my hair. "Here. If you want it, you can have it," I said, holdin' it out to Helenne. Givin' it back might break the spell, even if the sisters said it wouldn't.

Helenne snatched it from my hand, and Billy was on her like a burst of fire. He pushed her hard in the chest and snatched the ribbon from her hand. She fell into the wall, knockin' a picture of blue daisies that the Adairs give me to the floor. Kate screamed louder, scared by the loud thump and the sound of breakin' glass.

Billy and Helenne locked eyes, and then Billy held out the ribbon to me and commanded me to put it on. I did.

"See, Helenne? It don't matter whose it is. It matters who's wearin' it." And he came over, grabbed me, and kissed my mouth hard. "She's my witch, ain't you, babe?" he asked me, and he held my head back at a hard angle to look at me. I were more worried for my hurt neck than answerin' him, so I didn't. He didn't notice. He were in a fury at Helenne. And Helenne were in a fury at Billy and me. Billy's treatment o' me were rough too, rougher than he'd ever been before, and I felt scared.

"She. Is. No. Witch," Helenne spit, pushin' her black hair off her face. Then she stood up and left.

I were terrified but needed to tell Billy what I done. "Billy," I said. "I stole this ribbon from Helenne. You oughta know."

I thought he might treat me mean like he done Helenne. Instead, he smiled. "Then good," he said. "You a witch, so stealin' come natural, and I ain't gon' hear no more about it. I believe in the prophecy and that's all there is to it."

"I stole her destiny," I said.

"Yep. Everybody knows you steal the destiny of the person you steal from. I say, so what? It's yern now," he said and went outside to chop some logs.

I were quiverin' like jelly, but Kate needed me. Poor little thing. She weren't makin' sense o' this, and neither were I. What the hell was all that puttin'-on about? So much over a ribbon! And then I knowed. The truth come to me like one of them white doves in the Bible, comin' down from the clouds, sent by God hisself. Helenne and Billy were close, so he'd have tol' her about the Conjure Man's prediction. She'd bought that ribbon with her savings for one reason: She were in love with Billy and counted on bein' with him her whole life. When I come along and stole that ribbon, I stole her destiny, which were to be with Billy. But if she were supposed to be the one with the ribbon, she were also the one who were the witch. On the day she saved me from them wolf-dogs, she didn't see the ribbon before. Jes' afterwards. That's the only reason I were alive. It mighta been different if she seen the ribbon first.

And I knowed somethin' else. I had to be careful. Protecting both me and my baby was vital. I walked the floor with Kate until she quieted down and fell asleep against my jumpy heart. Once I'd put her to bed, I went back to the other room where Billy were sittin' at the end of the table eatin' some cereal out o' a bowl. I were mad at him, but I didn't know why. He'd stuck up for me, after all, and that were somethin'.

"Sit down," he said, and when I sat in the hardwood chair beside him, he put down his bowl. He took my hand, kissed it, put our hands to his heart, and seemed back to his ol' self. "I love you, Callie Moon. There ain't no one for me in this world but you. Don't you worry about Helenne. We won't care 'bout her. She'll come 'round from time to time. She'll spout off, but I will always—hear me now—always protect you. D'you believe me?"

His eyes was full of tears and he looked heartbroken for the upset he caused. It were such a tender moment—and a surprisin' one—that I hadn't had in such a long time that I said, "Yes. I believe you, Billy Mars. And you are my love, too."

CHAPTER 17

Those four days was a joyful time. Billy come back to me, and we made love every day. Helenne stayed away, and Kate didn't cry as much. Lookin' back on it, those four days was the happiest o' my life. On day five, I made us a tasty breakfast o' eggs and pig fat on bread. Kate were playin' in the corner, and Billy went up to the roof. There were a leak in the chimney near where it opened to the sky. I'd got the laundry together to boil in the yard when I heard a lot o' commotion and a hair-raisin' scream before the day went quiet. When I run out to the yard, Billy were lyin' on the ground bleedin' from his head and nose, the ladder lyin' on top of him. It were me who screamed then. I tore off the ladder, and patted him and called his name as Kate, still chewing on a piece o' toast, come out to watch us from the porch.

Billy were out cold. Without a phone, there weren't nothin' to do but grab Kate and run to Alister's house. He were closer than anybody else. He took us back in his car and examined Billy. His neck didn't seem broke, but Alister couldn't be sure. With no other choice, we loaded him into Alister's Range Rover, dropped Kate off at the Adair's, and drove Billy outta the high hills and over to Asheville, two hours away. There weren't no place to treat bad trouble anywhere else.

When we got there, we kept Billy in the car till Alister brung out some white-clad folks who loaded Billy on a rollin' cart. I ran behind as best I could, and they took us to a little cubicle with curtains. Alister and I tol' 'em what happened, and they tol' us to go out to the lobby to wait while they examined him. I cried. Worryin' my head off, I didn't know if I'd ever see Billy again, and there ain't much to do in a hospital lobby but fret. I watched people come and go—some was happy, some was sad, some looked as worried as me, their head bowed, their foreheads full of woe. The hours seemed longer than most when a nurse come out and said that we should go home 'cause there weren't gon' to be no news for a while. They had to do tests. So Alister give her his number and tol' her we'd go back to the mountain. I didn't have no phone, see, 'cause Billy never seen the use of one since we could walk to everythin'. So once Alister and me picked up Kate, he suggested we stay with him, which we did 'cause o' the phone.

Alister's house were pleasant. The rooms was big, but you'd never know it. Books and papers cluttered everywhere, but he were a big shot writer after all, so it seemed fittin'. What couldn't get crammed on bookcases, he stacked on the floor and tables. Scribblings was everywhere too. From big notebooks to little sheets of curling stick-on paper he'd put on his kitchen cabinets, his bedpost, and even his bathroom mirror. His furniture was large 'cause he were a tall man and required big things, and it were all leathery, tweedy, and masculine. I couldn't help but think he'd benefit from a plant or two to soften things up, and I set to plantin' for him to keep my mind off Billy.

I slept in his bedroom with Kate in the biggest bed I ever seen. Alister slept on his recliner in the livin' room, and he fed me and Kate like we was somethin' special: meat and vegetables, fruit, and little wrapped chocolates from a blue hobnail bowl. But when the hospital called, each piece of news about Billy broke my heart. They kept tellin' us that his brain pressure were elevated, and he weren't gettin' enough oxygen to his brain.

"What's it mean?" I asked Alister when he got off the phone.

"That there could be some irreversible brain damage. If his intracranial brain pressure is too high for a prolonged period—" he said.

"Did they say how long he got before it's irreversible?" I asked. That word "irreversible," didn't roll outta my mouth easy.

"He looked at me with kind eyes and said, 'Three minutes or longer.'

Well, I thought, we long since passed that mark.

Alister drove me over to Asheville every week so I could visit Billy. Billy always seemed outta it, and most times, he didn't know I were there. One *time, I walked in and Helenne were sittin' on his bed holdin' his hand. I stood starin', and when she saw me, she leaned over, kissed Billy on his lips, and left. She took her own sweet time about it, too, as if she were darin' me to say somethin'.*

#

It were April, six months later, when Billy come home, and a lot had happened. I were six months pregnant and gettin' 'round as best I could, although I were sick most days and didn't have as much energy to care for Kate. The Adairs helped a lot when they got back to Blood Mountain from their winter home in Florida.

By the time the doctors released Billy from the hospital, Alister, the Adairs, and Judge Stein had all chipped in and gifted me a ol' blue truck so I could pick him up from the hospital in style. I were proud that day. I had me genuine friends, and we mattered to each other. We had gotten closer since Billy's accident, and I wanted to tell Billy all about it—how they'd helped us, and how excited I was that his baby was growing inside me.

Right away, though, I couldn't talk to Billy 'bout none of it. He were wiped out and had a faraway look, and when we got back to Blood Mountain and I put him to bed, he stayed terrible sick for a long, long time.

#

"Three months later, after I brung Billy home, Kate and me was out walkin'. It were a warm July day with the sun beamin' down. We was lookin' for crawdads in the dancin' water o' the trout stream a good stretch of the legs from our house. But while I stood on the bank, a little spurt o' water trickled down my leg, and I felt the pressure of the baby comin'. There weren't no time to get back up to the house, the pains was too close, but Kate were four-year-old, and I'd tol' her about havin' babies and explained the happenings. She helped lay me down on the bank, and as the creek water burbled beside us, the baby come out in a gush.

It were a beautiful girl, with all her fingers and toes and skin as beautiful as the petal of a summer rose, and we named her Gilly in honor of all the little fish with gills that could breathe underwater and that swam in the creek beside us. Kate found a sharp stone, and together we cut the umbilical cord and tied it off so that Gilly were officially her own person. She were also Kate's, who wrapped the babe up in my shucked-off skirt, cradled her in her arms, and carried her to the house. I liked the name Gilly and hoped it would please Billy, since it rhymed with his name.

After that, I were exhausted, maybe more than I ever felt before, but after a couple of weeks, I regained some strength. Kate were always bringin' me bouillon from the Adairs and takin' good care of me, so I got up when I were able and went about tryin' to keep the young'uns quiet for Billy Mars. He needed to heal too, and he slept a lot, and we jes' couldn't have all the squealin', cryin', and yellin' that were part o' life with rackety children. Billy Mars healed in his way, but it took a year. Durin' that time, Kate and me exercised his legs for him, movin' 'em this way and that so they wouldn't shrink away. Gilly sat on her little side bed, entertained by all the doings.

Billy still slept a lot, and we missed the money he brung in from workin', so I went to work cleanin' house for the Adairs. Then Alister and Judge Stein asked me to come help them too. I liked the work. Maybe 'cause I recollected a time when there weren't nothin' to clean.

But Billy had changed. He were distant somehow, and he eyed me suspicious-like. Helenne came 'round all the time, sometimes with her wolf-dogs, which she'd leave outside and which kept me and the kids trapped. I'd hear Billy and her laughin' in the bedroom, some private joke the two of 'em shared, while I entertained the kids in the livin' area with a smile on my face, pretendin' not to care. When Helenne come, she'd often bring a bottle of somethin'. Hooch generally. Or better made moonshine. I asked her not to do it, but she did it anyway and seemed delighted that it upset me. Billy drank everythin' she give him, and on top of all the pills he were takin' from the doctors and some she brung him, the mix didn't serve any o' us. He were often mean as a snake, cursin' me, Kate, and the baby, and many a night, I went to bed cryin'.

I didn't say none of this to my friends on the mountain. I didn't want nobody feelin' sorry for me or thinkin' any less of Billy Mars. But it all came to a head one day in October when Alister Banks stopped by the house with a rose-colored vase full of pretty store-bought flowers. The kids was spendin' the day with the Adairs, so they wasn't with me.

"Hi," Alister said when I opened the door. "I brought you and Billy some flowers. Thought they might cheer you up."

I never had store-bought flowers before and thought they was the prettiest thing I ever seen. What I didn't know were that Billy, still weak and wobbly, had let hisself into the kitchen behind us and were hearin' everythin'.

"Why, ain't you sweet, Alister," I said. "I'm sure Billy'll like 'em too. Won't you come in and sit down?"

He come in, but as soon as he sat at the table, Billy Mars created a racket, bangin' two pots together like he were clappin' with 'em.

"This is what you're doin' while I almost died?" he yelled over the racket.

I froze. My chest felt caved in, and it were hard to breathe.

"He brung you some flowers," I shouted over the din, and I pointed to the vase.

"Naw, he brung you them flowers, not me. What's been goin' on here behind my back?"

My eyes hurt fierce from the pressure behind 'em, but I could think of nothin' to say. I jes' stared at Billy, wishin' he'd get hisself back to bed.

"Nothing's going on, Billy, I assure you," said Alister. "Callie works for me."

"Works for you? Doin' what?"

"She cleans house for me and for some other people on the mountain."

"So you've turned yerself into a servant girl. Some witch you are," Billy said.

"I guess I'd better go," said Alister, tappin' the table and gettin' up with a last look at me. "Come on up to the house if you need anything."

He walked out the door without lookin' back. Mortification filled me up. I felt like I were half-sunk in a hole.

"Why'd you do that, Billy?" I were standin' at the door, quiverin', watchin' Alister walk up the road. I couldn't make myself turn 'round and look Billy in the eye.

"You're my witch," he said and went back to bed.

"I ain't no witch," I whispered, but nobody heard that but me.

#

That night, I made a pot o' stew. Whenever I'm upset, I cook, and I were plenty on edge. The stew were rich with potatoes, carrots, celery, broccoli, and a good, hearty cut o' beef from the Adairs.

I went about tryin' to make everythin' extra nice: good food, a pretty table. Gilly were dancin' in the middle of the room and Kate got up and joined her. They eventually fell down laughin'. I pretended to laugh, too, and complimented them on their mighty talents. I didn't want the events of the day, and me and Billy's dark moods, to drown their fun. As I placed the flowers on the table, I thought o' my lost little boy, Jimmy. I hoped somebody someday would see his grave there alongside Big Jim's and put some flowers on it as pretty as the ones Alister brung.

I thought o' Big Jim. At heart, he weren't no mean man, just clueless, and I took a moment to wish him well wherever he were in heaven or hell. Billy differed from Big Jim. What Big Jim did were predictable, but Billy—I couldn't get no take on him. I jes' knew I had to beware. Maybe the love of *a good man weren't no thing at all, but jes' somethin' we tell ourselfs to keep us goin'.*

Callin' the family to the table, I strapped Gilly in her highchair. I served Kate a plate and made a nice big plate for Billy. I were dishin' up my own at the stove when Billy raised up his hand and flung his plate against the wall. Meat, vegetables, and drippings run down to the floor. My heart seized up. Gilly shrieked, and Billy raised his voice right over her.

"You know why I had to do that, Kate? 'Cause your momma tried to poison me. I smelled the poison in the stew, and that's why I had to throw it against the wall. She's tryin' to poison you, too. I wouldn't eat that if I was you."

Kate touched her plate and looked at me. She didn't know what to do, who to believe.

"Nothin' wrong with that stew," I said to her, but she just sat there. "Eat or don't eat what you will, Billy Mars, but don't you be denyin' my daughter," I said.

"Your ma's a liar," he whispered to Kate loud enough for me to hear. He then tore off a flower from Alister's bouquet and stuck it behind Kate's ear. "There. That's better." He threw the stem at me. It bounced off my cheek. Then he put his hands 'round the big vase and slammed it to the floor. Gilly started screamin' and cryin' even louder. Kate looked like she'd fallen down a well and expected to be at the bottom forever.

"Kate," I said, tryin' to stay calm for the girls. "Let's you and me take Gilly to the bedroom." So we got up, and I walked us out, half expectin' Billy to come after us. He didn't.

I guided Kate to her little bed and put Gilly in her arms. Scared to touch Kate, I was afraid she would feel me trembling and fear me as well as Billy. I crossed my arms to keep from reachin' for her and we jes' sat there, listenin' to Gilly wail.

Lookin' back on that time, I made a mistake. I should've tol' Kate everythin', but I thought she were too young to understand the complications o' Billy Mars and me. I kept mum, hopin' that one day, she'd figure it for herself.

CHAPTER 18

Word had gotten 'round about Billy Mars's treatment of me, and all I wanted to do were hide—though in a small community like this, it ain't possible. To their credit, my friends on the mountain said nary a word about it, but they upped their concern for me and the kids by comin' by with somethin' every day. Sally with a casserole. Ben with a couple of toys. Judge Stein sent his new nurse, Alice, who come over with a bunch of new pots and pans that were fancy and store-bought, right outta a box. Whoever come each day stayed as long as they could, requestin' a cup of tea or a biscuit to prolong the visit. They was there to scope out if the kids and me was all right. But I never saw Alister. He stayed away. Perhaps it were best.

Billy talked about me to anybody who'd listen. He'd say that I was a witch and a bad witch at that. This riled up that self-righteous Reverend Thatcher, and one day he, his wife, and a parishioner come to our house with Bibles in their hands. The preacher were tall and positively gaunt. His wife made up for it in the girth department. She looked like she hadn't had a lean day in her life and had worried every hair off her head. The parishioner looked gray and disgusted, like he were there to wash slimy stuff off the bottom of his shoe and it were me. Them people pushed their way into my house when I were there with the kids and weren't expectin' no kind o' trouble. Once inside, though, the Reverend grabbed hold o' me and forced me to the table.

"God knows you're a sinner!" Reverend Thatcher yelled, pushin' the side of my head down on the table and holdin' it there. Across the room, my kids run to the wall, holdin' each other and tryin' to be invisible.

"Christ our savior, I exhort you to come into this woman and drive the devil out!" the preacher yelled.

I tried to get up then, but he had me pinned. When I reached up to remove his hand from my head, he leaned over and put the full weight o' his arm across my neck, and his wife and the other man held my arms down hard against the table.

"Don't fight it, child," said the preacher. "The jaws of hell got you, and we must cleanse you for you to be free!"

"I ain't no devil!" I spat. "And nobody's got me but you!"

"Renounce the evil-doer and all his ways!" shouted the preacher, still holdin' me down.

"There ain't nobody to renounce!" I screamed back.

My neck hurt so bad that I yowled up a big 'un. I guess the Reverend thought he were killin' me then, so his hold relaxed, and he finally let go o' me so I could stand up and move my neck around.

"I think we've lost this 'un, Reverend," the parishioner said, shakin' his head. "We gonna have to watch her and slap down her every move."

"Let us pray," said the Reverend to nobody in particular.

I were glad to be let go of and hurried to my babies who was huddled together, their faces wet with tears and turned to the wall.

"Good and Gracious Lord," the Reverend prayed, "this woman is a sinner, a witch, a major flaw in your creation. We exhort you to punish her for her evil ways and blight out her kind from now until the end of time! We'll not pity the abomination, but drive her out of our hearts, and when she lies alone in a cold, dark grave, we will praise you! Amen."

And then they took their Bibles and marched out. Dumbfounded, I didn't even know what 'exhort' meant until Alister explained it to me on the day I went to clean for him. I still had a crick in my neck from the good Reverend's handling o' me, and Alister saw it. He were furious at that preacher and called him a 'nut job,' which made me laugh. I guess I were a failure at being exhorted, but I knowed one thing: I couldn't trust Billy ever again. He'd set us up.

After that, I tried to keep me and the babies away from Billy as much as possible. The children seemed to irritate him somethin' fierce, and he were always angrier 'round them. Billy and me was still livin' together, but that didn't mean we had to be in the same room, and I shuffled the babes and me around dependin' on where he were. I took them with me when I were cleanin', and other times I took them with me to have cookies and milk with Judge Stein and Nurse Alice.

Nurse Alice were a great asset to Judge Stein. She cooked for him and made him laugh. She were pretty and strong and always saw the positive side of things. I loved her. Judge Stein's health had gotten bad and where he used to occasional walk shaky with a cane, he couldn't do it no more. He leaned on Nurse Alice's pretty shoulders to move from wheelchair to bed to toilet. Judge Stein weren't no fool. He knowed he were close to the end, and Nurse Alice made it nice for him—and for me.

Those afternoons with Judge Stein and Nurse Alice, hearin' the kids happy and playin' outside in his garden near his ol' tool shed, was magical. His garden were shaped like a four-leaf clover, and it had a three-rowed fountain in the middle that lighted up at night. Flowers bloomed everywhere. There was roses, geraniums, dahlias, marigolds, and everythin' that you could imagine bloomin', bloomed there. I thought it must be what heaven looked like—the birds singin', the hummingbirds buzzin' 'round and makin' us laugh at their antics.

I were always in my best cotton dress for those afternoons, even though I knowed I'd be cold when the sun dipped behind the mountains and the shadows got long. We'd sit in the sun listenin' to the squeals of little girl laughter and those was happy times. Judge Stein recollected his famous cases, the highs and lows of his career, and most especially he'd remember the love of his life, his wife of fifty-two years, who he called Miss Monica. She died o' spinal cancer, a terrible death, some twenty years before. And then one day, as we sat in the autumn sun and remarked on the chill in the air, Judge Stein asked Nurse Alice to fetch a box for him from the big chifforobe in his room. She came back with it and laid it in his lap. He fiddled 'round in the box and pulled out a beautiful set of earrings that was dangly with green stones set in amongst the gold—and a dainty little pendant that fell to pieces in his hand.

"My dear wife loved jewelry. I bought her these earrings in the south of France, and this little pendant came from Italy. It's broken now. Oh, well. It's the memories that are important. We were in Venice when I bought it and nearly froze to death. That one day, Venice was cold as Alaska in wintertime, and we were there in summer clothes! And this one…" He held up a gold necklace with a heart hangin' off it. The heart contained a genuine diamond. "This was the first thing I ever gave her. I loved her from the first moment I saw her. A poor law student doesn't have a pot to pee in, at least I didn't, so I worked security at night to make enough money to give her this just for…love. It was just for love because it wasn't Christmas or her birthday."

He rummaged in the box some more. "Most of what's in this box is junk now. I've given a lot of it away to friends through the years already. But I've saved the best for last, and now the time has come. I want you to have this."

He held the necklace out to me, and I thought he were jokin'. When I saw he weren't, my breath hitched. "I can't," I said when I seen him wantin' me to take it. "It's too precious. I mean, I thank you kindly, Judge Stein. But I jes' can't." What I were sayin' were true, but I also knowed I couldn't explain the necklace to Billy.

"Hmm. Alice here said you probably wouldn't take it. You women have minds of your own. But here's the thing—show her where it'll be, Alice—and I want you girls to promise me that when the good Lord calls me home, you'll come in and get the jewelry I want you to have. Is that a deal?"

"Is Nurse Alice gettin' somethin' too?" I asked.

"Yes," said Alice. "He's giving me the earrings from France."

That made me happy.

"Is it a deal?" said the Judge.

"Yeah," I said, "But let's not talk about anybody passin' on."

I loved him and Alice, and I wanted to keep things jes' as they was forever. I didn't know how I'd get along without them, and I choked up thinkin' about how things might be different one day. Then we all went back to watchin' the children until the bright sun hid itself behind the clouds.

#

The girls and me dragged home as night were settin' in. My heart hurt again to see Helenne's truck comin' from our house and speedin' past us on the road when we was almost home. She almost hit Gilly, but for Kate grabbin' her outta the way. Helenne never even slowed down.

Billy were sittin' at the table, drunk as a skunk, when we walked in. I didn't say nothin', but turned to the sink in the kitchen to wash Gilly off 'cause she was dirty from makin' mud pies in Judge Stein's garden. I had jes' sat her up on the edge of the sink and pulled her ol' cotton shift over her head when he spoke up.

"You screwin' somebody other'n me?"

I turned to him and stared him in the eyes. *"Don't you be talkin' crazy, Billy—"*

"I ain't crazy! You stop callin' me that!" He staggered to his feet and pointed at Gilly. *"How'd I even know that's my baby? It don't look like me."*

My blood come up. My ears started poundin', and it were all I could do to breathe in and out. I come to a place, though, where holdin' back weren't possible. *"Look at yourself, Billy Mars! All you do is drink and yell and hurt us. What happened to the Billy Mars I loved?"*

Billy come at me like a wildcat then, his hands hittin', punchin', and pullin'. It happened so fast; I weren't prepared to fight back. He grabbed me by the waist and started haulin' me to the other room. Try as I might, I couldn't *get my feet to the floor, and I couldn't get my breath neither 'cause he were stovin' in my ribs. All I could think of were my baby sittin' on the edge o' the sink about to fall.*

"Gilly!" I croaked at Kate, who run for her sister and pulled her into her arms.

That were the last thing I seen of the girls as Billy threw me on the bed and unbuckled his pants. He were hard, and I didn't want him. I hadn't had him in a year, and this Billy Mars weren't no friend.

"No! You will not touch me!" I screamed.

Rollin' over, I scrambled to get up off the bed, but he caught the back of my dress and tore it. I grabbed the fabric in the front to cover my body. He spun me, his rough hands snatchin', and ripped the rest of the fabric away. I went at him then, trying to push him away from me. Ignoring my blows as if they was nothing, he pushed me down on the bed again and crawled on top of me. Then I hit him with everything I had, but in his rage, he were beyond feelin' anything I did. Holdin' me down with his chest and arms and the big bulk o' him, he tried to still my head as I were thrashin' to get up, and he pulled my hair till I could feel it tore out. Then he used his foot to push my panties down my legs and checked to see if they was off. When he looked back at me, I bit him hard on the jawbone. Surprised, he reared back and punched me in the face with his fist. He kept punching too. Then he grabbed what were left o' my hair and put his mouth to my ear.

"You try somethin' like that again, and I'll kill you," he said and bit my ear. He bit me again as if he was trying to tear the ear from my head. Finally, he threw my head down on the bed and pushed into me. He hurt me so bad I thought I was splittin' in two.

There were a spider on the ceiling. It were one of them bitin' spiders, so I hoped it wouldn't drop on me. Them spiders enter through the chinks of a plank house, and there weren't much to do to keep 'em out. Their bites would swell up big like a half dollar, and drive a body crazy from the pain and itchin'. Little Jimmy came to my mind then. I didn't want to die like he did. Living were hard, but I had babies to stay here for. I simply were gon' have to do somethin' about them bitin' spiders to keep the babies safe, and so I kept my eyes on that spider lest somethin' bad would happen.

When it were over, Billy rolled off me and sat on the side of the bed for a while. The spider had crawled off someplace, and I curled into a ball and stayed that way, afeared to move or call attention. Then Billy got up to scrounge around in the bathroom, probably lookin' for more pills to take. Eventually, the front door opened and slammed shut, and the blue truck drove off. I think I breathed then, for the first time in a while.

I set to shakin' then and my ears felt stuffed with cotton. I called to Kate 'cause I didn't trust myself to stand up. At first, she didn't come to me, and I got scared that Billy had drove off with the girls to hurt me. I willed myself to sit up despite me hurtin' everywhere, but when I called again, Kate showed herself standin' in the other room a distance away from the door with Gilly in her arms. Her eyes was as big as saucer plates, and there were no explainin' away what Billy done to me. It were then that I knowed I'd lost her. It were as if she were standin' on the moon, clutchin' her sister like a doll, but all by herself. I'd missed my chance to explain Billy Mars and me a ways back, and the chance'd never come again.

The girls and I slept together in the big bed that night. Gilly fell asleep in my arms right away. Kate lay a little way apart, watchin' me.

"Is he gonna kill you, Momma?" she asked.

"Naw, naw," I said, not believin' that he wouldn't. "You know how your daddy is. He says things he don't mean—"

"Is he gonna kill Gilly 'cause she ain't his?"

I knowed what she was thinkin': that she weren't his neither, and she were afeared for herself. "Now you listen here, Kate. He ain't gon' kill nobody. And Gilly is his. He were just spoutin'—"

"If you die," she said, "who's gonna take care o' Gilly and me?"

"I ain't goin' nowhere—"

"But if you do…" She were pressin' me, and I had to come up with a answer.

"Okay," I said. "Here's the way it is. If I ain't here, I'll send the moon to watch over you."

"What good'll that do? It's all the ways up in the sky."

Kate were too smart for her own good. "Okay…why don't I send a animal to protect you, to walk with you jes' like your momma would if I was here? What would you like me to send?"

"Mmm…" she said. "A dog. I like dogs."

"Then I'll send you a dog. Why don't I send a Carolina dog so you'll know it's me? Would you like that?" She nodded and there were the trace of a smile. I pulled her closer to me. "But I ain't goin' nowhere, honey," I said, hopin' it was so.

The three of us fell asleep, all nestled into each other. But 'long about three A.M., Billy come home, and I hurried the kids into their own little bed by the wall. I didn't know what were gon' to happen. As I was about to leave the room, Billy come in to find me. I backed away.

But he were cryin' and looked broke in two. His eyes was red and bloodshot. He walked with a stoop, and he come over and took my hand. I didn't want to give it at first, and I were ready to run, but there weren't no way 'round him.

He wailed out loud then and sunk down on his knees and held onto me through my nightdress. "What can I do to beg yer forgiveness? I did so wrong. Are you hurt? Did I hurt you? Forgive me, please forgive me… This ain't gon' happen ever again. Oh, Callie Moon, forgive me…"

I stood there in that dark room and tried to remember that his brain weren't right, and that were as close to forgiveness as I could come.

#

The next mornin', I didn't want to talk. Billy could change on a dime. I didn't trust him and didn't want to set off another row. I fed the girls breakfast and sent 'em outside to get 'em away from what might happen.

Billy were actin' like a fool. While I were washin' the dishes, he started to dry and sidled up to me, movin' into my space so that I had to take a step away. He had a stupid grin on his face like nothin'-at-all had happened the night before, and it were as if he expected me to cut up with him. I weren't gon' do it. There weren't no nonsense left in me.

He put down the dishrag and went over to the kettle on the stove and poured hisself a cup o' coffee. "Want some?" he asked, holdin' up his cup.

"No," I said.

Then he started whistlin' and sat at the table watchin' me. He stopped whistlin' when he took a swallow of coffee and then he started again. I'd had all I could stand, and I braced my arms on the counter to tell him what I had to say.

"Billy," I said, "last night you asked me what you could do to make up for hurtin' me. So I'm gon' tell you. Keep Helenne outta our house. I don't want to see her here again."

Billy smiled real calm and stood up like all his bones were creakin'. Then he threw the cup hard at my head. It glanced off my forehead and shattered on the floor.

"You disrespectin' me? Did I jes' hear you disrespectin' me, girl?" he asked. "Helenne tol' me you was doin' this. She says you been disrespectin' me for a long time, and she tol' me not to take any lip from you. So...you disrespectin' me? I can disrespect you, too!"

I knew better than to talk again. In a fury, he leaped over to the garbage can, reached in, and threw trash at me. Cans and bottles hit me over and over, and the stink were already on me by the time he turned the trashcan over on my head.

"Whatta you think about that? How's that feel? Huh?" he said to me, smackin' the can loud several times. "Huh?" When he was sure I were good and deaf, he took the can off of me and threw it across the room. Then he stood still for a minute with his head low. "You know, baby, you're a colossal disappointment. Where's my witch, huh? You promised me a witch."

He spit on the floor and left. Outside, the truck roared to life and peeled off the gravel. I were relieved he were gone, but I'd jes' got a earful. Whatever hurt Billy'd suffered in the accident, Helenne were behind what he'd become. She were gettin' even with me for takin' him away. Picking up the garbage first, I went to change my clothes. Then I mopped the floor and called in the kids. I packed some toys in a bag and took the babes and their toys over to the Adairs. I knowed what I had to do, and I didn't want the children anywhere near me when I did it.

When I got back, I walked up the mountain to Helenne's. Billy weren't gon' ask her to stay away, so I were gon' to do it. I were scared as a rabbit when I knocked on the little red door o' her white house. The wolf-dogs snarled and growled at me from inside.

"Helenne?" I called, but still keepin' my voice real calm. "Can you come out here? I need to talk to you." The door opened, and she came out with a wolf-dog on each side of her. She crossed her arms. I reminded myself again to talk low.

"You don't need them dogs," I said, hopin' she's put 'em inside, but she didn't. She jes' stared at me.

"What d'you want?" she asked.

"Helenne, I don't want you comin' 'round Billy no more. I don't want you bringin' liquor or pills to him. You ain't good for any of us, and I'm gon' ask you to leave us alone. I know you mess with his mind. He tol' me."

She smiled. "You think you've won, don't you?"

"What are you talkin' about?"

"You think he's yours."

"He is mine," I said.

"You're either very loyal or stupid," she said, and she started laughin' at me. She wouldn't stop laughin'. She laughed and laughed. There were nothin' left to do, but back away from her and those wolf-dogs and go home.

CHAPTER 19

I'd read most of the night, and it was now mid-afternoon. I'd promised myself that I'd read until I finished the book, but I just couldn't go on without a break.

There were a hundred thoughts igniting like matches in my mind. Most shocking was reading about Billy Mars's cruelty and violence. I felt fear for my mother, and I was equally frightened for Gilly and me as children. Perhaps I would have been even more traumatized had I remembered any of this, but I didn't. I simply felt an uncanny resonance with it, as if something hibernating deep within its den was finally stirring. As an adult, I'd had all the symptoms of having come from a home like this: high-risk behaviors, difficulty trusting, dissociation and memory gaps, difficulties being vulnerable and more. I saw, with clarity and no small amount of horror, that I was dysfunction's poster child.

I went to the kitchen to pour myself a cup of coffee. It might have been too late in the afternoon to drink caffeine if I wanted a night's sleep, but I needed it to clear my mind. There was a lot to process. I went digging in my bag for my notebook and a pen and started a list:

1. Alister—different than my mother described. What had happened to him?

2. Cup and Blue—eccentric old ladies, witches, or supernatural forces? My mother—a witch???

The two most likely candidates for that title were right under everyone's noses and yet few people knew them. Callie and I knew them. It sounded like Alister did, and Reverend Thatcher and his group knew them. Sal had lived here most of his life, and he didn't know them. And what about the sisters living in different houses? Is this why I couldn't find their turquoise home? And I didn't remember them or anything about living with them. Did they give me one of their special teas to wipe my memories away? Is there an elixir strong enough to make you forget what's important for you to remember? Or could the trauma that I saw and endured be the sole cause of my memory loss?

I balled myself up on Bruce's sofa. I stared across the room for the longest time, shaking my head at nothing. And my heart ached with longing to set this right for my mother, for Gilly, for Asa and me, and I struggled with the negative voice in my head that said it was too late.

I returned to my list:

3. Helenne—bad news. Still alive? Where?

4. Judge Stein and Nurse Alice. Judge Stein—probably dead. Nurse Alice? Find out if she stayed in the region.

I wanted to interview all the people my mother mentioned. I made a list of them: Alister, Cup and Blue, Nurse Alice, and Helenne.

What I'd read about my mother's life was shocking, and I saw that she'd had good reason to do the things she did. She'd been protecting Gilly and me. She'd been trying to keep us from the brutality of Billy Mars, and I'd sorely misjudged her. I re-read much of her book, and I could see that there was room for a mixed-up little kid to misperceive the things she said and did. What did I know of complex adult emotions when I was five? As a child, all I knew was if she was mean or nice. Now, I could see she wasn't impatient; she was frantic. Far from mean, she was stressed beyond belief. And she was never unloving; but many times, she'd reached her emotional limit and had nothing left to give.

I reminded myself that nothing could excuse the terrible act of selling a child, but I was open to the possibility that I might've even misunderstood that. After all, I'd had a wonderful life. Perhaps some terrible fate awaited me had I stayed with Billy Mars. He could have been a child molester. She might have been getting me away from that. I wondered if she'd also sold Gilly and Asa. How would I ever know? And how would any of this ever be sorted if there were no answers?

The walls around my old life were shaking with a vengeance. The childhood narrative I'd created had gone up in flames. I wasn't who I thought I was, and who I was becoming was anyone's guess.

I then thought about the dog. I wanted to go back to the vet to get the Carolina dog that had saved me from the bear. No, I didn't believe my mother had sent him. But perhaps, on some level, I *wanted* to believe it. I rationalized that having a dog would be a smart move if The Laundry Man came calling, as if I needed an excuse to love a dog. And I realized again, with some shock, that I was far more involved in my story than that of The Laundry Man.

I needed to read the rest of the book. My investigation began with the purpose of finding out who killed my father. I'd discovered my mother instead and that my father was Big Jim Moon, who'd committed suicide. And there was Billy Mars, a presence in the center of all our lives, a violent man who, I believe, I'd confused as my father. Having read thus far in the book, I feared for all the people in the story. *My* people. *My family.* Whatever had become of them, we belonged to each other.

Digging in the tissue box multiple times that afternoon, I was teary and restless. I came up with a plan that made me feel better: I'd track down the Carolina dog and bring him home the next morning. Wanting to keep him safe from future bear encounters, however, I knew I needed to train with the bear spray and the holster that still sat on the table. I took the items outside and practiced my "fast draw." It wasn't as hard as I'd expected, and I was confident that if I had to, I'd get a pretty accurate shot off to save us both. From that time on, I wore the holster and bear spray whenever I walked the mountains.

\#

The next morning, I went to the vet.

"I'm here to inquire about the dog I brought in two weeks ago," I said to the receptionist. "I want to adopt him. A bear attacked him. I paid cash and will be happy to pay you if there's money owed."

"Your name?"

"...Sarah Johnson...I think..." That statement didn't sound weird just to me.

"You don't know your own name?" she asked. A little smile.

"Well, it's been one of those days," I said as she typed my alias into her computer.

"I have the transaction here, but we don't have the dog," she said.

My heart sank. "You don't? Where is he?"

"We transferred him to the Humane Society. Don't worry. It's a no-kill shelter, but you're going to have to call them."

"Where are they? I'll just go over there," I said, and she gave me the address.

I drove into Bowden and went east on 64. When I arrived at the facility, I stated my business again, and again, a young woman entered the data into her computer.

"I'm sorry. We don't have that dog. He got transferred out of here."

"Can you tell me where you transferred him?"

"Looks like Anderson, South Carolina. Would you like the number?"

I took it and left. In the car, I called Anderson, told them about the Carolina dog, and said that I wanted to adopt him.

"Can you describe the dog?" the woman asked.

CHAPTER 19

"Easily. He has a very distinctive white mark running up his nose to his head. It looks like the end of a Milk-Bone dog biscuit."

"Sounds cute. But I don't remember seeing any dog like that."

"It's a Carolina dog—"

"Yes, you've said that. I see all the dogs that come through here, and I don't remember one like you're describing. I suppose someone could have adopted him before I put him in the system, but it's highly unlikely and against policy."

"If someone adopted him, could you check on that?"

"Only if he has a name. Does he?"

"No. I didn't name him."

"Then I don't know what I can do. We don't keep a record of what dogs look like," she said.

"But the Bowden Humane Society said they transferred him to you." I was distressed.

How could a humane society lose a dog?

"I'm sorry. We're as good as our records, and we don't have any record of the dog you're calling about."

I was heartbroken. The dog was gone. He had been adopted or lost during transport, but how could that happen? I blamed myself for being negligent. Then I blamed myself for blaming myself, and that made me feel worse. I was being stupid. If he had a loving home now, I wanted to be glad for him, and yet I was heartbroken because he wasn't with me. As I wiped away the tears, the phone rang. Salem. Feeling sad and vulnerable, I invited him to spend the night. He sounded happy about that.

"I'll be a late arrival, though," he said. "Nine? Ten o'clock?"

His schedule was fine with me. On the way back, I made an impetuous turn to go to Blood Mountain. I wanted to see Alister Banks. It was already dusk as I'd spent most of the day trying to track down the dog. I parked at the gate and hiked the rest of the way up the mountain on my throbbing foot.

When I got to his house, there weren't any lights on. I knocked, but he wasn't home. I walked back down the mountain in the dark, angry at myself for not having called ahead, and glad I'd strapped on my bear spray. With each step, my left foot felt stabbed by glass shards, and I reminded myself to breathe through the pain as I kept trying to hold my breath against the uncompromising agony. I chose my steps carefully with the help of the flashlight on my phone when, almost to the gate, I rounded a switchback and looked down into a deep ravine. There was a small white house at the foot of the dramatic slope, and multiple police cars, their rotator lights flashing, filled a parking area at the front of the house. Ramos had said the Thatchers' house was in a deep ravine, so I guessed that this was their place. Suddenly, I was frightened for Mrs. Thatcher, and in no small way for me, and I limped as fast as I could down the steep, curved drive. As I drew closer, I saw a familiar somebody, looking exceedingly world weary: Ramos. His face bore a pinched expression. When he saw me, he excused himself from the officers with whom he was speaking.

"What the hell are you doing here?" he demanded, coming at me like an irate bull. "You had orders to stay put."

"I was visiting a friend when I saw the lights…Is this the Thatcher house? What happened?"

"It's Mrs. Thatcher."

"The Laundry Man," I said. It wasn't a question.

"Kate, this is hard enough without you running around making yourself a target. Get the hell home," he said. "Lock your doors. You're going to see more police at the cabin. I called some units out. And for God's sake, stay inside."

"Can I speak with the Reverend?" I said. "I'd like to tell him how sorry I am."

"Well, that's gotta be one of your worst ideas." Ramos had just gotten the words out of his mouth when Reverend Thatcher, clad in black and red faced, came thundering out of his house.

"How dare you come into my yard! You did this!" he screamed at me as he practically fell down the wooden steps of his front porch, pointing a finger at me lest anyone mistake his target of blame. "Arrest her! Arrest her!"

"For what?" Ramos said. His tone implied that he wanted to roll his eyes.

"For bringing this curse on us! It ain't no accident my wife's murdered in the Lord's season! The devil chose the day! *She* brought this on us! She's a *witch*!" screamed the Reverend.

Ramos leaned into me. "He's misspelled the word," he said. Furious at me, his snide remark wasn't a joke. "Go back inside, Reverend Thatcher. Someone's going to take your statement in a minute," Ramos called.

"I'm giving you my statement now!" yelled the Reverend. "She's a *witch,* and she brought this grief on us!"

Ramos, who had perfected the art of screaming louder than anyone else, bellowed, "Go inside!"

The Reverend looked startled. He backed up several paces, turned, fell up the porch stairs, and went into the house.

"So… I'll convey your condolences, Kate," Ramos said. "Now go home. Let me finish up here, and then I'll come talk to you. Where's your car?"

I pointed. He had an officer escort me to it. When I got to the cabin, the place was crawling with the police. I nodded to one of them, who nodded back. In the house, I had a drink, but it did nothing to calm me down, and shortly thereafter, Ramos was ringing the bear bell. He had a man with him whose skin shone like polished mahogany. He had a lovely, but guarded, smile and compassionate eyes. I invited both of them in.

"Officer Stanley. Kate Adair," Ramos said. "Officer Stanley is going to be living with you for a while and you're not to go anywhere without him. He'll be on rotation with another officer, John Branch. Same rules apply. He'll show you his ID and there'll be a picture with it so you know it's our guy and not The Laundry Man. Capisce?"

"Oh, God," I said. This had gotten real so fast.

Agent Ramos helped himself to a seat on the sofa. "Can't be too careful."

I took a deep breath. "You want coffee?" I asked.

"Only if you dispense it through an IV," he said.

"Would you like to sit down?" I asked Officer Stanley.

"Thanks," he said. "I'm fine."

That worried me. It looked as if he anticipated an imminent assault on the fortress.

"What happened to Mrs. Thatcher?" I asked. "And shouldn't I be packing my bags and getting out of the mountains? This one's too close for comfort."

"I would agree, but someone killed her in Charlotte while she was visiting her sister, not here. There's no reason for us to believe this was anything more than another of The Laundry Man's random murders. We still feel you're safer here."

"But the killer did her laundry on Blood Mountain," I argued. "I think—"

"Kate. Stop. It's been a long day, and I'd appreciate you letting me do my job," he said.

I felt for him, but I needed answers. "Was this definitely The Laundry Man? What about Mrs. Thatcher's age? She was an old woman, not a young professional. What's caused this shift in his M.O.?"

"We're looking into it. That's all I can say," said Ramos. "I'll take that coffee now." I fixed it for him—cream, no sugar. Officer Stanley didn't want any.

Ramos downed his cup and got up to leave. "Just do me a favor. Stay here. Don't go out when the sun goes down. Don't walk anywhere, even in the daytime, without Officer Stanley. We want to keep you alive, Kate, and you're not being very cooperative."

"Okay," I said, meaning it this time.

"Well, duty calls." Ramos walked to the door. He nodded to Officer Stanley and looked back at me. "Good luck," he said. The remark didn't make me feel any better. Luck? Was that what living or dying came down to? I turned to Officer Stanley. His large brown eyes looked as if they'd seen things he'd like to forget.

"What's your first name?" I asked as I closed the door behind Ramos. "If we're going to be roommates, I should know."

"George," he said.

"Well, George, I hope you're not easily scandalized," I said as I thought of Salem.

CHAPTER 20

Sal arrived close to ten P.M. I'd fixed a late meal of chicken and dumplings for the two men. Sal and George ate with enthusiasm and talked about their travels around the country. I wasn't hungry and their inconsequential chatter was driving me crazy. There was a murderer on the loose, and the reality had hit home. I was a nervous wreck, petrified, flinching at the slightest sound. And I realized, too late, that I didn't want company; I wanted to be alone.

All of this put me in a terrible mood. After I'd cleaned up from dinner and said goodnight to George, I walked into the bedroom to find Sal stretched out on the bed, working on his laptop. He looked so relaxed that it infuriated me, and I stopped midway to the bed and announced sharply that I was going to take a bath. In the bathroom, he'd spread out his toiletries beside the sink—a meticulously laid out comb, brush, aftershave, razor, toothbrush, paste, and nail clippers. This was too much, and I stormed back into the bedroom to confront him.

"What the hell, Sal? Do you think you're moving in here?"

"What do you mean?"

"Your stuff is all over the counter by the sink. I didn't invite you to do that."

"Kate, I've got a meeting tomorrow morning in Asheville. I can't go looking like an unmade bed."

"You should have told me."

"I'm telling you now...Look, I'll pack up and leave with my tail between my legs in the morning, but I'm tired tonight. Do you mind?"

I was aware I'd overreacted and felt embarrassed about it. "Okay. I'm sorry. I'm just on edge," I said.

"Have your bath and come to bed, Kate," he said. He sounded condescending, but I didn't want another argument, so I kept my mouth shut and had a bath. When I crawled into bed beside him, his back was to me. I was hoping to sleep but didn't. Whenever I dozed off, I dreamed that someone was breaking into the house. Or people unknown were trapping me and would harm and kill those I loved. The nightmares left me feeling vulnerable and concerned that they might be prescient. It was a miserable night as I lay in bed beside Sal, and I had plenty of time to feel guilty about overreacting. By the time Sal woke up in the morning, I was ready to talk.

"I'm sorry for my behavior last night," I said.

"No need," he said. "Mind if I take a shower?" His eyes were cold.

"Sal, please forgive me. As I told you, I'm a nervous wreck. It's fine for you to leave your stuff here. It'll make it easier when you come and go. My feelings are all jumbled up, and I'm not thinking. I'm just reacting."

He smiled, and however reluctantly, came over and sat beside me on the bed. "I understand, Kate," he said, removing a strand of my hair and kissing my temple. His kiss lingered there. Then he excused himself, showered, dressed, and left for Asheville.

While George was speaking to the next officer on duty outside, I pried up the boards and retrieved my mother's book. After getting a cup of coffee, I settled down in the bedroom to read. I'd meet the new officer later. For now, I wanted to be closer to my mother.

I stayed home for two weeks, nauseated and sickly, but then I tol' myself to get up and do some work. I were late gettin' to Alister's that day to clean. When I got there and set to it, he pretended to fiddle at his desk, but I could feel his eyes on me. He put his arm up on his ol' typewriter and said, "Callie, would you be willing to tell me your story?"

"Naw…" I said. This extra attention, unusual for a workday, made me feel uncomfortable. "What story would I have to tell?"

"Your life, Callie. I want to hear about your life."

"Why?" I said. "I ain't nothin'."

"Where'd you get an idea like that? Everybody's something, Callie. We each have a story to tell, something to add to the collective…"

I didn't know what the "collective" was, but it sounded important.

"What would I have to do?" I asked.

"Just sit in a chair and talk. Come. I'll show you," he said, getting' up and takin' me by the hand. He deposited me alongside his desk, in the straight-backed wooden chair with a little tweedy pillow in the seat. "See? You'll just talk about your life, and I'll type what you say."

"Why would you want to hear about me?"

"There're a lot of reasons," he said.

I didn't ask what they was. I'd o' been too afraid to know in case I disappointed him.

Before long, I come to like this story tellin'. Even in the hard parts, I felt somethin' akin to hope. He were hearin' without judgin' me, and, gradually, I were relieved o' a burden he were willin' to share, so I didn't feel alone. Over time, I tol' him everythin': We laughed at some good times and then moved on to Billy and his meanness to me and the girls.

One cold mornin' after being with Helenne, Billy come home drunk. I usually heard the truck and could get me and the girls out of the house, but this time he walked home and surprised me. By the way he stood in the doorway, all pump and swagger, we was in for it.

"This place is filthy!" he said and pushed over the long, open shelves by the door. It made a terrible racket when it fell. Cans, food, and dishes went

everywhere. Glass jars broke and the beets I'd jes' preserved turned the wood floor red as blood. Gilly screamed her heart out. Kate grabbed Gilly and got behind me and I could feel 'em both clutchin' at my body and shakin'.

Billy went 'round breakin' things. Pretty soon, the floor were wet and nasty, and with his being drunk, he slipped and slid and cursed as he made his way all over the kitchen throwin' things down. Finally, he tore open a bag o' potato chips I'd bought as a special somethin' for the girls and he turned 'em out all over the floor. He did this while starin' me down, darin' me to say somethin'. I knowed better. All I wanted to do was get the girls out the door, but we couldn't go anywhere 'cause he were blockin' the way.

"Now, girls," he said. "Come out from behind your momma's skirts. You come on out now. Come on…" he said. I could feel their hands loosenin' on me, but when they stepped 'round, I put my arm up and held 'em back.

"What you want with these babies?" I said.

"Well, they gotta clean this place up," said Billy.

"No, they ain't. You made this mess, Billy. I'll help you, but you let the girls go."

He smiled. "Okey-doke," he said.

So I raised my arm, but before the babies could move past me, Billy swooped on me, grabbed me by the neck and hair, dragged me out the front door, and threw me in the yard. He slammed the door behind me and clicked the lock.

I run back onto the porch and pounded on the door. "Let me in!" I screamed. "Let me in, Billy Mars! Don't you hurt my children! Don't you hurt my babies!" Gilly were still screamin', and Kate set to whimperin', which were completely unlike her. She must o' been plenty scared, and it made me pound the door harder, but Billy wouldn't open it. "I'm here, babies! I'm right here! Momma's right outside! I ain't goin' nowhere!"

Runnin' around to the side yard, I picked up a log from the stack. I busted out the nearest window, and I were startin' to hoist myself through when a shotgun barrel come out of nowhere and poked me in the head.

"You ain't comin' in this house," Billy Mars said. "Now back off, or I'll kill everybody while you watch." I could tell he meant it, so I pulled myself away and went to sit on the floor of the front porch. It were a helpless, crushin' feelin' not being able to get to my babies, and I sat there rockin' and holdin' onto myself. I thought of runnin' to Alister's, but I were terrified that, if I did, Billy would kill my babies to spite me. There wasn't nothin' to do but stay put.

"Now, kiddies," he said, ranting. "You're gonna learn to do some ol' fashioned house cleanin'. You're gonna show that slovenly ol' momma of yern what real cleanin' is! Now move it!" he yelled. "You tarry and somebody's gon' get hurt!"

I got up. "No!" I screamed through the door. "No!"

"Don't listen to her. You do as your pappy says. Go on." And when they hesitated, he bellowed, "Go on!" and they got to work.

About twenty minutes in, it went quiet inside, and I peeked through the window to see what were goin' on. The girls was slavin', and Billy Mars sat there drinkin' a bottle of liquor with the shotgun 'cross his lap. A mighty hate come up in me as I sat there in my cotton shift, froze to the bone, waitin' for the babies to finish their disgrace. It were a couple hours later when Billy shouted, "Not good enough!" and I looked in the window, scared he were goin' after 'em, to see him rampagin' all over again, throwin' more mess on the floor and breakin' anythin' that weren't broke before.

"Now clean it up, and do it right this time!" he yelled, and my babies set to work.

I cried, promising myself that I'd never be this helpless to protect my children again. I would be on guard always, ever vigilant, and while Billy were 'round us, I swore I'd never sleep.

\#

I snatched the babies away when Billy got so drunk that he passed out and fell out o' the chair sideways. I took the shotgun, and the babies and me buried it deep in the woods. We spied on the house then and only when Billy Mars got hisself up and out, did we go home. I'm not sure why I took ourselves home. We coulda gone to Alister's. I could have broke into the Adair's house and hid us there—and they'd o' been glad for us to do it. But I went home— and took the girls home—right in harm's way. I were naïve, I guess. Stupid is more like it, like Helenne said I were. I were ashamed too and prideful, which is a sin, but didn't want my friends to know the worst. I didn't want 'em to think less of me, or pity me, or think I were more trouble than I were worth. And I didn't want 'em to help me and get hurt. Billy were capable o' anythin'. I felt all this, and yet, I jes' couldn't believe things wasn't gon' get better, that Billy weren't gonna wake up and come to his right mind. And I were afeared, if Billy were gone, that whatever were next might be a lot worse. And then again, maybe I wanted to matter to somebody so much, the only thing I knowed to do was stay true to the one I used to matter to.

In the spring, when the Adairs come back from Florida, it were a relief to leave the girls with 'em to spend the night. They give me a sack of food, and I felt safe 'cause Billy's truck weren't in the yard when I went home. I didn't see him much anyways. He stayed gone a lot and that were all right by me.

I were puttin' away the groceries, when right behind me, the light wavered funny like there were somethin' movin' behind me, and I turned 'round. Billy Mars were hangin' by his neck from the rafters. His eyes was closed, and his face were gray, looking as dead as they come. I screamed and screamed. Seein' Billy like that brung back all the worst of my life. I run, but I bumped into the furniture and sent dishes and pots clatterin'. It were like I were trapped in a room without windows and doors, and I couldn't find no way out. I ended up a squallin', bawlin' heap on the floor, losin' my mind and unable to help myself.

And then…laughin'. I didn't recognize the sound at first. My panicky yowls, which was all my ears could hear, had buried it deep. But the laughin' got louder and Helenne stepped outta the bedroom, and I turned back to look at Billy, and he were laughin' too and squirmin' outta the harness and noose.

My confusion give way to rage, and I run at Billy soon as he dropped from the rope. I hit him with everythin' I had, but he wouldn't stop laughin'.

"Go easy on him, Callie. Billy just got back from Death Valley," said Helenne, but I were so furious I couldn't stop poundin' him.

I had nightmares after that. Screaming and thrashing around, I'd wake up the kids up with my misery. I'd quiet 'em down, but stay up the rest o' the night, afeared to close my eyes lest the nightmares come again and take me away for good. And Billy and Helenne would bring this story up again and again whenever I seen 'em, how funny I looked so panicky, and how somethin' were wrong with me that I couldn't take a joke.

Another time, Billy showed up at three o'clock in the mornin' and smothered me with a pillow 'cause I didn't have no dinner set out on the table for him. I kneed him where it hurt and run outside with the children who knew it were best to jump up and run when I went screamin' for 'em day or night. Then I tried to make it a game for the girls and showed 'em plants to eat and plants to leave alone in the woods like Cup and Blue'd showed me. We slept in a cornfield that night and the next till Billy cleared out.

Being so open with Alister, I also tol' him about the day he brung the flowers, and Billy's rage, and how he'd hurt me. Alister stopped typin'.

"Leave him," he said. He was beggin' and tears rolled down his cheeks and made stains on the clean blue shirt he were wearin'. "Leave him please. He's going to kill you." I were feelin' kind o' queasy, so I reached out and patted his hand, tol' him the day I'd be comin' back to clean for him, and left.

As I got to Sally's house, I stopped and retched so hard it brought me to my knees. There weren't no water to clean the stink out of my mouth, so I wiped myself off and stood up, shaky, but holdin' myself upright. I had to get to Sally's. My girls'd spent the day there, and it were time to pick 'em up.

When I got there, they was watchin' a TV show and gigglin' like all get-out, so Sally steered me into the kitchen for a cup o' tea. Her kitchen were clean and neat most all the time, but today the dishwasher were open, and the racks was taken out and set on the counter. Dirty dishes were cluttering the counters.

"I apologize for the mess. Ben's fixing the broken dishwasher himself," she said. She threw up her hands, smilin' like she were sayin', 'What do you do with a man like that?"

We sat at the round breakfast table covered with red gingham cloth. There were a green fern in a little green vase in the middle of the table she'd been encouragin' to grow for a while. It looked puny, but I liked how she tried.

"How're things going at home?" she asked.

"They's goin'," I said, managin' a smile.

"You're a good woman, Callie," said Sally, and when I was gon' talk back, she held up her hand to shush me. "I've hesitated to say anything about this, but I feel like we need to talk frankly. Is that all right with you?"

I nodded. Suddenly, I felt frightened, never having seen her so solemn.

"Billy Mars is spreading word all over these mountains that you're a witch—"

"I ain't no witch—"

"That's not the point, is it?" Sally said. "The point is, he's disparaging you, sweetie. Not just that, but he's bragging that he's hitting you and the girls to keep you in line. Is that true?"

"Some of it. He's a big talker," I said. So far he were only hittin' me, but the less she knew the better.

"He's justifying his behavior! That asshole told Ben you needed the beatings," said Sally. I were aghast 'cause I ain't never heard her cuss before. "So here's a blunt question: Are you unhappy, Callie?"

"Unhappy?" I couldn't meet her eyes, but could feel her starin' at me.

"Many people are happy with each other. Ben and I are happy. It's possible," said Sally. "And it's none of my business, but I'm going to ask you to consider making yourself happy."

"How'd I do that?" I said, finally lookin' up.

"Leave Billy."

I felt struck down by lightning. Alister pleaded with me to do the same thing. I felt ganged up on. But I were too much of a coward to do what these folks was askin' so I froze with nothin' to say. Sally saw my reaction and took hold of my hand.

"Do you still love him, Callie?" she asked.

I sat for a good minute, thinkin', watchin' her hand rubbin' on mine. "I don't as yet know. But I'm gon' have his baby."

She pulled her hand away and nodded at me, and we said no more about it.

CHAPTER 21

Another June come by, and it were a fiery one. I were swole as they come with the baby about ready to pop in a few weeks, and me feelin' poorly. Kate and Gilly did for me. They cleaned the house, washed the cups and saucers up, and hid in the woods without me askin' when Billy Mars come home drunk.

Billy were sure the baby weren't his. He'd corner me, askin', "Who's the father of that new bastard? That ain't my baby. You're a slut, and I spit on you and the day I found you!" And I'd get spit on and slapped, but it didn't hurt as much somehow 'cause o' my new little baby who I loved so much.

At first, Billy focused on Alister as the father, but I were careful. I only give Alister my story when I were supposed to be cleanin' for him, and he paid me for my time so Billy wouldn't get suspicious. Billy come by to check on me from time to time anyway, and I'd hop up and pretend to clean and Alister acted like he were too busy workin' to even talk to the likes o' us.

So then suspicion landed on poor Judge Stein who were an ol' man and nothin' but kind to me. I didn't know why Billy blamed him, but I were sure Helenne were behind it. That ol' sweet Judge were gracious and nothin' else when Billy'd come by to glare at him.

It were that June that Sally and Ben asked me to sit down in their kitchen. They looked kinda stony-faced, and as much as I loved and admired them, I were worried about what they was gon' tell me.

"Callie, Sally and I want to tell you we're putting our house on the market. It's just too hard to have two houses and go back and forth to Florida like we've been doing all these years. It's a seller's market right now, and we'd be fools not to take advantage..."

I didn't hear the rest he had to say.

"Oh, no, please…" were all I could whisper. Losin' them weren't somethin' I could bear. They was family—good, trustworthy folks, the family I'd never knowed. It was some sort o' miracle that we'd found each other at all.

"We're deeding your little house and the surrounding property to you," he said and slid over an envelope. "You've done a wonderful job with it, and we want you to have it. The deed's in your name only," he said, emphasizin' the "only."

I cried, of course. Nobody gives nobody a house, for sure, but the tears come because I didn't want 'em to go.

Sally said, "We're not putting the house on the market right now, Callie. We'll stay to enjoy the season and the beautiful fall—"

"We probably won't offer it till November," said Ben.

I bawled harder. And they let me sit there until I cried myself out, bringin' me cups of tea and tryin' to get me to eat for the good of the baby.

#

It were a month after when I went into labor pains and they was bad. Billy'd been gone for two days, and I were glad to be alone with my girls without his makin' everythin' about hisself. Outside, a big storm were on top of us, and the rain come down like hell knew where we was—fallin' so hard the girls and me had to shout to hear each other over the thunder, lightning, and day-long pour. Kate were holdin' my hand as I lay in the big bed and set to screamin'. Kate shouted to Gilly, now two-year-old, to round up all the towels she could find 'cause the baby were comin', and I were bleedin' fierce. And then I seen Gilly, her short little legs runnin' 'cross the floor, her arms full of towels, happy to help her sister and me. Midway, she dropped one and stopped to pick it up.

There were a loud crack. We seen her sweet face look up as a massive pine tree come crashin' through the roof. It smashed on Gilly's head and my poor child went down. There weren't even time for Kate and me to scream. It happened too fast, and at that very moment, the new baby slid out, and he were screamin' for us all.

Kate cut the cord with a kitchen knife and tied it off like I tol' her to. She were jes' goin' through the motions, and when she finished, she left me and went to Gilly. She were determined to get to her sister, and pushed branches away that was too heavy for her to move. But when she uncovered Gilly, she took a good look, saw her little white neck broke, blood pouring from her nose and ears, and Kate knew she were gone. She covered Gilly with a piece of blue tarp Billy used for paint jobs to keep the rain off of her.

A few hours later, when I could stand, I got myself up to Alister's and asked for help. He come and picked up Gilly's body and took it away in his truck, and Kate went back to that spot on the floor and didn't move for three days. I couldn't get her to eat or sleep. She just sat there in the rain; I guess she were tryin' to understand somethin' that couldn't be understood by nobody.

The Adairs and Alister jumped in to help, bringin' food, hirin' folk to remove the tree, and rebuild the roof and wall that'd been damaged. Kate barely stirred out of the way, and when we had to move her, I tried to hold her, but she quickly removed herself, standing against the wall until the workin' folk finished and she could go back to her spot on the floor.

I felt like I coulda joined Kate there for the rest o' my life, but time don't stand still for the dead. With a child to give my breast to, I also had a child to bury and one to worry about. I never in my life carried anythin' heavier than my heart for those weeks, and I were numb to feelings. I had to remind myself to breathe to get anythin' done at all. And in the wee hours of those July nights, I sat in front of the cold stone fireplace, and rocked, and wondered how many babies I had to lose before I could see one speck o' mercy that the revival preacher were so sure were there.

Billy come home on day three. I were in the rocker and didn't get up. He went to the icebox and looked inside, and since nothin' were to his likin', he shut it with a loud thud.

"*You got yourself a baby boy. His name is Asa,*" *I said.* "*And your girl, Gilly, is dead.*"

"*Uh-huh,*" *he said.* "*Ain't there nothin' to eat?*"

I were ready for Kate to get up off the floor and hit him, but all she did was stare at him with dead eyes. I rocked and lowered my head and closed my eyes to shut him out o' the room, and Billy snorted and banged the screen door shut as he left again in the truck.

#

We buried Gilly in Alister's pasture, remote-like, where we knowed Billy'd never find her. Not that he'd be lookin'. Gilly were our baby, Kate's and mine, not his, and bearing the loss, we tried to get on with our lives, but it weren't easy. Kate and me was runnin' on empty, and we had a baby to care for. Little Asa wouldn't have us mournin' neither. He was dark-haired and wild, all brash and clang, and kept us hoppin'.

We burned the bloody sheets, but the mattress were ruined. I wouldn't throw it out. Billy would see it one day, and I wanted him horrified and sad for Gilly. It were the only thing I could think of to punish him for being gone, for all the times he'd been gone. I wanted him to feel bad for not being the man I'd hoped he were. So I left the mattress there on display and didn't get nothin' to cover up the blood, but when he come home, he slept on that bloody thing and didn't even notice or care.

I refused to sleep in that bed ever again. I slept with Kate and Asa in the little side bed, and we let ourselves feel some comfort when Billy weren't home. We couldn't show it when he were around. Whoever he were mad at, which were mostly me, he'd take it out on who I loved. I couldn't put the babies in no more danger, so I acted cold to 'em when he were there.

#

Before we knowed it, it were fall on Blood Mountain, the carefree red leaves rollickin' on the wind and shamin' the grief we still had in us. I'd been so busy with the new baby that I hadn't had it in me to go visitin', and one day I thought it were time. I wore the clothes I had and took Kate and the baby over to see Judge Stein. Kate and me wanted to show Asa off—and to talk to him and Nurse Alice about Gilly and why they hadn't seen us for so long.

As I got nearer his house, somethin' were dreadful wrong. Hard to describe, it were too still and reminded me of the day I found little Jimmy. There were a strange smell that hit me at the doorsill too, a smell like wet pennies, and the front door were wide open and that weren't no usual thing neither.

"You hold Asa and wait out here," I said to Kate and give her the boy. Then I went inside.

Despite all the sunlight streamin' through the windows, I didn't see nothin' at first. But roundin' the big table in the dining room, I seen Alice lyin' on the floor face down in a tarn of blood, and it were the blood that smelled. Sweet Alice lay in her white uniform with the nurse cap still attached to her head with bobby pins. There weren't no pulse. The wounds had bled through her uniform, ugly red stains dryin' brown 'round the edges, and her eyes was open wide, like she'd been surprised by what come for her. Somebody had pulled her nurse dress up past decency and her little white panties lay in a wad next to her hip.

"Oh, Alice…" I said, pullin' her dress down to cover her.

I got up and walked on, each step quivery and hard to take, knowing what I might find. Judge Stein were in the next room, tied to his wheelchair, his arms stretched behind his back, even the right one that didn't work. Whoever done this had strangled him with a red scarf and left it danglin' there over his shoulder as a final slight. I recognized the scarf. It were Helenne's.

I run from the house and snatched up the children. I didn't know where to go or what to do, but I knowed better'n to call the police over to Bryson or go to Alister before I could think for myself. Alister'd call the police, and I knowed what he'd say to me. He'd tell me to leave Billy and fill my head with what he thought, and I needed thoughts o' my own, even if I didn't know what they was yet. Besides, I was afeared that Billy and Helenne had it in 'em to kill us all.

If Helenne did this, that were one thing. If Billy was involved, that were something else again, and I had to know. I had to talk to Billy. I ran down the road as fast as I could, keepin' to the side so if anybody saw me, I could duck into the woods with the babies. Nobody come along though, and it were just as well 'cause I got lost. I can't explain why, but I got turned 'round on a road I'd walked a hundred times. And then up ahead, there were a bright purple house with a green door and Cup workin' out front in a yard covered with flowers. I were so relieved that I stumbled and cried, barely holdin' onto my babies when I fell into the yard. Asa went to bawlin'. Kate were her usual quiet self.

"Somethin's happened!" I cried.

"I know. Come inside," she said, puttin' her arm around me and makin' me walk fast.

As Blue calmed the children and entertained them with her crow, I sat at the big table with Cup and cried.

'Holy crow!' the bird said.

"Helenne killed 'em. I know she did. And maybe Billy did too." I cried some more. "She's a witch, you know. That's what she says she is—"

"Witch," Cup said with disdain. "Psychopath's the better word."

"Did you call the police, Cal?" asked Blue, lookin' up from jostlin' Asa in her arms.

"No. I were sure they'd blame me, and I ain't done nothin' wrong!"

"Calm down now. You're all right," Cup said pattin' my hand and rubbin' my arm.

CHAPTER 21

"But what am I gon' do? I don't know what to do!" I cried.

Cup smiled a sad smile and pulled herself back from me. "It's not our place to tell you what to do. This is your destiny and nobody else's, so you're gon' have to figure it."

"I can't—" I choked out.

"Don't give us that. 'Course you can. You're a smart girl. It's time for you to grow up and work this out on your own."

I lost it then. "I been figurin' things out all my life! There ain't been nobody here to help me! I've been doin' this alone my whole life! I been all alone forever! There ain't been nobody keen on helpin' me!"

I beat on the ol' trestle table until my hand hurt so bad I couldn't hit no more. Cup watched me. I looked 'round. The kids were starin' at me, mouths agape. Cup were right. I were jes' havin' a fit, and I were suddenly ashamed of me. I clutched at my heart with both hands 'cause this were where the truth were: Throughout my life, generous folk like Cup and Blue, Alister, the Adairs, Judge Stein, and Nurse Alice have always been there to help me. But what Cup were tellin' me were that I had relied on 'em too much, and not enough on me. I pulled myself together. It were time to get on with whatever come next.

"Can you and Blue look after the kids for me?" I asked.

"Of course we can," said Cup. "It'll be our pleasure."

"Okay, then," I said, getting' up and wipin' my face on my sleeve. "Where'll I find you when I come for my babies?"

"Why don't we stay right here in this house?" said Cup. "That all right with you, Blue?"

"A-okay," Blue said.

The crow said, "What? What?"

And so I left to do what I had to do, even if I didn't know what it were. I went back to Blood Mountain to talk to Billy, but he weren't at our house. The wind had picked up though, and it was blowin' this way and that without a clear direction, which made the climb to Helenne's harder. Sure enough, Billy's blue truck were there, and Billy and Helenne was talkin' inside. I didn't see no wolf-dogs, so I crouched down under a half-open window where they was, and sat on my haunches to hear what they had to say, my back braced against the white clapboard house.

"Easy as pie, wasn't it, little Billy?" said Helenne. "Life ain't all it's cracked up to be. You did the world a favor getting rid of him and that spinster nurse. What good were they? Some people are just a burden to society if you ask me."

"Let's kill 'em all!" Billy said. He was slurrin' his words.

"Drink up, baby," said Helenne. "But simmer down. We got to let all this rest for a while. Let the excitement die down. That's the smart way."

"And then it's back to killin'. I like it! Let me tell you a secret, Helenne, ol' girl. I feel powerful!" He howled like a wolf then.

"Well, you are powerful when you kill somebody," Helenne said. "You hold all the cards. Nobody can beat you, nobody can hurt you, nobody can tell you what to do. And today was a good start. Those two fools were weak. They weren't gon' to fight back. But the real challenge to killing is when you find somebody who will. Somebody with a lot to live for. Someone who'll fight you. You think you feel powerful now? Take somebody down like that, and you'll feel like the king of the world!"

"King o' the world! That's what I wanna be!" said Billy. "That's what I wanna feel like."

"You will, baby. You will." It sounded like she'd come closer and somethin' more private were goin' on. Her tone changed.

"Kiss me," she said.

CHAPTER 21

It were a knife to my heart. I raised up to peek in the window to see what they was doin' 'cause I just couldn't believe what I were hearin'. Helenne were straddlin' him and unzippin' his pants. She moved her body down and put him in her mouth, and Billy moaned with pleasure as she rocked back and forth and nursed him with her tongue.

"It's soon, baby, it's soon!" Billy screamed, and she mounted him again and crammed him into her, ridin' him hard.

I were sick and turned to vomit when 'round the side of the house them two wolf-dogs come growlin', most likely attracted by the sound of Billy screamin'. They saw me and stopped, starin' at me. I were sure to be torn apart if I moved or made a sound. And nothin' in the world were gon' make me scream.

Sinking down the wall again, I pulled my knees in, lowered my head to my knees, and placed my arms slow over my head. I brung my elbows in as tight to my body as they'd go. I were a big hunk of quake, scared o' them dogs and scared that Billy and Helenne would kill me if the dogs didn't. The wolves's wet noses and red-hot breath touched my skin as they pushed inside my denim shirt and sniffed me all over. They was decidin' if I was worth devourin'. They smelled bad too, like blood.

I mattered little to 'em in the end. They lost interest and wandered 'round the other side o' the house. When I thought they was gone, I bolted off the house and into the woods. Tripping over everythin', I kept goin', the nettles and silverthorne gougin' my legs all the way. I run to the top of Blood Mountain, my peaceful place, not so peaceful anymore 'cause of what my ears had heard, and eyes had seen, and I sat on my rock. I looked over the valley and cried, tryin' to make sense o' no sense at all.

Helenne had thought she'd won, and I knowed why: She'd won Billy back, poor dimwitted Billy. He were now exactly what she wanted, damaged like he were—somebody she could control and bend to her will. She knowed how to get him: through sex, drugs, alcohol, and promises to feel better and be somebody, and them tactics was as wily as they was effective. He were a sad mix of things now: brain injury and manipulation by Helenne, but his rashness—the thing I found so wild attractive in the early days—was in the mix too. Maybe there had been warning signs for what was to come. Maybe, maybe, maybe can torment a mind to death, and I knowed that the only thing that mattered were what I were gon' do next. Helenne had him and would keep him 'less I could think of another way. I didn't want him back, but I knowed if she had him, the killin' would go on and on and more innocent people would die.

I shoulda called the police. There wasn't no local ones, but county ones would be called for somethin' like this. The sheriff'd come. But I'd found me two dead bodies and I weren't nobody for the sheriff to believe. Helenne were a better liar'n me, and she'd blame the killings on me. That were an easy way to get rid o' me once and for all.

And Helenne and Billy wasn't gon' stop. They planned to kill again, and they'd murder Kate, Asa, and me. We was in the way—that is, if the sheriff didn't arrest me first. And without me to protect 'em, my children would jes' disappear one day with nobody to miss 'em or look for 'em, or ask about 'em, and that'd be that.

I stayed on that rock and thought all afternoon and into the night. I knowed it were up to me like Cup said, but I didn't have no plan in my head, just a million thoughts ricochetin' off the granite mountains. But when the lightnin' come and rent the sky, and the coyotes howled, and the eagles rode the wind, and the hoot owls blinked themselves awake to watch for prey, I let myself become what I were destined to be, and never looked back.

CHAPTER 22

That morning, the clang of the welcome bell on the front porch, loud and insistent, startled the living blazes out of me. I shut my mother's book and buried it in the rumpled bed linens.

A knock at the door. "Ms. Adair? You have a visitor. Simon Chase?" said an officer whose voice I didn't recognize.

I cracked the door. "Hey," he said. "I'm Officer Branch." He showed me his ID, and he looked just like his picture. Premature gray-white hair, blue eyes, chiseled jaw. He ought to have been in the movies.

"Hey," I said back. "You're George's relief. I heard you change shifts. Thank you for what you're doing." He nodded, and I walked by him and to the front door, where I found Simon waiting. Simon was facing away from me, and I could see him fidgeting. His hand kept hitting his thigh. He wore a navy parka over a white t-shirt and he was in khakis. He shifted weight from one leg to another before he knew I was watching him. When he turned, I invited him in.

"What are you doing here? An assignment?"

"No. I'm here to talk about something personal." He glanced at Officer Branch and then looked back at me.

"Okay," I said. "Let's go to the bedroom. More privacy."

When we got there, Simon shut the door.

"What's up?" I asked.

"I'm here to tell you I can't do this anymore."

"What do you mean?" I asked.

"Kate, I've worried about you and cared about you, and all you've done this whole time is dismiss my feelings and express a certain disdain for me—"

I started to interrupt, and he put up his hand.

"Let me finish. This may be the way you treat everyone who cares about you, I don't know. But I don't want to do this anymore. It's tearing me up."

"I thought we agreed that love wasn't part of this," I said.

He looked at the floor. "Yeah. Talk to the heart about that."

"Oh, Simon," I said, sinking down to sit on the bed. "I'm sorry."

It was sudden, this seeing the way he was, knowing I was responsible for the pain he was in. I hadn't wanted to take this kind of responsibility before. But now, I felt ashamed–a new emotion for the woman who said to hell with anyone whose perspective didn't match the image she liked to have of herself. And for the first time in my adult life, I was speechless. What do you say when you realize that apologizing for your behavior doesn't cut it anymore?

"I'll always care about you, Kate, but I'm going to stop feeling the way I do," he said. "You're the most talented and beautiful person I know, and I wish you well. But I'm done."

"That's it?"

I didn't mean to sound flippant, but I did. I wanted him to keep talking, to give me some idea of what to say that would turn back time and make us friends again. He looked so sad, but he smiled, as if he'd expected me to be flippant, and I didn't disappoint.

"Yeah, that's it," he said, sighing. "I'll use your facilities and get out of here. Won't bother you again."

He went to the bathroom and shut the door. While he was in there, I started shaking. Simon had always been there. Even when I pushed him away, he'd always come back. He was there at my door with a bottle of champagne when something went awry, and he was the friend who would sit up all night and laugh with me until dawn came and things looked better. I couldn't imagine my life without him. But this declaration had never happened before and he'd made it clear that we'd come to the end.

Simon came out of the bathroom. His attitude was all business. Despite that, I stood and thought of flinging myself into his arms, but he looked at his watch. "Five-thirty flight. I've got to get back to Asheville. Two-hour drive, as you know. Goodbye, Kate. Take care of yourself," he said, and walked out the door.

He mumbled his thanks to Officer Branch, and then he drove away. The sound of his car receding on the gravel drive broke my heart. I turned to the mirror over the mahogany dresser and stared at the fool I was and had always been.

#

I don't know how long I lay on the bed feeling sorry for myself, but it was a good long time. By midafternoon, however, I needed to get out of there. I put the bear spray in my belt holster and opened the door.

Officer Branch was having a cup of coffee when I came out. He had his sleeves rolled up and his elbows on the table. With the cup in his hands, his thick, muscular forearms showed he worked out regularly.

"May I ask your first name again?" I asked.

"John," he said.

"Oh, yes. Forgive me. I remember…John, could I get you to go on a hike with me? I know a peaceful spot, and I could use some peace right now." I found myself trembling. John saw it too.

"Of course."

I went for my car keys hanging by the door.

"Uh," he said. "Why don't you ride in my car?"

"Because there's an arsenal in there?" I asked.

"That. And snacks," he said.

I went for the snacks. As we drove over to Blood Mountain, we munched on caramel corn and made small talk. "Are you married, John?"

"Yep," he said. "To one very smart gal. She's studying to be a radiologist."

"Do you have kids?"

"Sure do. Two. That's why the caramel corn. They got me hooked."

"What are they?" I asked.

"A boy and a girl. My wife says they look like me. God knows, I hope they grow out of that," he teased. A few moments passed before he asked, "Things didn't go well with your friend?"

"You could say that. I got dumped."

"Ouch."

"It's probably for the best," I said, trying to turn sour milk into chocolate pudding.

"Maybe I don't have it in me to give people what they need."

"Don't underestimate yourself, Ms. Adair."

"Please…call me Kate," I said.

"Kate," he said with kindness.

I smiled. There had once been a time in my life when I would've made a pass at John, the radiologist student be damned. Back then, emotions that I didn't know how to deal with would throw me over the edge, and I'd reach for something or someone to soothe me, numb me, and distract me. I wasn't that woman anymore, and I found myself happy that—after John's stint with me was over—he could go back home to a wife who he was proud of and a family who adored him.

We turned to drive up Blood Mountain and stopped at the gate. "We're going to have to walk the rest of the way. I'd like to show you the top," I said.

"No problem," said John.

He opened the driver's side door and put on the hiking boots he'd stashed in the back seat. The pain in my left foot had made me want to avoid going up to the top of Blood Mountain at all, but mother's book made me feel like I wanted to see it again, maybe to feel closer to her and what she thought was beautiful. Blood Mountain was now a comforting thing to me, and I knew I needed to connect with myself now that Simon was gone. Losing him made me feel as if I'd lost a limb, and I was searching for something to hold on to so I didn't fall, metaphorically, into the dark, familiar well of self-recrimination and misery. For whatever reason I justified to myself, I wanted to see the very top of the mountain.

We pushed our way through tall weeds and over gnarled tree roots and fallen branches. We slipped on shifting scree, and we stretched our stride to climb large slabs of granite that rose from the ground defiantly and challenged our path. The mountain smelled of pine, earthy moss, and decomposing summer flora. The air, saturated and promising future rain, was moist on the skin. All the while, I struggled, limping full-out now and not minding who saw me.

"You all right, Kate?" John asked. "You look like you're in pain. What's the deal?"

I hesitated, but only briefly. "I have vasculitis, and my left foot folds under like a claw."

"Ow. That sounds painful," he said. "Let me know if I can help."

John was a good man. He wasn't solicitous or hovering. He was a man who allowed me to keep my dignity, and I found myself glad to have him along as I planted my foot in a safe spot and kept going. Pine needles shifted under my weight and made the climb more tedious, and I concentrated intently on not falling. It got hot fast in the spots where the tree limbs parted and sunlight blazed down, and the heat dared me to keep going and not return to the car and run the air conditioning. Halfway into our climb, however, we were high enough and the temperature plummeted. We both felt relief.

The coolness allowed us to appreciate our surroundings. The view through the foliage was astonishing: Blue, green, gray, and purple mountain ranges stretched to infinity. An affable breeze blew and gave me the feeling of being apart from reality and in the middle of it all at the same time. The odor of the mountain was tantalizing: a mixture of balsam fir and sweet, fertile earth. The scoop of certain leaves held rain, and myriad birds—juncos, chickadees, towhees, and cardinals—partook of refreshment. It was a contrasting experience to when I first arrived, sick with disappointment and wallowing in misery. Today, it felt like a Disney movie.

I came out of my reverie and smiled at John. We were too high in altitude for mosquitoes, and the season for gnats had passed, so all we had to focus on was taking deep breaths and getting ourselves up the hill. At one point, we stopped to take a drink and John stuck his head under the cold water pouring from a rock.

"Mother Nature's water fountain," said John, shaking his wet head and showering me.

"God, John! What are you? A labrador retriever?" I said.

"Oh, I'm sorry!" he said, and we laughed like children. In truth, the spray felt good. "I love these mountains. Do you?" he asked.

"They've grown on me," I said.

When we broke through the trees at the top, the experience was surreal, which is how I felt every time I'd ever been at the top. The rocky ledge jutting out over the valley was terrifying, with a cliff's edge reserved for nightmares. But the view was spectacular: mountain ranges one after the other, the colors startling, and no two hues alike. The lakes below were a glimmering sapphire, the sky cerulean blue, the colors of the valley awash with the slow fade of fall.

A bald eagle, his head and tail the whitest of whites, circled below us. Low-hanging clouds covered the mountain tops to our left and laced in and out of the time-worn hills. Fog lifted in plumes among the evergreens straight in front of us, and small branches snapped as an animal, a rabbit or a raccoon, foraged for an early dinner.

"This is…" John trailed off, as there were no words for it.

"I agree," I said.

I looked back in the direction we'd come. At the edge of the trees, there was the big rock pile I'd hidden behind as a child. It was smaller than I remembered. I moved forward, away from the memory, and went out onto the overhang where my mother dared to sit.

"Be careful," John warned.

"Don't worry," I assured him.

I wasn't brave enough to go all the way to the point as mother had, so I sat a respectful distance from the edge, hugging my knees. John stood some distance back.

"Don't you want to come sit down?" I asked, patting the cold stone beside me.

John hesitated. "Damn it, Kate," he said. "I'm afraid of heights," and I could swear he blushed.

I smiled. Big, brave guy hired to protect little ol' me, and he's afraid of heights. We stayed there—him standing, me sitting—for a while. I breathed and meditated and tried to feel what my mother might have felt here. It had been such an enormous journey for her, one of courage and endurance. She'd had no safe harbor. For her, there were few places she could feel at peace and never for very long. I felt a surge of emotion that filled my eyes with tears.

And she'd lost so much, Big Jim, Jimmy, Billy, Gilly, Judge Stein, and Alice. She thought she'd lost me too, and I wished I could tell her she hadn't, that I was fine, that I'd made my way back to her at last. I found myself profoundly grateful, breathing in what I can only call "peace."

I listened for the sounds of traffic from the highway across the abyss, but I couldn't hear anything. Nor could I see any people at the overlook; it was too far away, and they couldn't see me either. I felt alone and lonely, but not empty, and I thought of Simon.

"Want to tell me about him?" asked John, sensing my mood. Ordinarily, I wouldn't have talked about something so personal, but at some point in recent weeks, I'd moved past "ordinarily."

"He's a wonderful man," I said. "I didn't treat him the way he deserved. Once, when I had the stomach flu and was vomiting my brains out, he called me on Zoom from Barcelona and read me poetry for three solid hours. Another time, he took me on a tour of every cheesy tourist attraction in New England. Ever been to the Equinox Hotel in Vermont where Mary Todd Lincoln still walks the halls?"

"Missed that one," he smiled.

"And more than once, he listened to me moan and complain and rage and feel sorry for myself, and then there were all those times he literally and metaphorically held my hand when I said I didn't want him to…but I did."

"And what did you do for him?"

"Well…" I stopped, words drying up in my mouth. My first thought was that I'd done nothing–or at least not nearly as much as he had. But that wasn't exactly true. I delighted in cooking for him. His abusive mother was a mess until the end of her life and when he couldn't attend her, I was more than happy to. I'd always adored the way he looked and how he smelled, even after a grueling workout. No matter how sweaty, I liked it. I'd loved how he put me first, as if I were the most important thing in the world to him. His emotional honesty was beautiful and unusual and we talked about everything, and I was always struck by his self-awareness–and that he cared about me even if I was behaving badly–which was a lot of the time, I realized now. All this boiled down to one thing and I considered saying it out loud before I actually did. "I loved him," I said.

"Did you tell him?" he asked, working the ground with the toe of his boot.

"In so many words?" I asked. I shook my head. "I didn't dare," I said.

"Well, Kate, that was then. This is now. What're you going to do?" I didn't know. I didn't have a clue. "I'd pat you on the shoulder and be comforting, but no way I'm coming out on that ledge."

We laughed. And then the inevitable feeling of loss settled over me. We sat listening to the shriek of an eagle, the chirp of a bird, the whistle of a breeze passing through the fissures of the cliff. John didn't hurry me, nor did he act bored to tears, but the time came when we agreed to hike back down to the car. We took care, because if anything, my foot hurt worse on the trip down the mountain than it had on the way up. By the time we got back to the cabin, I was bushed and excused myself to my room after telling John goodnight. He was about to be relieved of duty anyway, as George handled the night shift. In my room, I pulled my mother's book from its hiding place, got in bed, elevated my left foot on a pillow, and began reading.

#

I had to do this right. I went back to Judge Stein's house. Flies had found him and Nurse Alice and was beginnin' to lay eggs in their eyes. Pullin' their bodies out of the house, off the back porch, and into the garden, I were shaky and clumsy. I messed up their pretty flowers good, trompin' all over 'em, but I had to hurry as best I could. I didn't know if Billy and Helenne would come back for somethin', and I were afeared they'd catch me. Anyway, I buried the Judge and Nurse Alice as deep as I could so wild animals couldn't get 'em. It took me diggin' all day and into the next, and when it were done, I stood over their graves. I had to say somethin'. I were the only one who could.

"God, if you're listenin'," I said, "give the Judge and Nurse Alice that speck of mercy you had reserved for me. Amen," I said and hoped it were enough.

Next, I went to Sally and Ben's house and had a talk with them. I tol' 'em as little of the truth as I could. First, they'd have worried 'bout me. Second, they'd call the police 'cause they lived in a world that tol' 'em that if somethin' bad happened, the police'd fix it. That jes' weren't my world.

We sat at their breakfast table, the kitchen smellin' of fresh cornbread and country butter. In fact, they put it on the table for all o' us to enjoy with little plates decorated with yellow flowers, but this weren't no friendly visit, and I pushed the plate away. I had a plan to lay out and eatin' were the last thing on my mind. It were important to upset 'em jes' enough, so they'd do what I wanted, but I couldn't upset 'em so much they'd go to the police.

"It's a shock, I know, to hear what I'm gon' tell you, and I'm sorry for that. I hold you dear people in such esteem, and I know y'all will respect what I have to say and not go runnin' off to no sheriff. Can I count on that?" I asked.

They nodded. But I'd frightened 'em and it showed in their eyes.

"Okay. So here's what I need to say: I can't keep Kate. Part of it's the money. She's older now and eats more." I could see they was acceptin' o' that. It weren't true, but I had to make a case for things they'd understand. "But

the other thing is…it's bad at my house. Billy hasn't yet, but he might go after her."

I didn't say a word about Judge Stein and Alice. Sally and Ben couldn't know.

"Oh, my God," said Sally, puttin' her hand to her mouth. Ben reached over and held her other hand.

"So here's what I figure: I want to send Kate with you to Florida. You can adopt her if you want. Asa's too little. He's still nursin' so he'll stay with me."

Ben let go of his wife's hand and went to wringin' his own in front of him. "The police need to hear about this," he said.

"No, no, they don't. If the police get involved, Billy Mars'll lose his mind. I think he'd come after me if he gets scared enough, so I need y'all to listen to me and do what I'm tellin' you to do. I've thought it through. If you do what I say, we can set this right."

"But we can't take your daughter away from you—" said Sally.

"Yes, you can. It's her one chance, see," I said, "I'm givin' her to you 'cause you love her, don't you?"

Sally and Ben nodded.

"She'll have a better life with you, and she'll be safe, see? You can give her a education, and someday, she might be somebody. You know how smart she is. Please, please don't say no, please…" I were about to cry. I shut down the emotion I were feelin'. The words I were sayin' don't mean nothin', I told myself. They was the language o' somebody else.

Sally and Ben looked at each other. "We love her like our own child," said Sally.

"We do," said Ben.

"And one more thing—" I said, "and I hate to ask you this—but once I give you Kate, you gotta leave these mountains right away. And I got to ask you to never, ever come back to Blood Mountain, or it won't be safe for nobody. Can you do that?"

"Well, we were going to sell the house anyway—" said Ben.

"We could just move the timetable up. We can do it. But if it's so bad at home, why don't you come with us?"

I shook my head.

"Why not?" asked Ben.

"What's holding you here, honey?" Sally said.

Even though I couldn't tell 'em, I knew, knew without a doubt, that there was gon' be more blood spilt. And I were terrified that Billy and Helenne would murder them too. I had to get 'em to go away.

"Some things is pressin' so I can't come for a while. But here's what we're gon' do 'cause we gotta focus on right now," I said. "Let's meet tomorrow mornin' at the top of Blood Mountain. Billy ain't likely to find us there 'cause it gives him the creeps. Meet me there at nine o'clock sharp. He ain't up that early neither, and it'll be safe to give you Kate." I tried to swallow then, but there were a lump the size of a grapefruit in my throat.

"And then we'll leave the mountain immediately—" said Sally.

"Yeah," I said, "Can you be ready to go by then?"

"We'll be selling the furniture with the house, so there's nothing to move but a few sentimental things—" Ben said.

"And our clothes," said Sally.

"We can pack it all up in the car tonight and be ready," Ben said. "I'll call the real estate agent from Florida."

CHAPTER 22

"Then please…be there. The top of Blood Mountain," I said and got up from the table.

"Wait," said Sally. She looked like she weren't there no more. For the first time, her skin hung off her face, gray, and as lifeless as wet cardboard in the rain. Ben noticed it too.

"We don't have to get involved, Sally. We don't have to do this," he said, clutchin' at her tremblin' hands again.

"Yes, we do," she said, lookin' at me. I stared back and left before they could change their minds.

I went to pick up the kids at Cup and Blue's. I wanted 'em with me, even though I lay awake all night afeared Billy would come home, and we'd all have to run. He didn't show.

I lay in that little bed with Kate and Asa pressed up against me all night and thought my life were over. All I wanted to do were call everythin' off, keep my babies close, lose not one. But then I thought o' Billy and how he'd changed, and how he and Helenne would come after us forever. Hidin', with no place to go, they'd find us and murder us all. Kate had to leave. There weren't nothin' else to do.

#

It were frosty the next mornin'. I got up early. Leavin' Kate in bed asleep, I carried Asa, and some formula for him, back to Cup and Blue's, prayin' Billy wouldn't catch me and scared he would. Runnin' myself back home, I woke Kate and had her dress in as many layers as she could. She was slow and mad at me for hurryin' her, and uncomfortable with all them clothes on, and I suspected she didn't sleep well the night before either, being as I were so restless. She were movin' like cold molasses, so I grabbed her arm, and hauled her up the mountain. It were already eight-thirty, and the climb took a good half hour.

We slipped and slid goin' up. The rocks was slick. Kate almost fell twice on the fleshy, wet leaves. Each time, I caught the collar of her coat and pulled her back to her feet. I couldn't have her hollerin' 'bout a scraped knee and alertin' Helenne and Billy if they was within earshot, and more'n once, I tol' her to hush up.

The mornin' air smelled of loam and pine needles, and I kept tellin' Kate to breathe deep as we both was out of breath from the straight-up climb and all the scurryin'. There weren't no view to distract her. Fog socked us in, and I tried to entertain her by tellin' her that only special people got to see the inside of a cloud like we was doin'. She knowed what I were sayin' were a pack o' crap though, and my child were as distressed as me, but without knowin' why.

When we got to the top of Blood Mountain, I tol' her to wait behind a pile o' rocks. I didn't want her to see me hysterical, and I were afeared I would be. Sally and Ben was already there on the cliff. In the night, I tol' myself that I were doin' the right thing, and I were plannin' to take some mornin' time to assure my little girl that I loved her and explain the situation. But I messed up: The foggy climb had taken way too long, and I were panicky, sure we was gon' to be discovered and killed. When we got to the top, the time for niceties were gone. I couldn't explain to Kate and Sally and Ben kept trying to comfort me. There weren't time for any of this! Nobody understood the urgency.

"You're doing the right thing," said Ben.

"We're going to take good care of her, Callie, don't you worry," said Sally. "She'll go to the best schools and have the prettiest clothes, and lots of new friends."

I were sobbin' my eyes out and kept lookin' to the woods for danger.

"Oh, please don't cry. It's hard enough as it is," Sally said, puttin' her arm 'round my shoulders. But all o' us was cryin', and I couldn't bear no more talk. I wanted it over, so I broke away and called Kate down from the rocks. Hearin' me so frantic, she hurried, fell, and slid a good ways on her poor little hands and knees. Cut up and limpin', she come to me bloody. My brave girl didn't even cry.

But this had to be over. I had to get 'em away from Blood Mountain before Billy and Helenne killed us all. Jumping at every sound, my jaw ached from clenchin' it, and my muscles hurt like I'd been liftin' stone. This hand-over were takin' way too long! Ben and Sally was talkin' too much, and I imagined Billy on his way to find us. "I'm givin' you to the Adairs," I blurted out, frantic.

Kate give me a surprised look. She liked the Adairs, but she knowed somethin' were bad wrong.

"For how long?" she asked.

"For forever," I said, stumblin' over the words.

"No," she said back. "I ain't goin'."

"Listen to me, Kate," I said. "These people are gon' take care of you now and give you a better life."

"No," she said, crossin' her arms and pullin' away from me. I couldn't have her actin' like that, so I grabbed hold o' her and tried to put her hand into Sally's.

"No!" she screamed again, jerkin' away.

"It's for the best!" I yelled.

"No!" she yelled back.

I stepped away from her, glancin' first at the woods and then starin' at this stranger who was my daughter. She were burnin' with defiance. I knowed what I had to do to make her go. With all my soul's might, I didn't want to do it, but I slapped her in the face as hard as I could. She fell into Ben, who held onto her.

"Stop actin' like this! Don't you see? I don't love you no more!" I said. We stared at each other, and I tried to keep myself iron hearted. "You ain't nothin' but trouble, girl! You cost too much money, and I don't have it to give! I don't want you no more, don't you see? I don't love you! Surely you ain't too dumb

to realize that… *You ain't no daughter to me! You're a sack of burden that I'm finally puttin' down and good riddance!"*

She got away from Ben then and made a dive for my skirt. "Stay away from me! Get her off me! Get her away from me!" I screamed. She were screamin', too, and kept grabbin' at me, calling "Momma! Momma!"

"Get off of me! Get away from me! Take her! Take her!" I cried to Ben. I tore her off me and pushed her, and she landed on the hard rock at Ben's feet. She'd fallen on her tailbone and sat there stunned, and Ben grabbed her. He hoisted her up on his shoulder and carried her down the mountain. I can still hear her screamin' for me. Her screams come from inside me now and they ain't gon' stop.

Sally held out some money for me. "I know this wasn't part of our agreement, but take this, Callie. Please. Ben and I want you to have it," she said. At first, I didn't hear her. "Please. You must. Look, you take this money and when all this is over, it'll buy you a plane ticket to us in Sarasota. You can bring Asa and come get Kate. It'll help with the down payment on a little house. It'll be a better life for all of you."

I seen it then, that this weren't the end. I'd go down to Florida. Kate'd be older and maybe she'd forgive me. I'd have Asa, and we'd get ourselves a house by the calm blue sea. But, despite them pretty thoughts, I felt like I were dyin' inside from a heart shredded and tore to pieces. I had to get away to be by myself, to outrun the sound of the meanness I had in me, and the sound of Kate's yowls, so I grabbed the money and run.

I spent most of the day hidin' in the woods and cryin'. But when the shade of the day started turnin' itself into shadows, I got myself up 'cause there were work to be done. Returnin' to our house, Billy's and mine, I seen he still weren't there. Taking a cardboard box o' kindlin' and puttin' it in the middle o' the floor o' the main room, I turned the sticks out, puttin' the box on top of them. I took me the dish towels and washrags and all our clothes and piled 'em high on the logs, all the while purely terrified that Billy'd come home and kill me. Finding the stubs of candles that we used when the lights went out,

I lit 'em, and poked 'em in the pyre. They caught right away. Pretty soon, the fire spread, and I stood there, froze, in pure horror at what I done.

In no time, the fire licked up the walls and across the ceiling. Wires and sockets exploded as they shorted out. At first, it smelled like a big ol' bonfire, but when the flames hit the plastic toys that belonged to the children, my nose, throat, and lungs started burnin' somethin' savage, and it were time to run.

Outside, I gulped in the healin' air I'd always relied on, but for a while, I couldn't breathe. Then, after I finished wheezin' and chokin', spittin' out ash and phlegm like they was all I had in me, I moved to watch the blaze from across the road. Sparks danced on the natural air drafts and the ones created by the fire, and I thanked the good Lord that all the woods, which was drier than usual and vulnerable to a forest fire, was a safe distance away. It were jes' the house that were burnin', and I watched until the wood walls warped and the roof beams caved in. I walked 'round to the back of the house as the window panes exploded. Then, as I looked through a bedroom window, our double bed caught fire, flames leapin' into the air, burnin' all the memories away. All the good times and bad, the violence and the love. It were all over, to never come again. I watched until the inferno took all o' me and Billy, and what the children loved and feared, and turned them things to ash.

#

For two days, I waited in the woods. Living off what I found in the forest, I ate blackberries, kudzu, dandelion greens, and burdock root, though I didn't feel much like eatin'. I were waitin' for Billy to come home. I heard him before I saw him, whistlin' his tune, then walkin' all jaunty like nothin' could bother him. When he saw what I done, he stood stock-still on the road in front of where the house'd been. It were still smokin', the vapors risin' and the wind whippin' 'em away. Vexed, his fists workin' themselves tight over and over, and I come out of the woods and up behind him.

"Hey, Billy," I said. "How you like the house?"

He turned and backhanded me across the face with everythin' he had in him. I fell in the long grass. I weren't surprised to find myself there.

"Why? Why'd you do it?" he screamed at me.

"I did it for you," I said, wipin' the blood off my mouth.

"You burned up every goddamn thing I owned!" he yelled.

"Yeah," I said. "And the children were in there too. Aw hell, Billy. You wanted a witch. Now you got one."

"You burned up the kids?" he asked.

"Yeah. You didn't want 'em anyway."

He turned and looked at the house again, and I seen his shoulders shake. At first, I thought I'd read him wrong. Were he cryin'? No. When he turned 'round, he were laughin' like I'd said the funniest thing.

"You burned up yer own children! Yeowee! I got myself a witch!" he roared.

"Yeah, Billy boy. You finally got your witch. And I want you to take me right here and now," I said. Shuckin' off my blouse and flingin' off my skirt, I laughed when the wind blew the skirt away. It looked like it was gallopin' off by itself. I surprised him again when I went up to him, pulled down my panties, and stepped out of them.

When he took me in the long grass, I didn't feel it. He touched my breasts, and I looked at the sky and thought about what it must be like to be a bird, flying away from the anguish and soreness o' livin'. Afterwards, we lay there, and he touched me sweet all over. I let myself feel that. It were almost like the beginnin' o' things again. Maybe it were the beginnin' o' what we'd become. Our hands entwined, and we held them up to the sun and laughed.

And then I said to Billy, "You killed Judge Stein and Alice, didn't you? I found 'em and buried 'em."

He got up on his elbows with a start. "Now don't you go lecturin' me—"

"I'm glad you did it," I said, cuttin' him off. "You got gumption, and I'm glad to see it. You's powerful and strong again."

"I am, ain't I? I'm good at killin'. Helenne tol' me so."

"And I'm tellin' you too," I said, not to be outdone.

"Am I more powerful and strong than before?"

"Before the accident, you mean?"

He nodded.

"Yeah. Sure," I said. "Way more than that."

He smiled and lay back.

"And I'm glad Judge Stein and Alice is dead. They was a drag."

"Yeah..." he said. "Why's that?"

"Well, I been thinkin' about it. They had what I always wanted."

"Like what?"

"Money. Lots and lots of money," I said, laughin', as I squeezed up against him. "And jewelry."

"Yeah?"

"Billy, why jes' kill folks? Don't you want what they got? Don't you jes' itch for it?"

"I guess so..." He looked uncertain without Helenne tellin' him what to do.

I played with gettin' him semi-hard again. "Judge Stein showed me a necklace one time. It belonged to his wife, and I know where it's hid. It's a gold necklace with a little diamond in a heart. I want it, and I want you to give it to me. It's something I really, really want. And if you get it for me, I'll be so pleased that I'll give you a hard-on you ain't never comin' down from.

What d'ya say?"

He pulled away and sat up, shakin', stuffin' hisself in his pants. "I can't do that. You know I can't do that."

"Why, baby?" I said, playin' with his hair.

"Cause I'd be stealin' somebody's destiny," he said.

"Oh, I've heard that ol' wives' tale, too, and used to believe it. I since changed my mind. It's a bunch of hooey and everybody knows it."

"I don't know it," he said.

"Then know it from me now," I said, mountin' him and stickin' my hand down his pants.

I worked him until he come again in my hand. I laughed. "And that were your proof. That ol' wives' tale is bull, and you know it or you couldn't have been able to concentrate like you jes' did. And I'd say you concentrated jes' fine."

"Yeah, yeah…" he said.

"I want me that necklace, Billy, and I want you to get it for me. I ain't never had no fine jewelry from a real man before, and I got myself a real man now. You get me that little heart, and I'll wear it forever because I'm yours, Billy boy. I'm yours," and I kissed him long, hard, and deep, grindin' my body into his.

And when he were good and worked up, I didn't give him no more until he got up to go to the Judge's house with me. We held hands along the way like ol' times, and Billy skipped flat stones 'cross a pond and acted proud, like he didn't have a care in the world.

When we got to the Judge's house, I held back. "Billy, you go in," I said, as nice as could be. "In Judge Stein's bedroom, there's a chifforobe. The box is on the third shelf down and the necklace is in the box. Get it for me, baby," and I kissed him.

"You make me dizzy," he said after the kiss.

He went to get the necklace, and only then did I walk in to make sure he got the right thing. The house still smelled like blood, but not as bad. I looked 'round the dusky room. There were a picture o' Miss Monica on the bedside table. There was ol' man pajamas hangin' up on a hook behind the door, and there were Judge Stein's wheelchair.

"This what you want? Billy asked, holdin' up the necklace.

"That's it. Put it on me, will you? Billy Mars, you're such a big man and so brave! You stole this pretty thing from that ol' judge. You wanted to steal it, didn't you?'

"I did. I sure 'nough did," he said, proud of hisself, and we looked in the chifforobe mirror as he put it on me.

CHAPTER 23

I read until I fell asleep and a book page fell forward and hit me in the face. I awoke enough to put the page back in its box and, surprisingly, fell asleep again, slumbering through the night. In the morning, I found I hadn't done my usual tossing and turning, nor had I left the bed linens looking like a war zone. I went out to get a cup of coffee and said good morning to John, then headed back to my room. I got back in bed and picked up the book again and re-read what mother had written about the seduction of Billy Mars. Then I turned to the next page. It was blank. At first, I thought it was a printer mistake, the extra catch of a page. But, on further inspection, I realized that all the remaining pages in the box were blank.

The book had ended, and it had been put on top of a stack of blank copy paper to fill up the box. I looked through every page again, trying to find something, some word about what had happened to my mother. There was nothing.

Frustrated, confused, and panicky, I paced. To be thwarted after all this time was unacceptable. Then the tears came, unapologetically. I looked through the box again, but there were nothing but blank pages.

I thumbed through the part I'd read. My eyes fell on how she'd seen my bleeding hands and knees on top of Blood Mountain, and suddenly, it was as if the emotional floor had dropped away, and I was standing in a deeper place, on a different level of being. For the first time in my life, I felt—no…I *knew* my mother loved me. Really loved me. My heart burst with compassion for her, and I felt what it must have taken for her to give me to the Adairs, to walk away from a bleeding child, to hit me and scold me, and make me hate her so that I would live. The realization broke me, and I got down on my knees and cried.

When I had exhausted myself, I wiped my eyes, blew my nose, and got up. Where was the rest of the book? I had to find out. Despite the pain in my foot, which was excruciating, I grabbed my bag and jacket and limped to the front door. John stopped me.

"Where're you going, Kate?"

"I've got an errand to run. You've got to let me go."

"No, ma'am. Ramos chewed me a new one about our hike, and my orders are that you can only leave the house for essential errands, and only with me."

"Look. This is essential," I said, but I could see he wasn't changing his mind. "It's so 'essential,' John, that I won't take no for an answer. And if you resist, I'll drag you with me kicking and screaming—or you'll have to shoot me. I've got to go, and that's all there is to it."

"Good God, you're tough," he said. "Okay, let's do it. But not a word to Ramos."

"Deal," I said.

He drove us again in his car, and I directed him back to Blood Mountain. On the way through Bowden, we chatted to distract me from my distress. "Tell me about your kids, John," I said.

"Well, let's see, you know I have a boy and a girl…"

"One of each. That's nice. Ages?"

"Scott's seven, and Peaches, his sister, is four."

"Peaches?" I asked.

"Yeah, her real name is Marguerite, but…you know," he said, embarrassed to be a sucker for his kids. It was sweet. "There's a picture of them in my wallet there. You're welcome to look."

His wallet lay in an open pocket on the dashboard. There was a picture of Scott with a soccer ball under his arm, and one of Peaches, posing formally, all smiles, porcelain skin, and dimples.

"They look like you," I said.

"Yeah…"

"God, I hope they grow out of that," I said.

John guffawed, and I reminded him we were almost at the turn to Blood Mountain.

We parked at the gate. "Another hike?" he asked.

"We're not going to the top this time," I said. "I'm going to introduce you to a friend. Sometimes he's not very nice, so—"

"I have a gun," he said.

"Do you shoot people for being jerks?"

"For less," he said, chuckling.

We walked up through the woods and over the rocks to Alister's house, avoiding the main road that would have taken us the long way around. I limped, of course, and expected nothing less than monumental pain. The foot didn't disappoint, but John was the perfect gentleman, putting out his hand to help me when the going got rough.

When we arrived on Alister's porch, I was ready for whatever mood the old curmudgeon was in, but I hoped he wouldn't use his shotgun to greet us. John went around me and knocked on the door.

Alister's weary voice called, "Come in."

I made introductions when we entered, and the men nodded to each other.

"A bodyguard, huh? You're that precious?" Alister asked me as he flopped in his old tweed recliner.

"I told you he was charming, John," I said as I sat on the sofa. John sat on a scratched up leather ottoman to my left.

"What do you need now?" Alister asked.

"I've read through the book," I said. "And it just ends. Where's the rest of it?"

"That's all there is," he said.

"But it isn't the end. I still don't know what happened to my mother and Billy Mars."

He shrugged. "That's all there is. Now you should fly away home. Go back to New York where you belong."

There was something in his tone. "Why? Why do you say that?" I asked.

"Maybe you're in danger here," he said.

"Are you making a threat, Mr. Banks?" John asked, sliding to the edge of the ottoman.

"Of course not. Relax," Alister said. "I'm no fool."

He wasn't a fool. But he *was* a protector. He'd been protecting himself and his secrets all along. It occurred to me he might have been protecting me, too. "It was you," I said. "You wrote the poison pen letter telling me to get out."

He was silent.

"It was you, wasn't it?" I said, intolerant of any more secrets or lies.

He hesitated. "Yeah. That was me."

"Why?" I asked.

"Because you're in danger here."

"From whom?"

"I don't know. But you're asking questions and stirring up ancient history. Nobody ever investigated the crimes you read about, and there haven't been any arrests. Alice, Judge Stein, maybe others died. Look, you've read the book. Everyone around here keeps their mouths shut. That's how you stay alive." I knew he wasn't telling me everything, and my face showed it. His response was, "Look, I'm telling you what I know."

"So, did you shoot the man who attacked me as well?" I asked.

"I don't know what you're talking about." He had a blank expression. "Someone attacked you? Who? When?"

"Sir, do you own a Winchester?" John asked.

"What the hell are you talking about? Look, you know I own a shotgun because I shot over your head the first time you came. Hurt my oak tree doing it. That's my one gun, and it's not a Winchester. It's in the closet there," he said, gesturing, inviting John to look.

John rose, but I stopped him with my hand. I believed Alister, and John sat back down.

"Why the sudden end to the book, Alister? What happened to my mother?" I said, getting back on track.

Suddenly, there was a surge of emotion, and his eyes turned watery. He pursed his lips and worked his jaw. He rubbed his chin and pulled on an ear. The tears came then, and he said, "He killed her." Then, to John's and my mutual horror, Alister put his head in his hands and sobbed.

I touched his heaving shoulder. There had always been something in his communication style that was strange, an automatic sinking into a heavy heart in the unguarded spaces between words. I finally understood. "You were in love with her," I said, but he didn't respond. I said it again, more certain this time. "You were in love with her."

He looked at me and nodded slowly, his face a portrait of anguish. "She was my dearest love. I begged her to stay with me, live with me, marry me, move away someplace with me. But she wouldn't have it. Every day she returned to that scumbag. We kissed once, the last time I saw her. Pure as unsullied snow, that was us. She wouldn't have it any other way."

"What happened?" I asked.

"She walked in that day and announced she needed a break. Why she needed one, I didn't know. In retrospect, I thought maybe she was tired of talking to me and hearing me beg her to leave Billy Mars which I probably did too frequently. Whatever the reason, I supported her taking a break. But I had no idea it was the end."

"Alister," I said, "how did Billy Mars kill her, and what happened to both of them?"

"Kate—and I'm telling you the truth—I don't know how it all went down. I just know that one day she was sitting in that chair over there, and then she got up and kissed me on the lips, a warm, chaste kiss, and one that surprised and delighted me. Then she thanked me—for what, to this day, I don't know—and walked out the door. I begged her not to go as I did every time she left, and I never saw her again. After a while, I knew she was dead, and that bastard must've killed her. She would have come back to me, see? If she'd been alive, she would have. And that lowlife, Billy, disappeared around that time too—so what does that tell you?"

I glanced at John, who was sitting on the ottoman with his head bowed. I looked back at Alister, sunk even deeper into his chair, or maybe that was just my perception. "We're never going to know the truth, are we, Alister?" I said.

"'The truth,'" he scoffed. "Good luck with that. But if you stay here and keep searching for it…you're putting yourself in danger."

I raised my voice in frustration. "But from whom?"

"You've read the book. You know as much as I do!" he said.

"Where's Helenne?" I asked.

It was as if I'd hit him in the face. Shocked, he lowered his voice. "I don't know. And nobody ever proved anything. All we know is your mother's version, and she hated Helenne. After all these years, she's probably moved away. It's a waste of your time to look for her."

We stared at each other. "Okay," I said. "So I'm going to have to figure this out by myself."

Alister rolled his eyes at my obstinacy. "Why am I even talking to you?"

"Alister, was my mother wearing the heart necklace the last time you saw her?"

"The heart necklace? I remember something about that…I don't know…It was so long ago…"

"I understand," I said and got up. I was there for another important reason. "Gilly's buried somewhere on your property," I said. "Would you object to me seeing her grave?" I asked.

"Go out the back door, and where the pathway forks, go to the right. She's up there at the top of the hill looking over us all."

I explained to John who Gilly was and what had happened to her as we walked to the grave, which was under an ancient oak tree. There was a small headstone, but no name, and a low wrought-iron fence separated it from the rest of the hillside. I suppose I was expecting something overgrown, but someone had planted a brilliant red sedum over her grave. Probably Alister had done it, a tribute to my mother and the child she loved.

"Gosh," said John. "What kind of plant is that?" "It's called Dragon's Breath Sedum," I said. "But don't ask me how I know."

John walked away, giving me some time with Gilly. I kneeled in the thick grass near the blank headstone. I'd wondered what I would feel if this moment ever came. Now that I was here, it just felt surreal. At first, I felt too numb to feel anything. Then neither the tightness in my chest, nor the constriction in my throat, would ease until the tears came. And they came. And then they poured.

I'd loved this child, and she'd loved me, and in my mind's eye, I could see her still. Blond ringlets, blue eyes, a crooked smile, and Dragon's Breath Sedum worn jauntily on her head as a hat—and I suddenly realized that I was remembering. I remembered Gilly on a fine autumn day and how I'd laughed as I washed the dirt out of her beautiful golden hair that the sedum had left behind. I sat by her grave, stunned. Gilly had sent me a memory, and I wept, then with gratitude. I took my time there, me a blubbering mess, but eventually, I rose from the ground, and John helped me walk back to the house. Alister met us at the door.

"I...I've decided to show you something," he said, opening the screen. "I have a picture of your mother. The only one I have. I took it the last time I saw her."

"What? A picture? You have a picture of her?"

He handed me the old photograph and flopped into his chair again. Wrinkled, the photo appeared to have been handled a lot, with finger grease smudging the image and curled, yellowing edges.

John came over and stood beside me to see it. There was my mother from the chest up, her flaming red hair spilling over her shoulders, her large, sad eyes revealing the depth of the pain she was in. She was wearing a small necklace with a little heart that contained a diamond. She was exquisite in her vulnerability, a fragile porcelain figurine, a pre-war Dresden without the lace. I was speechless.

"Is that the necklace?" asked Alister.

"Yes," I said. "This picture helps me with the timeline. Billy stole the necklace for her before this picture was taken."

"She was sitting in the chair she always sat in, and the sun was glinting off her hair. She was so beautiful that I wanted to capture her," Alister said.

"How was she that day?" I asked. "She looks sad in this picture."

"Or peaceful. Maybe a little determined."

The word surprised me. "Determined about what?" I asked.

"I don't know," he said, shrugging. "Just a feeling."

"Do you know where she came from, or where she was going when she came to you that day?"

"I think she said she'd been with Cup and Blue," he said. "But I could be wrong, and I don't know where she was going."

I stared at the picture again. I remained struck by the sadness in her eyes. "Do you think she could have killed herself, Alister? Maybe Billy Mars didn't kill her."

"I wouldn't want to think so. I guess anything is possible."

"What about her living Helenne's destiny for stealing the ribbon? Could something like that be true?"

"It isn't whether it's true, Kate. It's whether Callie believed it. And she did. She was…" He looked as if he'd cry again, but he waved his emotion away, the wordsmith unable to find words for someone so ineffable. He pulled himself from his chair with effort and started walking us to the door.

"In the book," I said, "mother wondered if love lasts. I wish I could ask her about that."

"That's not a question for her, Kate," said Alister. "That's a question for the people who loved her. And the answer is 'yes'."

I looked down at the photo. "Can I…?" I was going to ask for a copy.

"Keep it. I have it all in here anyway," he said, tapping his heart. "But be careful, Kate. Somebody out there has secrets, and they don't want you finding out what they are."

John and I said our goodbyes, but I turned back at the threshold. "Alister, where's Asa? Is he still alive?"

Alister looked like I'd struck him another blow. "Know nothing about that," he said and shut the door.

#

John drove us back to the cabin. Along the way, he asked, "Do you want to talk about any of this, Kate? I'm a good listener."

"Thank you, John, but I'm all right," I said. "Appreciate it, though," and we were silent for the rest of the trip home.

Back at Bruce's, I went to my room. I was feeling a depth of emotion I'd never experienced. I was grateful for the audience with Alister, but also grieved. To have come so far in understanding my mother and to have hit an insurmountable block devastated me. I was involved with this family, *my* family. I wanted to locate my brother, and the thought of never finding him left me emotionally shattered. Tears sprang to my eyes as I realized so much of my effort had been for nothing. Holes in the story, questions I'd never have answers to, missing people, an unfinished symphony of longing, pain, misunderstandings, and murder.

Some investigative journalist I am. The story had unraveled like an old sweater. I thought about having a drink, but knew I was reaching for it out of habit and didn't want one. And when I asked myself what it was I wanted, the answer surprised me: I wanted to sit and be present with this new me, even if it made me feel like a child in the middle of a lost and found who knew no one was ever coming for her.

CHAPTER 23

I kept staring at the picture of my mother and crying. It was, as I expected, a long, sorrowful night.

#

I stayed close to home the next day. I re-read what my mother had written, and found being alone with myself was, if not comforting, at least comfortable. George and John took good care of me, and I took good care of them, finding a cookbook in Marjorie's stash that inspired me to cook a Greek-style ravioli.

I'd decided something, and finally being off the fence about it had brought me a grudging peace. Laundry Man or no Laundry Man, I was going back to New York.

I called Da to say I was coming home after spending the day packing. That night, I planned to have dinner with Sal. I wanted to update him and thank him for being there when I needed him. Before Sal picked me up, however, I tried to convince George to go home, and after a phone call to Bud Ramos, who said "absolutely not" to my wanting to be alone with Sal on an actual date, George went to the restaurant with us and sat, discreetly, several tables away.

It was a small, intimate eatery in the middle of Bowden. There were nine tables, well-spaced, so no one was going to overhear us. Elegant sconces on ivory walls hinted at romance, and a red-headed server attended to every culinary desire. Sal had dessert, a Napoleon cake about which he waxed poetic, and I waited until after the server brought us coffee to tell him what I had to say.

"Sal, thank you for everything you've done for me since I came here."

"Uh-oh," he said. "That sounds ominous."

"Well, I've decided to go back to New York."

"What? Why?" I'd never seen Sal so thrown as he was at that moment. "Why?" he asked again. "They haven't caught the killer. It's not safe. I don't want you to go."

Despite Sal's lack of emotionality, I was fond of him, but he wasn't saying the very words that would've made me reconsider. I'd pushed love away once. I told myself I wouldn't do it again. But I saw, in all its exposed glory, the nature of our relationship. There was no love here, and while I couldn't determine what it was we had, I knew now that it wasn't what I wanted.

"I don't know what to make of this story, Sal," I said. "I've tried my best here, but there're too many unanswered questions. In these mountains, my mother is alive and a breath away at every turn, and yet I can't reach her. I can't even find out what happened to her and how she died. There isn't even a grave to visit. It hurts being here without those things. I want to go home, Sal, serial killer or no serial killer."

"I see," he said, his eyes darting around the room. He took his napkin from his lap and placed it, neatly folded, on the table.

"So what does that mean for us?" he asked.

In the past, my automatic response would have been, "There is no us." But there was no reason to say that now.

"Let's play it by ear once I'm back in the city," I said.

Sal said, "This is where you say, 'We'll always be friends' or 'It's not you, it's me.'" He stared down at his empty hands, upturned on the table.

"Well, perhaps that's all true," I said, thinking of Simon.

Sal spent that night with me. He made love to me with a certain urgency, as if he'd never have another chance to hold me. I thought perhaps he was right. And in the morning, we said goodbye.

CHAPTER 24

I would fly from Asheville that evening, and so far, only Sal knew I was returning to New York. Ramos wouldn't want me to leave, of course, so I'd call him when I was back in the city. Then I'd talk to Bruce. It was so nice of him to volunteer his cabin, and I wanted to thank him. I didn't know if I'd work for him again, but I was hoping so. I expected Dr. Marsh would be pleased I was back, and I'd be glad to be under his care. Crippled, which was alarming enough since a serial killer was after me, I also didn't want to end up needing crutches or in a wheelchair.

The Laundry Man, now active again, had killed two more people in the last two weeks: Frances Furness was twenty-three, a single black woman who'd just gotten a big promotion at IBM. When she didn't show up for work at her new position, someone found her at the end of the subway line. She looked like she was sleeping on a bench, except the blood from her throat was seeping into her Burberry scarf and coat. She'd found folded laundry four months before and had bought a handgun. It was still in her handbag when someone found her.

His second victim was Gloria Rios. Beautiful, Hispanic, and shattering the glass ceiling as a news anchor for NBC. Getting married the following week, she had countless little girls looking up to her. She was in her cubicle, dead and slumped over her desk, people all around. She'd bled out over the story she was pulling together on The Laundry Man and his murder of Frances Furness. Gloria, too, had found the murderer's calling card, her underwear washed and folded on her bed, two weeks prior.

Ready to take my chances, I wasn't going to be afraid anymore. Backing down was not an option, and neither was cowering. I'd be smart. If I needed help, I'd ask for it. And seeking medical attention for my foot was paramount. I refused to be one of those slow-moving animals that gets singled out from the herd by a predator. Neglectful of my condition, I was now paying the price as the pain was unrelenting. I was out of options.

With the packed suitcases hidden under the bed, John would find out about my plans soon enough. There'd be an argument, but with the car service waiting outside to whisk me away, there was little he could but call Ramos, who'd probably have someone meet me at JFK to put me in protective custody. Ramos would fly in and curse me the hell out, and I'd tell him about the vasculitis and he'd forgive me. At least, that's what I was counting on.

I sat on a porch rocker for most of the morning. I had mixed feelings about leaving, and I was sad to say goodbye to these wonderful old mountains that had become my friends. Then the phone rang.

"Good day, Kate!" said Sal.

"And to you," I said.

"Kate, I've been remiss: What time's your flight?" he asked.

"Six fifteen."

"Don't worry about getting to the airport," he said. "I'll drive you. As I recall, I owe you one. But first, I've got exciting news."

I didn't tell him I'd already booked a service to take me to Asheville. I made a mental note to cancel it. I tuned back into the conversation. There was a strange thrill in Sal's voice.

"I've found your mother's grave!" he said, sounding triumphant.

This astonished me. Because with all the unanswered questions, the grave was more important to me than ever. It was a connection to my mother, an actual place to honor her and all she'd been through. A place I could count on, a place I could visit.

Now I was thrilled. "Where?" I asked. "Where is it?"

"At the top of Blood Mountain," he said. "I know I promised to stay out of it, but I found it, and I thought you'd want to know. Shall I meet you there?"

"When?" I asked.

"No time like the present. Will you bring John?" he asked.

"Yes, he's still with me."

"Well, see you there," he said and rang off.

Someone had given my mother a last resting place on the mountaintop she loved. It was a fitting place. But who'd buried her there? Perhaps Cup and Blue. They really were the most infuriating, withholding women.

I chastised myself for not looking more thoroughly through the dense undergrowth at the top of the mountain. I didn't know how long I'd be at her grave, so I changed into my travel clothes and put the bear spray into the belt holster for the last time. Then I went out to convince John that this was important to me and invite him along.

He must have heard the excitement in my voice because he didn't mount any objections. We put on our coats and boots and went to Blood Mountain. As we hiked to the top, John supported me when I couldn't keep up. I was no longer intimidated by my disability and even felt a remarkable peace about it. I was going to live with or without my condition. Time would tell which one it was going to be.

The woods were beautiful. Now that I was leaving, I relished everything about these hills. When I was pushing for answers, I didn't see the glory, but Blood Mountain was a phenomenon like no other. Exuberant ferns unfurled everywhere. Gnarly, insistent tree roots zigzagged up the path and reminded me of modern sculpture. The scent of my own sweet sweat mixed with the odor of the soil's fertile dampness. I breathed it all in with deep, enthusiastic breaths. I couldn't get enough of it. Lizards darted over the loam to hide under crisp leaves. Deep in the valley, a dog barked somewhere, and in my heart, I hoped it was a Carolina dog. The wind picked up and turned my hair into a red mess, but I didn't care. I embraced it all. I was approaching the consummate end of my journey, and even though I'd always have questions about it, I could still appreciate and be grateful for whatever resolution I'd found.

Sal was waiting for us when John and I walked out of the woods. It was much colder at the top of the mountain than at Bruce's, and the wind howled like a banshee in an old horror movie. Sal had brought a folding chair, no doubt to get me off my aching foot and make me comfortable at my mother's final resting place. I appreciated the gesture and was about to thank him when the telephone rang in my pocket. Surprised, I jumped at the vibration and the sound.

"Kate?" It was Simon's voice. I signaled to John and Sal that I needed to take the call.

Then Sal said, "John, why don't you go back into the woods and stand on the path to be our lookout? Just an extra precaution. From there, you'll see anyone coming up the mountain, and we can give Kate a little privacy."

"Okay…" John said, looking at me. I nodded at him and gave him a "thumbs up" and he jogged back into the woods. Sal gave me a little space too, although not as much as I would have liked.

"Kate, I've got something important to tell you. Please don't be angry," said Simon.

"Angry? I'm just so glad to hear from you!" I wanted to say, "I'm so glad it's not over," but I didn't have that assurance.

"Listen to me," he said, and it was then I heard the urgency in his voice. I knew instantly this wasn't a personal call, and I felt wary without knowing why. "When I was at the cabin with you, I took some hairs out of the hairbrush by your sink. I assumed they were Sal's."

"They were," I said. Was he mad about Sal's stuff being there?

"I had the police run DNA on them. They match The Laundry Man," he said.

I staggered on the uneven rocks. Simon went on. "We should've had the results in a timelier manner. Somehow, someone routed them to Washington, where they sat on somebody's desk for a week." I said nothing. "Do you understand, Kate? I know you don't want to hear it, but Sal is The Laundry Man."

I glanced at Sal. He watched me like a raptor focused on prey. His eyes had turned so dark that even in the daylight, I couldn't see his pupils. He might have been guessing that I knew the truth, but playing my last card, I tried to smile, and project cluelessness. Unfortunately, my cheek quivered, and he saw it. I rapidly went through my options. Running wasn't one of them. I had John, though, and he had a gun. If I could just get to him—

"Kate? Kate?" Simon asked.

"I hear you," I said, trying to sound lighthearted. Then I turned away from Sal and hoped I'd dropped my voice enough so that he wouldn't hear what I was saying. "The FBI profile—"

"Was wrong..." he said. He paused. "You sound strange. Are you okay?"

"No. No, I'm not..." I said. I wanted to cry, but there was no time for that.

"He's there," Simon said. "Oh God, Kate, get out of there!"

"Um…yeah. Thanks for calling," I said and hit 'End call.'

My brain was spinning with possible excuses as I turned to face Sal. Which would he buy? "I'm sorry, Sal, but that was Agent Ramos. I've got something to tell John. Pardon me a moment…"

My legs were rigid as posts, and I could hardly walk to go to John. Taking a few steps in that direction, a woman, wrinkled, with white, pixie-cut hair, dragged herself from the woods in front of me. She was panting and bent over. She stopped in my path, an enormous wolf on either side of her. Knowing who she was, I suspected that the two animals were descendants of the ones that had threatened my mother and were just as deadly. Judge Stein's advice to my mother echoed in my head: "Don't scream." I didn't know whether this advice still applied, but I had little time to think about it as I was standing face-to-face with the woman and the animals, just as mother had. This was the woman from the liquor store and from the Emporium, and she had a name: Helenne. Frightened, I no longer tried to hide it.

She was as I imagined from my mother's book. Her eyes were dark, too, and like Sal, I couldn't see her pupils. Her eyebrows were heavy, her face shriveled, not just by exposure to the sun, but I guessed by a lifetime of hatred and revenge. When she walked toward me, each step brought her more upright until she stood directly in front of me. She had gotten her breath by then and she smiled.

Terrified, I shuffled around her, giving her and the wolf-dogs a wide berth. "John? John!" I called, keeping my voice low, even in a piping hot panic. The dogs growled and watched me with glacial eyes. I entered the woods but didn't have far to go. John lay on the path, his throat cut, choking on his blood. The cut was expert, deep and long. The wound would have cut the windpipe and the veins and arteries that went to the brain. This was how The Laundry Man worked. I'd read about it pragmatically, pouring over each case, and for that, I felt shame. These were people, as real and dear as the friend I gathered in my arms. "John! John!" I cried. He opened his eyes and managed the smallest smile, his last acknowledgment of anything. His chest heaved for air and the rattle in his throat drowned out my pleas for him to stay. Red bubbles foamed and popped where Helenne had cut him. His breathing grew shallow, and he gave up trying to stay alive, the effort too much. His beautiful blue eyes paled and stared fixedly as the light left them, and after all the horror, his dear, gentle spirit just left. I held his body tight to me as if I could absorb his goodness and his courage.

"Get up," Sal said behind me, irritated by my hysteria. His voice had changed. It was gruff and guttural. The transformation was hideous to see, the mask discarded. "Don't think about running, not with that foot."

I was so terrified I couldn't move. I stayed clasped to John. Impatiently, Sal clamped his hand on me and yanked me up by my arm. I stumbled as Sal forced me to leave John's body behind. Sal took me back to the bluff where the white-haired woman was sitting in the folding chair that was meant for her. She was relaxed; her legs crossed, the knife I hadn't noticed before still bloody and dangling from her hand and a wolf-dog sat restlessly on either side of her. I felt rage, seeing her sitting there so smugly, but I held myself back from expressing anything. I had to be smart, to listen, to be aware if I were going to live.

"Kate," said Sal. "I'd like you to meet my mother—"

Mother…That explained a lot. "I know who you are," I said.

She looked far from demented, as Sal had once described her. Everything he'd told me had been a lie. Helenne was a focused and dangerous wild creature sitting in the chair. Hanging from her neck was my mother's necklace, a small heart with a diamond in it. I was sure she'd put it on for the occasion. Sickened, I turned to face Sal.

"And you're The Laundry Man," I said.

Mother and son laughed, refined chuckles, all things considered.

"Not him, you stupid girl. *I* am. He just helps me. A recent touch of arthritis in my arm," she said, rolling her shoulder.

I felt like a fool. It surprised me that she was The Laundry Man, but it was consistent with her character. How could forensics have been so wrong? "We had a profile," I said, shaking my head at all the clues law enforcement and I had missed.

"I'm familiar with your profiles. But I was smarter than all of you. You thought I was a man. And you thought I was an organized killer, which I am, but I left little disorganized clues when I had the time. A pinch of pot here and a smidgen of coke there. Mutilation. Overkill. I wore men's size twelve shoes too, so I didn't mind leaving prints. I threw you off, didn't I?"

"Yes," I said. "You did." But a part of the profile was correct. Helenne was a toxic narcissist and toxic narcissists like to hear themselves talk. "You killed my mother," I said.

"Oh, for Pete's sake. You're what? Forty years old and still whining about your mother?" She looked at Salem and rolled her eyes. They chuckled again as Salem walked over to sit on a rock. "You want to know what kind of person your mother was? Well, I'll tell you. I followed Billy to his house the day your mother burned it down. He was high on killing, and I wanted to make sure he didn't do anything stupid. After they talked, I even watched them having sex in the field across from their place, and heard what she was saying to him, that she was a witch now, and that she'd burned the children up in the house. I knew she was lying.

"I couldn't figure out what she was up to, though. Following them to Judge Stein's house, I watched until she left. Then I went inside to confront Billy, because he was being an asshole falling for her tricks. I found him on the floor, screaming that he was in pain, saying he couldn't walk anymore, or move his right side."

I thought of the blue ribbon that had started all this mess and the idea of stealing the destiny of the person you steal from.

"He begged me to help him. He pleaded. Billy was always such a drama queen. I asked him what happened to him. I asked him if your mother had hurt him. Confused, he was hysterical. His mind was all over the place. He said, 'yes' and then he said 'no.'" She shook her head. "Well anyway, he told me, that right after your mother left, he just collapsed. He accused her of witchery. Ain't that the pip? Bullshit. She wasn't a witch. I thought she'd poisoned him, but he was sure she hadn't. I asked if she'd hit him over the head. He said no to that, too.

"You know what he thought? He thought, since he'd stolen this necklace, that he got Judge Stein's destiny, so he had to be crippled. 'Shut up!' I told him. 'There's no such thing!' But he was a cretin and always had been, and I told him that Callie was messing with him. 'Grow some balls, and get the fuck off the goddamn floor!'" she thundered. I tried not to wince.

"Oh, well. Compassion isn't one of my strong points," she said, stretching herself.

"Billy said he couldn't work his legs. Really, he believed the stupidest things. I'm the one who graduated from high school, you know. Billy had no ambition. He was younger than me by three years, and he stayed young in his head, you know? Even before the accident. Some people do. Anyway, let's you and me look at this logically: Billy had a stroke. He was probably on the verge of one for a long time because of the accident..."

She fell silent and pursed her lips tightly.

"Did you help him?" I asked.

She gave me a menacing look. "Who's telling this goddamn story?"

I shut up.

"Did I help him..." she mused. "Maybe I did. But I left him on the floor." She slid to the edge of her chair. "I had a better idea, see?" she said. "I told him I was gonna leave him where he lay. We needed to see what your mother was up to, and he was good bait for us. I mean, if she'd wanted him dead, she'd have finished him already.

"He didn't like my idea. 'Helenne, you can't!'" she mimicked. "I told him to quit his sniveling and man up. We had to see what she was going to do." She held up the knife that had killed John. She wiped his blood on her pants and then held it up again. "I've liked knives all my life. I always have one with me, and I had a little four inch on me that day with Billy. So I slipped it to him and he hid it up his sleeve. Then I left him where I found him and waited in the bushes for your momma to come back."

She settled back in her chair. I glanced at Sal. He pointed at me and then pointed at his mother, like I was a child who wasn't paying enough attention to the teacher. "It took her a while, but she returned. Just like I predicted. I looked in the window to watch her. God, your momma was brainless! Thought she could reason with Billy. I coulda told her otherwise." Helenne spat on the ground beside her. Even her dog seemed disgusted and shifted away. "She told Billy that she wanted him to be good and not hurt people anymore, and Billy promised and listened to her with the most innocent expression on his face. He had a talent for sarcasm, that boy. She kept begging him, saying that she didn't want to hurt him, and that all he had to do was mend his ways. She said that, even though he was sick in the head, she might learn to love him again once he did his time for killing Judge Stein and Alice. Oops. Big mistake bringing up prison. Your momma, of course, told him that jail time was the 'decent' thing to do." She repeated the word with disgust. "*Decent*. Where we come from, that ain't even a word."

"Hmm." She took a few seconds to get herself back on track. "Billy hated prison, see? He'd stolen cars when he was a kid and got caught and put in the hoosegow. I can imagine what happened to him there, a good-looking, crispy boy like him with a tight little ass. Easy-pickings. Anyway, when he got out, he swore he was never going back, so when he heard your momma was gonna turn him in, or make him turn himself in, he didn't like that. He pretended he was all for it, though. You shoulda seen his performance.

"I guess your momma thought he'd 'seen the light,'" Helenne raised her arms and closed her eyes. Moaning, she was a grotesquerie of rapture. "And then came the struggle to lift him up into Judge Stein's wheelchair—Billy was all muscle and dead weight—she got him in there, though. But when she leaned over to take the brake off, he plunged the knife in her side. Aw, you shoulda been there for that! Hot dang! It was great!"

Helenne jumped out of her chair, too excited now, too manic. She wiped her sweating face on her sleeve. "Well, your poor ol' momma couldn't believe it. She fell on Judge Stein's bed, holding her side and looking at the blood on her hand. 'Why'd you do that, Billy?' she said. 'I loved you...'" Helenne mocked, thumping her hand on her heart. "Cue the violins," Helenne said to Sal, who laughed.

"And then, she wheeled him out of the Judge's house. Your itsy-bitsy momma headed up the mountain pushing that wheelchair thing. She huffed and puffed and stopped along the way, bleeding all the while. A real mess.

"At first, Billy shouted at her something fierce. He said things like 'What are you doing, Cal? Why ain't my legs workin', Cal? What you done to me?' And then after a while, when he didn't get any answer, he got right nasty. 'You ain't nothing but trash! You're a born loser! Soon as I get out of this wheelchair, I'm gonna smash your nose into your brains! I'm gonna slit your ugly throat and kill everybody you know! I'm gonna piss into your miserable guts when I slit you open!' He was a mean talker. Personally, I think you catch more flies with honey, don't you?"

Helenne smiled and shook her head as if she were remembering something pleasurable. She sighed. "Well, you get my drift. But I still didn't know what your momma was up to. She was concentrating so hard on trying to get Billy up the hill she didn't even notice me following her. She had pluck, I tell you, and she was so small! I don't know how she did it."

This was some sort of triumphal moment for Helenne. I didn't understand it. I looked at Sal, hoping he'd explain, but he was busy kicking at a loose stone. When I looked back at Helenne, she was taking in the view. The wind was picking up considerably, and it was hard to stay on my feet.

"Billy hated the top of this mountain. Did you know that? I don't think he feared heights as much as he respected what falling could do to him." She chuckled at her cleverness. "Anyway, your mother pushed him out to the point. By that time, Billy was terrified and calling out for me to save him. I was hiding behind the rocks and didn't come out. I didn't want her to know I was there. Your momma pushed him all the way to the ledge and stopped, waiting for him to be quiet. Billy was worn out from screaming his ass off and he sat there red-faced and panting, scared shitless. And your momma said, 'Goodbye, Billy' all quiet-like, and pushed him over the edge."

I was furious. "You're a damn liar, Helenne. I have it on better authority than you that *he* killed *her*!"

"Who's been filling your head with that? It's nonsense. You're gonna die, so why should I lie to you?"

It was revelatory. Helenne, for all her vileness, was telling me the truth. It was Alister who didn't know the complete narrative, and in my mind, the story was now coming together. I looked at Sal, disgusted. "And you're Billy's son."

It took a moment, but he bowed. "Well, look at that, Helenne," he said to his mother. "She has a working brain cell."

I saw the whole thing: my mother confronting Helenne outside her house. Mother, naïve and confused, backing out of the yard, frightened of the wolves, while Helenne wouldn't stop laughing. Helenne *had* won Billy Mars: She'd been pregnant with Salem. The humiliation, mother's and mine, engulfed me. I brought a shaky hand to my forehead and shook my head in disbelief and absolute fury.

"It shocked me to see Billy go over the bluff," Helenne said. "Didn't know your mother had it in her. Then I got mad. How dare she do that, you know? Take away something that was mine."

Billy was the one who died, but to Helenne, it was still all about her.

"That sniveling momma of yours was hysterical. She cried all the way down the mountain. I followed her. What *was* she going to do next? She was full of surprises. Well, she went to somebody's house and got the baby. I knew it! I knew she hadn't killed him! But what had she done with you? You were alive somewhere, I could sense it, but where? And then you showed up looking just like your mother, but with a different name, on the front page of *The Express*! And you were writing about me! Of all the ironies! What luck, wouldn't you say? It was *you*! I just couldn't believe it was *you*. *You* who I'd been looking for all these years."

"We lost you for a little while," Sal said. "You disappeared. We expected you to stay in New York."

Never to be outdone, Helenne took back the conversation. "And then, of all the mother-loving places for you to come, you turn up in the liquor store. Where I work!" She looked at Sal. "You can always count on a lush, son. Never forget that. They're as reliable as clockwork."

I'd played right into their hands. Salem inserted himself in my life to spy on me, to watch me so I wouldn't disappear again, to play with my emotions, and possibly to kill me. I couldn't help myself. I laughed.

Helenne advanced on me. "What's so funny?"

"Me. Picking the wrong men," I said, shaking my head.

She looked at Sal. "Oh, he's not so bad," she said.

"Never had complaints before," he said.

It was bizarre, standing on this mountain, hearing the truth about my mother's life and my own, being entertained by murderers. *Might as well go all the way*, I told myself. "So fill in the blanks for me," I said. "You killed Judge Stein and the nurse. What did you do to my mother and Asa?"

She tilted her head. "You seem to know a lot about all this, and you were such a little girl. I shouldn't think you'd remember anything. Where're you getting your information?"

I was silent as Helenne studied me. No one knew about the book but Alister and me. Perhaps one day, after I was dead and moldering in dense woodland, maybe someone would find me, or someone would rebalance the staircase, find the book, and put pieces of the puzzle together. It was the only hope I had for justice, and I wasn't about to tell Helenne and Sal about my mother's book. I'd face death protecting it.

"Never mind," she said. "Who cares now? It doesn't matter. Do you want to hear the rest of the story? What happened to the sainted Callie Moon?"

I said nothing.

"Well, she came out with that goddamn baby in her arms. And she went to Judge Stein's and stayed in the old tool shed on the property. She turned on the light bulb by the string hanging down, and I watched through the dirty window as she brushed away mouse poop and made a little bed for the baby out of some drop cloths. She used a bag of rags for a pillow, and I waited until she turned the light out and was asleep before I sneaked in. I had to avoid the security light the Judge had installed outside. It went on automatically, surprising me once when I was still outside, so I stayed in the shadows, watching, until your mother went to sleep. I didn't have to wait long. Then I sneaked in.

"I knew what I was going to do. Kill her baby boy. An eye for an eye. But when I picked the kid up, it started squalling, and your mother woke up. I think she said, 'Helenne, no!' or something like that. Frankly, I didn't pay much attention. I grabbed the boy and ran.

"At first, I didn't know where I was going, and she was right behind me. I mean, I hadn't exactly thought through the details. It occurred to me she wasn't in that good of shape from pushing Billy and that wheelchair up the hill, and having a stab wound to boot, and I was sure she couldn't manage another run up the mountain. So that's where I went. Straight up to the top again.

"But your momma was in better shape than I thought. About the time I approached the ledge, she showed up. 'Helenne, please…Please don't hurt Asa. He ain't done nothing. I'm the one you want!' She was pathetic. Played it like a bad actor."

"What did you do?" I spoke slowly and deliberately, trying to keep my voice from quavering. I feared what she was about to tell me.

She smiled. "I took the kid by the leg and slung him off." She showed me how she did it, a horrific movement, as effortless as a golf swing.

"Oh, dear God…" I said. I could've imagined a lot of different endings to the story, but this—this was too tragic. Staggering, my foot went into a fissure and took me down. I sat there with no desire to move, and surrendering to futility, I covered my face with my hands.

Helenne and Sal stood, impatient, as I wept. Then Helenne came over, grabbed my hair, and yanked my head back so I was forced to look into her face.

"And you wanted to know what happened to your mother? She went right after him."

Helenne threw me forward and I landed on my face. Unexpectedly, this ignited something in my gut. It was as if I wanted every piece of information she could give me. I wanted to know of her savagery in its entirety. If I was going to die, I wanted to go down hating her with everything I was capable of feeling.

I glanced at Sal to see if he noticed the change in me, but he was looking at his mother. I turned to Helenne. "So," I said. "You killed her."

"Nope. Didn't have to. She ran after the boy as if the mountain air was going to support her. It didn't, by the way." She trumpeted a noise like a cartoon, demonstrating with a whistle and a splat at the end. "She sailed straight off the mountain, didn't even fumble for a branch to save herself. I guess she thought she could catch him or break his fall, or maybe she just wanted to end it all. Anyway, I didn't look for the kid. I'm sure the bears enjoyed the snack. But seeing your mother stony-white and dead, what a treat—and taking her jewelry! I went back for it once the worms had cleaned her up." She fingered the necklace. "This was hers. I guess I should give it to you, but I like it. And I don't want to go rooting in the woods for it a second time."

A tear rolled down my cheek. A tear for us all. Mother, Asa, Gilly, me. Why did all this happen? What purpose did it serve? Were all our lives just random pieces of muck to slog and suffer through and for what? To be tossed off a mountain or eaten by bears? It was almost too absurd, and I suddenly laughed. I must have looked like a crazy person, my despondency turning into peals of laughter echoing off the hills, but the witnesses to my madness were a couple of psychopaths, so what the hell did it matter? I was still chuckling when I looked at Sal.

"You're an asshole," I said. "It's hard to believe somebody like you exists."

"Fun while it lasted," he said.

"Why haven't you killed me before now? You've had plenty of chances."

"Yes. Well, we hired poor ol' Boris Purdy to do his worst, but he was such an incapable, useless piece of detritus that when I had a chance to kill him, I did."

"You were the man with the rifle."

"Crack shot," he said.

"And you didn't come to help me."

He looked at me like I was being ridiculous. "Why would I?" he said.

"And my mother's grave isn't here on the mountain."

Sal said nothing but cocked his head at me like I was the biggest fool alive.

"Ah, young love," Helenne said. "So tragic!" She was getting bored with me. Her movements were faster, as if every nerve was twitching and gearing up for action. She took a few steps nearer. "You want to know why I didn't kill you sooner? Well, for one thing, I only saw your picture in the newspaper recently. I mean, really...Who reads *The Express*? And when I found you, I decided to play with you, wanted to see you confused, make you suffer, have you feel the fear that most people can't even imagine. You were the one who got away, see? Sal will tell you I'm a sore loser, and I'm sure you'll understand that as long as you're alive, I can't declare victory. I haven't annihilated everyone your mother loved. That's just a burr up my butt."

"But the other women? Why them? Why'd you kill them? And Mrs. Thatcher?" I asked.

She raised her chin and cracked her neck. She sighed as if I were too stupid to explain it to. "I like a challenge. Women who have a lot to live for, who think they're better than me, who have more than I ever will. Killing them makes me more powerful, don't you see? People who're considered smart and who try to fight back. I can't tell you what a charge it is to conquer somebody like that! And Sal, being in corporate America, knew these people or knew of them. He traveled for business. He was my scout. As for the Reverend's wife—"

"I killed her. I wanted to rattle you, and she was convenient," said Sal.

"Collateral damage. She was a sanctimonious cow anyway, so killing her was fine by me," Helenne said.

She then smiled at Salem and raised her eyebrows, an agreement between conspirators to get on with it. She went back to sit in her chair. Knowing what was about to happen, I struggled to free myself from the fissure. Shakily, I stood and backed away, tripping over rocks and rolling on branches. The wolf-dogs jumped up. Changing their weight excitedly, they longed for action, and waited for the command from Helenne to attack.

But it was Salem who was on me like a lightning strike. He grabbed anything he could of me and started pulling me to the drop-off. I punched at him, bit his arm, but he delivered the *coup de grâce*. He stomped on my left foot. An excruciating explosion of pain shot through me. I whimpered, fell, and almost passed out. He took my arm and started to drag me closer to the precipice, Helenne egging him on.

"Brilliant!" she said. "That's my boy!"

I resisted, and grabbed onto anything I could. He stopped, walked up to my head, and slammed it into the rock. Dazed, I curled myself into a ball, but he started dragging me by the feet. There was no time to think or plan. I had to move and fight with everything I had. I kicked him in the knees until he dropped me. Then I flipped and crawled forward with my elbows and sunk my hands and forearms into a large fissure in the rock. There was nothing to grab onto in that hole, so my effort simply shredded my arms as he pulled me out. I then made myself dead weight to make it harder for him to drag me and I grabbed onto every rock I could. That slowed him down, but not enough to prevent him from getting me closer to the cliff's edge. When he leaned over to grab me around the waist, I turned and punched him in the nose, clawing his face. I tried to gouge his eyes, but he grabbed my hands and held them. This gave me leverage to scramble up where I tried to kick him in the groin, but missed, and succeeded only in unbalancing myself. Falling hard, despite him holding onto my hands, I kept kicking at him with my feet, striking at nothing. While he was busy dodging my assault, I got my hands away from him and turned, digging my fingers into another rocky fissure, and when he tried to hoist me to my feet, I turned back to him and hit him in the temple with a palm-sized rock in my hand. Furious, he knocked it from my grasp with his left hand and backhanded me with his right. Still on the ground, I felt him trying to drag me, so I again gave him dead weight. The wind whipped at us and made resistance more difficult. It was as if I were fighting two men, one of substance and one of air.

He tried to pick me up again to move me to the ledge faster, but when I got to my feet, I tried to run. Sal caught me around the waist. I bucked wildly toward the woods as he pulled me all the way to the point. I used my dead weight to sink down again and lie on my stomach. I held onto anything I could as he tried to kick me toward the descent. My ribs cracked, but I held onto a fissure that had a substantial lip. Cursing, he dropped, straddling my back, stretching to loosen the grip of my hands. He got my right hand free and pinned my right arm under my body, which he held down with his weight. He then tried to free my left hand and when he did, he flipped me over to hit me. I didn't resist. My right hand had found the bear spray, and I sprayed him full in the face with it before he could land the punch. He let go of me immediately, stood up, put his hands to his face, stumbled blindly to get away, and silently fell off the cliff. He didn't scream.

But someone did. The sound spiraled in the wind and was shocking and primitive, that of hell on earth. I turned to see Helenne, standing with her wolf-dogs. The animals looked as surprised as I was. The scream had come from their master, and they sat up, ears alert, confused about what to do. Helenne, her eyes fixed on the spot where Sal had gone over, then turned to me. Holding the knife, she made a few unsteady steps in my direction, and I braced for the inevitable attack. Not trusting my legs to hold me, I crawled on my hands and knees to get off the ledge and away from her. But when I looked back, she wasn't following me. She'd stopped a few feet short. Looking at me then, she did the unthinkable. She screamed again with all her might. A wild, frenzied, maniacal, demonic roar. And the wolf-dogs knew what to do.

When Helenne realized her mistake, it was too late. For a moment, genuine terror surfaced in her eyes. And then it was gone as the wolf-dogs lunged first for her throat, then for her abdomen. They were so thoroughly fixated on her destruction that I could pull myself up and back away to hide behind the rockpile where my mother had told me to wait as a child. I collapsed there, and as I went down, I remember reminding myself not to scream.

But there had been a moment, as Helenne's eyes stared into mine, when she passed onto me the horror that was her life, her scream being the last bitter, desperate call for someone to understand the anguished, unloved child she'd been, to bear witness to all she'd seen, and how it warped the person who could have been. I felt, in that ghastly moment, chosen to bear witness, and it would change me forever. That one moment had united us, and I knew that there, but for the grace of God, was I.

CHAPTER 25

Someone found me, an unconscious, crumpled heap behind the pile of rocks. I woke up in the hospital days later. I remember only a little about those days. The nightmares primarily. Horrible wolves ran after me. One of them, his red mouth gaping and bloody, pulled out a baby's intestines. It pulled the child into the lightless woods where, to its screams, the wolf devoured him. I dreamed of a dog that kept being run over in the road, or I had lost my shoe in the street and was getting hit by a bus trying to retrieve it. In my nightmares, people were breaking into my house, filling me with drugs, holding me hostage, and killing the people I loved. The hallucinations worsened because the hospital administered morphine when I regained consciousness, to which I now know I'm allergic—and there was no relief from the day or night terrors until the doctors switched medication.

After the hospital sedated me with something kinder to my constitution and the horrific episodes stopped, I experienced a period of disorientation. During that time, I didn't know if I was asleep or awake. Real or imagined friends spoke to me in hushed tones, and for a long time, it wasn't in me to answer back.

When the doctors deemed me strong enough, they allowed the FBI and the police to see me. I told them everything, even about my mother's book and where to find it. I made them promise to give it back when they'd finished their investigation.

After a week, Bud Ramos and Officer George Stanley came to visit. Ramos, looking older and more tired than usual, stood by my bedside; George, his hands in his pockets and studying the floor, stood with his back to the wall near the hall door.

"Kate, I want to tell you…" said Ramos. He cleared his throat and started over. "I think you're a damn clever and brave woman." His ears had turned bright red.

"Or just stupid," I said.

"Well, that too," he said.

We smiled at each other. "Sal had me fooled," I said.

"Yeah, we've all fallen for the wrong people sometime."

I was aware of Ramos's last divorce, but I knew nothing about his current private life. "Are you married, Ramos?" I asked.

"Only four times," he said. "Fifth time's the charm, huh?"

"Bud, you're asking the wrong person," I said.

"Well…" he said, giving my arm a pat, "I'm just glad you're around to give me bad advice. Come on over here, George."

I teared up as Officer Stanley took Ramos's place beside the bed.

"I'm sorry, George," I said.

He took my hand. "For what?"

"For leading John Branch into all this," I said.

He patted my hand. "That's our job, Kate. We know the risks."

"Are you in touch with his family?"

"I'd better be. He was married to my sister," he said.

"The radiologist?"

"The very one."

"Tell her…" I couldn't get the words out.

"She knows. She's very proud of him. He'll receive a National Police Service Medal from the Governor General if Ramos and I have anything to do with it. Perhaps you'll come to the ceremony."

"I'll be there," I said.

After they left, I called Da to hear his voice. I still missed my old Da, the one who would have gotten on a plane and come to me. When he answered, he sounded distracted.

"What are you looking at, Da? Am I interrupting something you're doing?" I could imagine him sitting there in his corner chair. In the background, there was chatter, the nurses taking down old decorations and putting up new ones.

"There are hearts hanging from the ceiling," he said.

"Yeah, Da? They're not on your sleeve?" I don't think he got the joke, but he laughed anyway.

"That's right, that's right," he said, his voice fading away, caught in the intoxication of hearts.

"I'll be home soon," I said.

And then he said, "It's cold outside, so don't forget to wear your toothbrush."

I knew exactly what he meant.

\#

Leaving the hospital in February, none other than Bruce Weatherstone picked me up curbside. This touched me, and I loved him more than I ever had. I tried to tell him what I was feeling, but he waved my words away.

"Yeah, well, I'm just so glad it's over and you're all right," he said, grasping the steering wheel a little too tightly.

We sat there until he could pull himself together and drive us back to the cabin. My "fan club," as Bruce called them, must have seen us coming. Before I could get out of the car, Cup, Blue, and Alister poured out of the house to greet me and help me hobble in on my crutches, where I collapsed in a chair.

"Watch out, Bruce. Your house is feeling like home," I said and he smiled.

Simon wasn't there. I was enormously disappointed about that. If a life-or-death situation couldn't bring him to forgive me, nothing could.

I pushed myself more upright then and concentrated on all the people who *were* there. They hurried around, taking off my coat, giving me something to put my foot on, and remarking on my hair, which was a bit of a mess. They went about setting the table, too, and preparing food.

"We invited a guest. I hope you don't mind…" said Cup. I hoped it was Simon, but when the welcome bear bell clanged, it wasn't him.

"Am I late?" the young man asked, coming in and taking off his hat, coat, and scarf. He hung them on the coat rack near the door. "Something smells great!"

At first, I thought he was someone's nephew or son. He wore a black eye patch like a pirate, but there was nothing else very buccaneer about him. He had the sensitive demeanor of a poet, but one with a keen sense of humor. I could tell by the sparkle in the eye I could see.

"Hello," he said, coming over and extending his hand. "You're the woman of the hour, I hear. I'm Asa."

I sat there like a dullard. "What?" I asked.

"Let me introduce you to your brother, Kate," said Bruce.

In utter stupefaction, I thought I might be dreaming.

"Where're the deviled eggs I just put out?" asked Blue.

Asa pulled up a chair next to me and took my hand. We sat there for a little while, me crying, him smiling his wonderful, intoxicating smile and squeezing my hand gently from time to time.

"Would you like to know what happened, Kate, and why I'm still here living, breathing, and causing trouble?"

"Yes," I said. "Please tell me everything. I thought you were dead."

"Just thrown off a mountain. That's different from being dead. And I was lucky. I landed in a thick fir tree and fell from branch to branch until a hard landing. I was plenty scratched up, and I lost an eye and had a mass of broken bones."

"The doctors called him a miracle baby," said Blue.

"I can see why," I said. "But mom died, right?" He nodded. "Then who took care of you?"

"Cup and Blue," he said.

"Am I dreaming?" I asked everyone.

"Nope," he said. "I was never in danger growing up. Helenne thought I was dead. And Cup and Blue changed my name."

"To Michael Anton," said Blue. "So romantic…"

"And they kept you a secret from me. I only found out about you yesterday," he said.

"Neither of you could know about the other," said Cup.

"Or Helenne would have killed us both…You're a musician," I said, realizing why he looked so familiar. "You played guitar at the Leaf Festival in the park in Bowden. And Cup and Blue were dancing. I saw all of you when I first got here."

"That's right! And I've been living about thirty minutes from here all along," he said.

"Am I delirious?" I asked, doubting my sanity.

"You're in your right mind, Kate," said Asa, "but it must be a lot to process."

"Truer words…" I said under my breath.

"Tell me when you're ready for more," he said.

"There's more?" I asked, settling myself more deeply into my chair.

"Okay. You look ready," said an ebullient Asa. "You see, this is where the story gets weird. Mother believed in 'The Pure of Heart Spell'."

"Okay," said Bruce, slapping the tops of his thighs. "This is where someone offers me a bourbon."

Alister brought over two whiskey glasses and a bottle. He poured Bruce two fingers of bourbon and plopped down next to him on the couch. "Bruce, as a summer resident, you're a bit of a virgin concerning the eccentricities in these hills, but stick around," Alister said as he poured four fingers of the amber liquid into his own glass.

"The Pure of Heart Spell was in a book of ours," said Cup. "When Callie was a little girl, she overheard Blue and me talking about it. I think she believed in it, but we didn't know

that—"

"Who knows what kids are thinking?" said Blue.

"The spell states you can save somebody from dying if the person you're trying to save is pure of heart. And—this here's the catch—you have to sacrifice what matters most to you," Cup said.

"And you have to perform the spell right before the person dies," said Blue.

"So when Mother jumped off that mountain after me—" Asa said.

"But wait a minute. *You* mattered most to her. She didn't sacrifice you. I don't understand," I said.

"Maybe she found out *she* mattered on the way down. Maybe she found out how precious life really is. In fact, a lot of people find out things on the way down, wouldn't you say?" said Cup, looking pointedly at me.

"And the spell worked, didn't it?" said Blue, gesturing to Asa. "Here's living proof!"

Asa leaned against me and lowered his voice. He's already made me a conspirator. "Blue conveniently forgets I landed in a fir tree," he said.

"However it happened, that's what happened," said Cup. "But you should know the rest of the story. Your mother came to us bleeding when Billy stabbed her. It was a pretty serious wound, and we treated it—"

"But she was hysterical—" said Blue.

"Full of remorse for killing Billy," Cup said. "Quite inconsolable."

"Wanted us to make it better, but there weren't nothing we could do," added Blue.

"Gotta make your peace with what is," said Cup. "As for what happened after—"

"Here's what happened," said Blue, taking over the conversation. "Callie Moon hit the ground first. She was heavier, don't you know, and the fir tree was slowing the baby down. She deliberately activated the Pure of Heart Spell to save her boy, and you ain't gon' tell me anything different," said Blue, glaring at Bruce.

"I wouldn't dream of trying, Madame," he said.

"But, Cup, she loved you and Blue," I said. "Why didn't mother just stay with you? Why take Asa and run away? She would have been safe if she'd just stayed with you."

"She was too upset to listen to us. And she had a pattern of taking her babies and running. I mean, that's how she came to Blood Mountain. So she took Asa and left."

"Fled. The word is 'fled,'" said Blue. "She took the boy and fled when we tried to get her to stay."

A heaviness had fallen over the room. Asa broke it up.

"Do you feel up to a quick ride? I'd like to show you where I live," he said to me. When there was a great outcry from Cup and Blue in the kitchen, he said, "I'll have her back in time for lunch."

#

I said yes to the ride. I'd have gone anywhere with this brother of mine. We got into his Outback and drove to his place. His car was neat, but not overly so. Half a cup of cold black coffee sat in the cup holder. There were muddy boots behind the driver's seat where he'd been hiking. I felt the car ride a little too keenly, the rough gravel of the road traveling through to my feet now. I had yet to be treated for Polyarteritis Nodosa and I'd become more sensitive, but I absolutely refused to give in to the pain. Not on this day.

We clattered over an old, covered bridge as we turned into his gravel driveway. "I love this bridge," Asa said. "I can hear it from the house, and it always alerts me when I'm about to have a visitor, so I'm not caught in my skivvies."

Asa's house was charming, rustic, and a little messy. A log cabin, beautifully chinked. We walked into a combined living room and kitchen, which was off to the left of the entrance. Coats, hats, and scarves hung on a horizontal row of hooks by the door. A red sofa faced a wood fire. Glowing embers lay in pillowy ash at the bottom of the hearth.

"This is lovely," I told him.

"You all right?" he asked me.

"You bet."

"Then there's something I want to show you outside. It's not a far walk," he said. "Can you make it?"

I left my crutches leaning against a chair and took his arm. We walked into the beautiful, bright noon. The backyard was an enchanted garden. Dried, unraked leaves billowed around us. There was a small meadow filled with apple trees, and a view of distant blue mountains aglow in the deep golden sun. It was a warmish day for February, and a groundhog came out of his den to forage. He sat straight up, looked at us, apparently didn't approve of the company, and tottered back in.

I laughed.

"That's Douglas The Groundhog. Antisocial personality disorder," said Asa. He stopped and pointed to a small tombstone. "She's there," he said.

Callie Moon 1965-1990

Beloved mother of Jimmy, Kate, Gilly, and Asa

For whom love lasts

It was too much, and I got down on my knees and wept. Asa kneeled beside me and handed me a semi-clean tissue he fished from his pocket, and I laughed again. Touching the soft brown earth that covered my mother's grave, I finally felt profoundly connected to her.

"I planted her grave with a whole slew of dandelions. They were really pretty last spring. They'll be popping out again in a few months," said Asa.

"She would have loved that," I said.

"I told her all about you." I must have looked puzzled. "When I found out about you yesterday, I came out here, and we had a good, long talk."

I couldn't tell if he was being serious. "And what did she say?" I said, playing along.

He looked a bit surprised I would ask. "Why, that she loves you, and she's glad you've found your way home."

CHAPTER 26

As promised, we were back at Bruce's house for a late lunch and sat down to a delicious meal of backstrap venison in a Cumberland sauce and quail with wild mushrooms. Bruce now seemed not just relaxed, but fitting right in with my eccentric friends, perhaps through the blessing of bourbon. He laughed and joked with Blue in particular, and she harangued him until he promised to put her recipe for ol' possum stew on the front page of the newspaper. To my knowledge, the world is still waiting for it.

Bruce had hired me back part time, so I had four more months to heal from everything before I went back to the newspaper and resumed my regular duties. But there were ulterior motives on Bruce's part, too.

"So now that you're working part time, you can write your book," he said while we were still at the table. "She's writing a book called 'Swan Songs' about all the women The Laundry Man murdered. I'm sure it'll be a big hit with true crime aficionados."

"No," I blurted out, a little more intensely than I'd intended. "I've decided not to write it."

Everyone around the table seemed shocked.

"Why?" said Bruce. "Why wouldn't you? You've done all this work. You've lived through it yourself. You're the expert."

But I knew why. "Because they're not dead," I said. "At least not to me."

I couldn't explain this to anyone. My feelings about this were deeply personal. Everyone, except for Cup and Blue, looked bewildered. But

Blue uncharacteristically leaned over, cupped my neck in the crook of her arm, and gave me a big, wet kiss on the cheek.

#

I was sorry when the party broke up. Cup, Blue, and Asa seemed in a hurry to go; Bruce had to make a plane; and Alister was Alister, the introvert, ready to go back to his papers and books. Bruce had insisted I stay in his cabin for at least another day, which puzzled me. I would have thought him eager to have me in New York at my desk, even part time.

There was the usual chaos of goodbyes and good wishes, hugs and kisses, and the sorting out of coats, hats, scarves, and gloves. When I finally opened the door for them to leave, it was as if they vaporized in some sort of Smoky Mountain mist. And when it cleared, there was Simon, his long legs crossed at the ankles, leaning up against his old green Subaru. Gasping at the sight of him, the frigid air hit the back of my throat so hard that tears came to my eyes. I wanted to rush into his arms, bury my face in the warmth of his neck and shoulder, but I didn't. I was aware of our last conversation when he was all business. Of course, we were discussing a serial killer and the fact that I was his next victim, so I suppose that warranted solemnity. Still, I was cautious.

"Hi," I said.

"Hi," said Simon. "I thought you might need a ride home."

"I do," I said.

"Then I'm your guy."

Trembling, I walked closer and stood in front of him.

I told myself not to shy away. Not again. "You *are* my guy," I said. He looked confused. "Simon, I'm sorry. I've been such an idiot. I have been, but I'm not now. You mean a lot to me. I…" I thought I dare not say it, but I did. "I love you," I said.

He teared up and changed the subject.

"I've been looking at property," he said. "I'd like to make this area my home once New York is done with me."

Perhaps my declaration made him uncomfortable. Maybe he even had somebody else by now. I felt a brick in my stomach, and I looked at the ground.

"Find anything?" I asked.

"Not yet," he said.

"It'll be there," I said.

"Yeah." He was still leaning against the car, shuffling his feet. He rubbed his hands against his blue jeans.

"Are you ready to go?" he asked.

"I have to pack," I said. "I'll be ready tomorrow."

"Okay." Then he whistled—a shrill, incongruous blast of sound that startled me.

A Carolina dog with the marking of a dog biscuit on his head careened, full tilt, from around the back of the car. I couldn't believe my eyes.

I got down on my knees as my little friend wriggled with joy.

"Where did you come from, boy?" I looked up at Simon. "Did you get him from the Humane Society?"

"No. I found him on Cullowhee Mountain Road, so I named him 'Cully'. Do you like dogs? I don't think I've ever asked."

And I laughed. I laughed so hard, I fell on the ice cold, hard gravel driveway. I wanted to fling my arms wide and yell, "Yes! Yes, I believe it all! Bring on the magic! Bring it on, you miraculous, crazy, ridiculous life!" But instead, I rolled on my back and hugged Cully, and submitted to having my tears licked away by a warm, velvet tongue.

"Need a hand up?" Simon asked. He found our silliness amusing, and I could tell he was having fun, even though he didn't understand it.

"I guess so," I said, sad that I would have to remove the dog that now lay on top of me, stem to stern. But Simon didn't help me up. Something was bothering him, and he crouched beside me, unsure.

"Kate...why love me now? I'm the same I've always been. I haven't changed. So if you're not sure...I don't want my heart broken again."

Propping up on my elbows, I said, "I'm sure."

"But why now?" he asked.

"Let me see," I said, taking the front of his jacket and pulling his lips down to mine. "Because now you have a dog," I said, and I kissed him with a passion that I'd never known for anyone else.

\#

On our drive back to New York, we stopped at the overlook to Blood Mountain. It wasn't tourist season, but a small caravan had pulled off the road, and a family was taking pictures of their children in front of the faded mountain. As Simon and I stood with our arms around each other, a little girl about seven years old skipped over to us and asked, "Are you guys from around here?" and, not giving us a chance to answer, she went on, "What's the name of that mountain?" she asked.

Simon and I looked at each other. Perhaps he was concerned about what I was going to say. I'd told him the story of my first day at this overlook.

"I think it's called Strawberry Hill," I said.

"Lovely," the child said precociously, and skipped off.

EPILOGUE

Simon finished with New York before it was finished with him.

Seven months passed before we stumbled upon a log cabin on Bruce's lake that suited our tastes, so we bought it and settled in. We brought Da with us, and he seems delighted to be back in the mountains. He has a new girlfriend, too. Both live in a lovely, assisted living community near Bowden. Asa visits not only us, but Da, impishly giving him dating advice which delights Da to no end. As for Alister, he's moved into this century, writing a blog on diet tips because he says overweight Americans look like snacks for other countries.

Dr. Marsh is still treating me for my condition. I became a vegan, which has helped lower my inflammation. Simon pretends to like the food, but I can tell he misses bacon as much as I do.

These days, I find myself grateful for everything, even the diet. I'm grateful for the way the ephemeral daffodils poke their hopeful heads out of the soil in the spring to be struck down by an inevitable chill before warm weather comes. I'm grateful for the mighty wind that whips and moans around the cabin. It's an agreeable companion to my restless mind when I can't sleep at night. I'm grateful for the all-day rain, the sun when it breaks through the clouds, and moonlight so bright through our bedroom window that it causes me to turn away and face a dark corner. And there's Simon, sleeping beside me, his light snores music to my ears. We wake in the night to check on each other, and at those times, Cully comes to sleep in the middle of us, his warmth and love so comforting, we go back to sleep. I'm grateful for all the answers I've received, and for the mysteries that remain, particularly this one: Who *are* Cup and Blue? I think of them often, yet I haven't seen them since the party.

But this is the way it is, and perhaps, the way it ought to be—that some things should be mysterious, fleeting, and never resolved. Perhaps only then do we keep questioning and searching for that elusive thing we want to find—whatever it is—and in this, hold our minds open to change, growth, and the absolute, transformative power of love.

The End

MEET THE AUTHOR

Martha has published two niche-market books of nonfiction, *The Life You Want* and *The Teacup Prophecies*. The latter is a book, but also an app for iPhones. She is a corporate coach specializing in empowering human potential. National magazines such as *Fast Company* have written articles on her as someone who brings about significant and pioneering transformations. She also is a therapist. As a screenwriter and a playwright, Martha has written for Scholastic and PBS and was runner-up in the S.E. Theater Conference's New Play Project for a play on Oscar Wilde called *A Feast of Panthers*. She also is an actor, a theater director, a dialogue and accent coach for movies, and a voice talent. Her experience includes being a columnist for *The Conscious Life Journal,* and she hosted a radio show called *Real Talk with Martha Novak* on Blog Talk Radio. Her shows are posted all over YouTube. Martha lives with her loving husband in the beautiful mountains of North Carolina.

Printed in the USA
CPSIA information can be obtained
at www.ICGtesting.com
LVHW021337161124
796821LV00043B/1115